"Did you stay away because of me?"

Dallas asked.

Rachel gazed at him a long moment before answering. "That was a big reason. I didn't want your name tainted—or my son's."

He stared at her, and a wanting engulfed him. And, although she didn't move at all, he almost felt her leaning toward him. And then their lips brushed, lightly, warmly, sweetly.

Rachel knew she should step back, but the emotions swirling inside her held her in place. Finally she managed to nod and turn toward her horse. "Thanks for all you've done for me, Dallas."

Gratitude? Was that all she felt? Stunned, he handed her the reins, then held the horse while she mounted.

With a jerk of the reins, Rachel turned the mare and urged her into a canter. She didn't really see a thing ahead of her, for her mind lingered on the man she'd left behind.

A man who could never be hers.

* * *

For generations of Cordell men, love
and trouble have always come hand in hand.
This June, watch what happens when
Love Finds Yancey Cordell
(Silhouette **Special Edition** #601),
also by award-winning
Curtiss Ann Matlock.

Dear Reader,

Welcome to the Silhouette **Special Edition** experience! With your search for consistently satisfying reading in mind, every month the authors and editors of Silhouette **Special Edition** aim to offer you a stimulating blend of deep emotions and high romance.

The name Silhouette **Special Edition** and the distinctive arch on the cover represent a commitment—a commitment to bring you six sensitive, substantial novels each month. In the pages of a Silhouette **Special Edition**, compelling true-to-life characters face riveting emotional issues—and come out winners. All the authors in the series strive for depth, vividness and warmth in writing about living and loving in today's world.

The result, we hope, is romance you can believe in. Deeply emotional, richly romantic, infinitely rewarding—that's the Silhouette **Special Edition** experience. Come share it with us—six times a month!

From all the authors and editors of Silhouette **Special Edition**,

Best wishes,

Leslie Kazanjian, Senior Editor

P.S. As promised in January, this month brings you Curtiss Ann Matlock's long-awaited first *contemporary* Cordell male, in *Intimate Circle* (#589). And come June, watch what happens to Dallas Cordell's macho brother as . . . *Love Finds Yancey Cordell* (#601).

CURTISS ANN MATLOCK
Intimate Circle

Silhouette Special Edition

Published by Silhouette Books New York

America's Publisher of Contemporary Romance

To Leslie Kazanjian,
who knows how to encourage the best from me
and to take that and make it better.

SILHOUETTE BOOKS
300 East 42nd St., New York, N.Y. 10017

Books by Curtiss Ann Matlock

Silhouette Special Edition

A Time and a Season #275
A Time To Keep #384
Last Chance Cafe #426
Wellspring #448
Intimate Circle #589

Silhouette Romance

Crosswinds #422
For Each Tomorrow #482
Good Vibrations #605

Silhouette Christmas Stories 1988

"*Miracle on I-40*"

CURTISS ANN MATLOCK,

a self-avowed bibliophile, says, "I was probably born with a book in my hand." When not reading or writing—which is almost constantly—she enjoys gardening, canning, crocheting, horseback riding, and motorcycling with her husband and son.

Married to her high-school sweetheart, the author is a Navy wife and has lived in eight different states within a sixteen-year period. The nomadic Matlocks finally settled in Oklahoma, where Curtiss Ann keeps busy juggling two full-time careers—as homemaker and writer.

Named 1989's Oklahoma Writer of the Year by the University of Oklahoma, Curtiss Ann Matlock recently made her debut in the historical fiction arena with *The Forever Rose*, linking it by multigenerational "family ties" to two contemporary novels, *Intimate Circle* and *Love Finds Yancey Cordell*. Each novel stands alone; together they create a unique family saga.

CORDELL FAMILY TREE

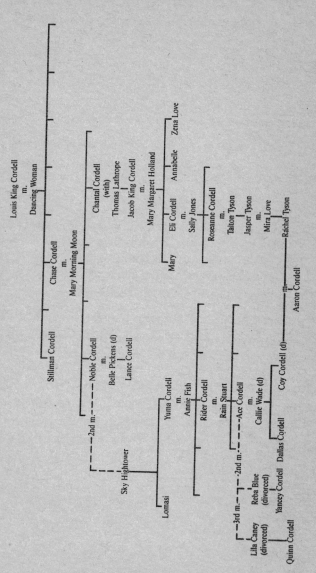

Chapter One

Holding the colt's lead rope, Dallas stopped just short of the horse trailer and decided to try one more time. Not that he'd ever known Ace Cordell to change his mind once he'd set his course. Nor had Dallas ever known his father to admit to being wrong, which he was this time.

"Dad, it would be best to wait." He looked over the colt's neck at his father. "You haven't been over to the Golden in forty years. You don't have to go this afternoon. And you know it."

Seldom, if ever, did Dallas question his father, much less censure him, more because he knew it did little good than because he thought the older man infallible. More also because of the fierce loyalty he held for the old man.

His father sent him a sharp glance, then turned his attention to the colt and rubbed the animal's sleek rump. "I got a right to welcome my grandson home." His voice was deep, though not loud.

"Yes...but you don't have a right to stir up trouble."
Dallas fixed his father with a firm gaze.

Ace's dark eyes flashed with defiance. Looking every inch
the proud warrior of his heritage, he said, "There'll only be
trouble if Jasper stirs it, not me."

"Aaron is Jasper's grandson, too," Dallas reminded
gently.

Though his father's weatherbeaten face remained characteristically stoic, Dallas recognized the jealousy burning
within the older man. His father didn't want Jasper Tyson
making inroads with their mutual grandson before he got a
chance to compete for the boy's affection. Pity tugged at
Dallas. Ace Cordell was all the things he appeared: a mighty
man, proud, unbending, even obnoxious. But what few saw,
and Dallas knew, was that his father also had a vulnerable
need buried deep within him that craved adoration from his
family.

"Aaron will be coming here, too, Dad," Dallas said.
"Plenty. He loves it here. He loves you."

Stepping back, Ace placed a rough hand to the leather
belt that rode low on his hips. His dark eyes shot fire.

"My grandson is coming today. My one and only grandson, I might add," he said with obvious censure. "Since he
isn't comin' here first, like by all rights he should be, I'll go
there." Though bent slightly now from numerous riding
accidents over his long years, nevertheless he was a big man,
six foot four, with a shock of thick silver hair and a way of
speaking that could cut like a knife. When Ace Cordell
spoke, people were given to listening. "Are you goin' to get
this colt into that trailer, or am I goin' to have to get him in
myself? Drive myself?"

Equally tall as his father, Dallas met the older man's hard,
cold stare. There'd been a time when that stare sent a chill
down his spine, but not anymore. And he complied now
with his father out of choice, not coercion.

"I'll take you, Dad."

Without another word he led the paint horse into the trailer. The colt's hooves clattered up the ramp. He was a high stepper—high stepper and feisty, same as Dallas's father.

Anger smoldered within Dallas. He didn't want to go over to the Tyson place. It was a rude thing to be doing, when Jasper and Mira were undoubtedly looking forward to a private family welcome for their daughter and grandson. They didn't need intruders, least of all the Cordells.

And Dallas had pretty cold feet about seeing Rachel, especially around the others.

Rachel coming home. The fact stirred memories long buried. Would she be very changed? Would he feel that electric fire when he looked at her?

He paused, held to the trailer door and took a deep breath as remorse and guilt swirled up to haunt him. Once upon a time Dallas had loved Rachel, his brother's wife.

In the same way he slammed the trailer doors in place and fastened the catch securely, he slammed the lid on his swirling speculations and locked them away. Those feelings were long gone, he told himself. Turned to ashes by all that had happened and the years that had passed. For both of them.

He adjusted his black Stetson on his head, then pulled the keys from his pocket as he strode to the driver's side of the truck. He was the eldest son and as such felt a strong responsibility for the old man. Driving wasn't easy for his father anymore; his eyesight was failing, though Ace refused to admit it. Besides, Dallas suspected a cooler head would be needed for the coming confrontation. Though each of them was on the down side of sixty-five, Ace Cordell and Jasper Tyson remained as explosive as ever when they came together. There was small doubt that Jasper would be mad as hell about this intrusion.

Dallas shifted into high gear and watched the dust of the road, a product of the dry winter, billow up behind them. It was past the middle of February, and they'd received little snow and weren't likely to get any more. Ranchers like himself could only hope for heavy spring rains to bring up the grass.

He reached for the mobile telephone.

"Who you callin'?" Ace asked.

"Mira."

"Mira! Damn it, Dallas..."

Ignoring his father's blustering, Dallas spoke to the operator, having her put the call through for him since he didn't know the Tyson phone number.

"Don't know why you have to go and call them," Ace grumbled. "They'll know we're comin' when we get there."

"Mira? It's Dallas."

Her answering voice was soft and cultured, extending polite pleasantries, as if she spoke to him every day—not the rare, quick times they'd happen to meet somewhere.

Dallas glanced over at his father's fuming expression and had to chuckle. "Fine, Mira, thank you . . . yes, that's what I wanted to tell you—warn you. Dad and I are headin' over. Dad can't wait to see them, and we're bringing Aaron a welcome-home present."

There was a short pause, no doubt one of shock, before she extended a polite welcome. Mira was a lady of the highest sort and, no matter the circumstance, conducted herself with grace. For an instant Dallas thought of Rachel, who was as beautiful and graceful as her mother. In Mira's voice, he heard Rachel's. Then he pushed away the wandering thoughts and listened to Mira's assurances.

"Thanks, Mira," he said, and hung up. He kept his attention on the road as he directed the pickup out onto the county highway, refusing to acknowledge his father's disapproving scowl.

The main house of Jasper Tyson's Golden Rose Ranch was less than fifteen minutes away. A good part of the Tyson land on the south bordered Cordell land on the north; it had been so since the Cordells had first come to Oklahoma in the 1800s. The sweet water spring that began on the Tyson ranch drained out and down through the Cordell spread. The Cordells and the Tysons were also related, something that seemed to aggravate the elders of both families as a burr under a saddle did a horse. The ancestor who had begun Jasper Tyson's ranch had been a Cordell, and through both families ran blood from the same Chickasaw clan.

The rivalry between the two families, as old as the ranches themselves, had begun when the Cordell who homesteaded the Golden Rose ranch land refused to join forces with the Cordell who built his ranch to the south. Later there'd been a killing between the two families and, later still, numerous arguments over Spring Creek. As the years passed, there cropped up boundary disputes and power struggles in regards to running the county. It was the classic story of feuding families such as many a Hollywood film had been made about.

Until it had come to Dallas's brother, Coy, and Rachel Tyson, Jasper's only child. Coy and Rachel had borne the seed of change when they'd fallen in love, dared to marry and together had produced Aaron McKinley Tyson Cordell.

Dallas turned into the graveled driveway and drove beneath the massive arched entry proclaiming the Golden Rose Ranch. The elaborate concrete arch was a new addition that year, and etched into it were the shapes of blooming roses with sweeping stems—the symbol of the place. On either side of the driveway were rosebushes. Their stalks were bare now, but in a few months they would bloom profusely with yellow blossoms. The first bush, a yellow rose, had been planted on the ranch over one hundred years earlier, and legend had it that the original bush remained, was tended to religiously by Jasper.

"Jasper's getting pretty highfalutin these days," Ace wrinkled his nose with distaste.

"About the same as someone I know who built an office building last year and named it after himself." Dallas kept the smile from his lips as he reminded his father of the new

high-rise office building up in Oklahoma City that housed
the Cordell Oil Company offices, among other tenants, and
had been christened the Cordell Plaza.

His father raised a bushy white eyebrow but refrained
from commenting.

Jasper and Mira stepped from the courtyard of their
rambling, Spanish-style ranch house just as Dallas pulled
the pickup to a stop in the curved driveway. It was a polite
way, Dallas knew, to keep from asking the Cordells into
their home. His father wouldn't have gone inside in any
case.

Jasper Tyson was tall like Ace, but more rotund. Traces
of red still tinged his curly white hair. Mira held his right
hand. She was seventeen years younger than Jasper and the
love of his life—something quite evident. The affectionate
respect with which Jasper treated Mira had always invoked
Dallas's admiration. He'd rarely caught a sign of such
emotion between his father and any of Ace's three wives.

Mira spoke first. "Hello, Dallas. Ace." Her tone held
warm invitation.

"Hello, Mira." Dallas allowed his gaze to apologize.

Jasper nodded at Dallas and shook his hand, then slowly
extended his hand to Ace. "'Lo, Ace."

Ace firmly shook the offered hand. "Jasper."

The greeting between the two old men, who'd been at
odds since birth and had tangled often throughout their
school years, went remarkably well in Dallas's opinion, due
mostly of course to Mira's graceful presence. She let the two
men know immediately, if subtly, how hurt she would be if
they were not civil to each other. And no one ever wanted to
hurt Mira.

"Seen your archway, Jasper." Ace pushed his wide-
brimmed hat back at an angle. "It's quite a grand sight."
There was nothing in his tone or manner to indicate sar-
casm.

Jasper's eyes narrowed. "It's meant to be."

"Well, you succeeded," Ace replied politely, sounding not at all like himself. The atmosphere was definitely strained.

Mira sent Dallas a speculative and amused expression. There was polite conversation about how long it would have taken Rachel and Aaron to drive out from Phoenix, about how dry the weather had been, and speculation on badly needed spring rains.

Dallas couldn't help thinking of Rachel as he looked at Mira and listened to her speak. Her voice was soft, melodious, Rachel's had been like that. He could hear it still, calling for Coy, or a dog, or himself.

Mira was about half-Chickasaw Indian, with elegant, finely chiseled features. Her hair was sleek and black, wound in a knot and fastened at the base of her neck. Her smile came mostly from her warm brown eyes. Rachel was a replica of her mother, with creamy ivory skin being the only thing she'd inherited from her white-skinned, red-haired father. Dallas wondered whether her dark hair would still hang down her back.

It took less than five minutes to get around to the subject of Ace's present for Aaron. Immediately Jasper scowled, and Dallas sensed the smoldering fury of an annoyed bull.

"I got horses here for Aaron," Jasper said.

"Not one like this," Ace countered immediately, and stepped toward the end of the trailer. "Get him out, Dallas. I want him to be the first thing Aaron sees."

"Now hold on, Ace." Jasper's voice rose. "I got a present for Aaron, too. A blue Australian pup. The boy shouldn't be getting everything at once. It'll confuse him."

"Jasper..." Mira sent her husband a look of caution.

Dallas noticed Jasper caught the look, and he at least lowered his voice. "A green colt isn't safe for a boy as young as my grandson."

"Aaron's of an age to start learning about horses. *My* grandson and this colt can grow together."

"I think you should have consulted Rachel about that. Likely she'll feel the same as anyone with a lick of sense—a feisty, high-blood colt isn't what a young boy should begin on. And besides, no one asked you to come buttin' in over here, Ace."

"I don't think it could be considered buttin' in for a man to want to see his own grandson."

"It's buttin' in when you ain't invited! And when you start bringin' horses."

"You're selfish as ever, Jasper Tyson, and I don't have to take it."

"Dad . . ." Dallas reached out to touch his father's arm. Then the next instant he involuntarily ducked as Jasper's fist came swinging through the air.

Though he blinked and didn't see Jasper's fist connect with his father's chin, he heard it, and his father went stumbling backward and smacked into the trailer.

Letting out a mumbled curse, Ace came back punching. And Dallas found himself right in the middle of two fiery giants.

Rachel's eyes kept straying to the countryside they passed. They had left behind the flat plains thirty minutes ago, and now the road dipped and rose as it moved through the hills of cleared pastures and blackjack oak, hackberry and sometimes walnut and pecan. Branches were bare and grass brown at this time of the year, but winter was short here, and in only a month or so green buds would begin to show.

Here was where the tribes used to roam freely and take the valuable buffalo. Here was where the Chickasaws had finally pushed west to settle, where Stillman Cordell had dared to be the first to carve out a homestead in the domain of the fierce Plains Indians—the homestead that had become the Golden Rose. Here was where Rachel's ancestors had raised cattle and driven them north to Abilene.

Her father loved to tell of history, most especially that of his own family. Since she could remember, she'd heard the stories of her Chickasaw forefathers and the white people who had intermarried with them in what had once been Indian territory. She hadn't realized until that moment how much those stories—most probably greatly exaggerated but carrying a grain of truth nonetheless—meant to her. They helped to define her being, somehow, helped her to understand who she was and what she was. She missed home more in that instant than in all the years she'd spent away.

She glanced from the road over to her son. His face was intense with growing excitement. Her heart tugged. She had high hopes that her decision to return home to live would mean the best future for him.

"Is that the cemetery where Daddy's buried?" Aaron asked suddenly, screwing his head around to glance at her while pointing out the window at the same time.

Rachel nodded. "Yes . . . I'm surprised you remember." She slowed and looked at it. More cleared land than had previously been there surrounded the cemetery, but the bare stalks of wild climbing roses still graced the old wrought-iron fencing at the front. She thought of the yellow roses at the ranch, one of them dating back well over a hundred years. Such hearty bushes could still be found on old homesteads throughout the West, brought by pioneers who came building a new life.

"I don't . . . not really," Aaron murmured. "It just seemed familiar."

"We'll visit his grave soon so you can see. There's a whole section of Cordells."

"Your side of the family, too?"

She smiled. Her son shared with her a love of reading cemetery stones. "A few," she said, "but most of our direct family are buried at the private cemetery on the ranch."

He nodded and focused his gaze ahead, as if trying to see all the way to his grandparents' house. Though Rachel had never asked, she'd learned by casual comments he'd made that Aaron's true memory of his father was hazy. What he knew came from pictures and things she'd told him, and she was always careful to tell the good. She'd let the bad be buried with Coy.

Aaron flashed her a quick smile. "We're almost there."

"Yes," she said, and reached over to brush the dark, thick hair from his forehead. "Excited?"

He grinned and nodded. "Grandpa J. said he has me a present." His smile widened. "So did Papa Ace."

Rachel sighed. So it began—no, so it continued. Since Aaron's birth, her father and father-in-law had vied for her son's attention, his love, as if neither believed the boy could love them both with all his heart.

"I'll bet it's horses," he said. "From each of them."

At Christmas, Ace has sent Aaron a .22 rifle with a stainless steel barrel and a carved wooden stock—for a ten-year-old boy who lived in the city. Her father had visited and brought a complete personal computer.

"They love you, Aaron. They can't seem to help but get carried away by giving you so many things. Please don't encourage them."

"Aw, Mom, I know, I know. I understand." He made a face and spoke with the impatient patience a child employs when tired of hearing something repeatedly.

Rachel smiled at him, and his expression brightened. His unruly dark hair had fallen again over his forehead, and his crystal-gray eyes twinkled. *So much like Dallas.*

She'd tried to forget Dallas, had succeeded in putting aside her feelings for him. But Aaron was a constant reminder of the man, as strange as that was, for Aaron resembled his uncle so much more than his father.

Coy's hair had been dark brown, almost black, but Aaron's was just a shade lighter—the exact shade of Dallas's and straight and unruly like his tended to be. Coy's eyes had been the color of a dark coffee bean, but Aaron had been born with blue ones that had turned a luminous gray-blue. Like Dallas's. And therein had lain the suspicion for Coy, leading to the accusations.

Her stomach tensed, as it always did when she remembered. Coy's accusations had been false. False! She had never slept with anyone but him. But even so, she hadn't been innocent. For at one time, while married to one man, she'd fallen in love with his brother.

That was all over, Rachel told herself, left behind in a past that couldn't be changed. What she must do was let the past lie. Today was the day to live.

"Well, my goodness..." She slowed for the driveway ahead and gazed at the new archway.

"That's neat!" Aaron said.

"Your grandfather mentioned they'd had a new entry built. Oh, Aaron, look at the roses carved in it." Roses had always been a symbol of the ranch. Her father had an enormous greenhouse where he experimented with cultivating them. Roses, history and his family were Jasper Tyson's passions.

A swift glance around revealed that nothing else had changed since the short two-day visit home she and Aaron had made a year and a half earlier—only the second visit in the five years they'd lived in Phoenix. There was a deep wood on one side of the driveway and Herefords feeding in the pasture on the other. Far out in the pasture the rocker arm of an oil well pumped slowly. The oil boom at the turn of the century had provided the base upon which the family had built its later fortunes in retail trade stores. Now the Tysons owned two of the largest, most prestigious western wear, tack and gift stores in the world, which also marketed its goods through a glossy paper catalog.

A glance to Aaron showed his face alight with anticipation, and Rachel's heart was touched with the same emotion. In that instant she knew for certain she was doing the right thing. Oh, how glad she was to be coming home!

The road curved around a group of trees, and the house came into view. Cold surprise and dismay sliced into Rachel's happy eagerness, for there, right in the middle of the driveway in front of the house, were Ace and her father grappling with each other in the manner of angry king crabs locked in battle. And sandwiched between them was the one person she hadn't counted on seeing right off—Dallas.

Rachel jammed on the brakes. Tires slid and gravel crunched. Her mother's startled face swung around to stare at her, and the three big men came to an instantaneous halt. Both the older men's faces were flushed red, their hands clenched into fists. Ace had hold of her father's collar; Jasper's big fist stopped in midair. Dallas's face was a blur as Rachel skimmed her gaze past him, unable to meet his eyes.

She glanced to Aaron and saw a confused and uncertain expression on his face. He knew of the hostility between his two grandfathers, had heard the tales of their outrageous behavior on a goodly number of occasions. But this was the first time he'd ever seen them actually fighting.

Anger flared within her. Into their sixties, and these two men carried on like obnoxious five-year-olds! And right in front of their grandson on his homecoming day!

For what seemed a long and silent ten seconds, no one moved. Then, seeing her mother start forward, an expression of composure on her face, Rachel turned off the key and took a deep breath, determined to follow her mother's lead and smooth over the troubled waters. She bit back her ire, promising herself both Ace and Jasper would hear of it later.

She cast Aaron an encouraging look. "We're here, sweetie," she said, and opened the car door.

While Ace and Jasper hastily swiped at their disheveled hair and called eagerly to Aaron, Rachel and her mother embraced. "Oh, it's so good to see you."

"You, too." Even as Rachel greeted her mother and noticed, as she always did, how small her mother's shoulders felt, she was singularly aware of Dallas. She focused on him over her mother's shoulder and found him staring at her.

A solitary, odd thought struck her. *His eyes, they're still the same.*

Then her attention shifted to Aaron. He was returning his grandfathers' greetings and trying to spread his attention to both men equally.

"Daddy?" she called, forcing Jasper to turn his attention. She opened her arms and moved forward.

"How's my girl?" The sweetly familiar feeling of her father's fleshy, strong muscles and scent engulfed her as he hugged her right off her feet.

"Fine, Daddy. Just fine." It felt so very good to be touching him. They pulled back and smiled broadly at each other.

Then there were greetings and hugs with Ace, and lastly with Dallas. She didn't have time to think of wanting to speak to him or to touch him. In their fleeting embrace and mutual hellos, Rachel felt his hard shoulder muscles and caught a whiff of familiar cologne and tobacco. She sensed his uncertainty, which mirrored her own, as if they were doing something not quite right. She didn't meet his eyes.

The glances her father and Ace gave her were those of two boys who'd been caught smoking out behind the barn. Ace adjusted his hat; Jasper straightened his string tie. Rachel met their sheepish gazes sternly but kept her voice and manner congenial.

While pleasantries were exchanged with Rachel and Aaron about their trip from Phoenix, Dallas stepped aside and lit up a panatela. Covertly he studied Rachel. He hadn't missed the flash of fury that had crossed her face when she'd arrived and found Ace and Jasper trading punches, but none showed now. Either it was gone or deliberately set aside. And she'd betrayed no emotion at all on seeing him. Why should she? he asked himself caustically.

Her large black eyes dominated her pale face. Silver discs dangled from her ears and caught the bright sunlight as they moved with her head and the breeze. Her silky, dark hair remained long, falling in a single braid down her back. A bulky sweater of bright colors on a black background reached her hips, hiding her shape, while tight-fitting denims hugged her slim thighs. Soft leather moccasins were tied up to her knees. They were elaborately decorated with beads, work she'd most likely done herself. He'd heard she'd become quite an artist with such work.

And she still had that smile he remembered. One that came slowly, almost secretly, as if she savored amusement first within herself before revealing it on her lips or in her eyes.

She was the same and yet different. Before, she'd been a girl. Now she was a woman possessed of a certain poise and assurance...and graceful movements to captivate a man's attention. A slow heat stirred within Dallas.

"Open that trailer!" Ace called, drawing his attention. The time had come to show his grandson his precious gift.

For an unguarded instant Dallas's gaze flew to meet Rachel's. Concern flared in her eyes. He felt the connection with her, without words or touch, just as they used to. At the same self-conscious moment, they both broke the contact.

Dallas moved into the trailer to bring out the colt, while his father and Aaron waited eagerly. Seeing the rapt glee on his nephew's face, Dallas recalled the first colt he'd had as his very own, and warm pleasure stole over him.

Rachel slipped her arm through her father's and leaned close. He smiled at her, then fastened his frown back on Ace Cordell. This was hard for her father, she knew. Many years ago her father had suffered the acceptance that he'd never have other than her—a daughter, not a son to carry on the family name. And she was his only daughter, Aaron his only grandson. This, she thought, was the reason he clung so tenaciously, a lion protecting his territory. It had been so very hard on him when she'd defied his wishes and had married Coy, the son of his sworn enemy.

The colt was a young yearling paint, a beautiful white and chocolate color with snow-white mane and tail. Aaron oohed and aahed and gave a smile wider than the Red River at flood season. At first concerned because the colt was obviously high-spirited, Rachel relaxed when she watched Dallas remain in firm control of the animal.

"When can I ride him?" Aaron asked, his voice high with excitement as he stroked the animal's neck.

"Oh . . . not yet, son." Ace draped an arm around the boy's neck, and beside Rachel, Jasper tensed. "You're going to have to work with him, train him."

"Me? Train him?"

"Sure, you. I'll show you how."

Rachel saw the light in Ace's dark eyes, and her heart tugged. She knew he missed Coy, his second-born son, his favorite, if the truth be told. She understood and sympathized with her father there beside her, but couldn't ignore and not understand what Aaron meant to Ace, as well. As always she was squeezed between the rock and the hard place.

"I think we need to get Rachel and Aaron inside for something to eat and some rest," her mother interjected in her soft but clearly audible voice. "They've come a very long way."

"Yes . . . I could certainly do with a cup of coffee and a place to put my feet up." Rachel cast her mother a grateful glance.

"And I have a surprise for you, too, Aaron, boy!" her father boomed. "Let's get a soft drink and head out back."

Aaron cast the colt a reluctant look. "Do I get to keep him here, Papa?" he asked Ace.

Ace shook his head. "I'll keep him over at the ranch, and you'll come every day to work with him. That way we can work together."

Rachel had known it. It was Ace's way of making certain Aaron would come regularly to the Cordell ranch. He had to feel in control of the situation, couldn't trust that Rachel would see Aaron got there as often as possible—without coercion.

"It's best, sweetie," she said, searching for words to soften the blow. "Papa and Dallas can help you a lot, then."

"And I got several horses here you can ride now, fella," Jasper said. It was Ace's turn to frown. "We'll let you pick one out tonight."

Aaron's face lightened, and he nodded. When he moved with Dallas to load the colt into the trailer, Rachel called, "No...Aaron, wait!" She knew well the dangers of feisty colts.

"I've got him, Rachel," Dallas said, drawing her gaze. And then for the third time she found herself looking into his crystal-gray eyes. "I'll show Aaron how it's done."

She stared at him and watched a slow, small smile trace his lips as his teeth clamped upon his thin cigar. His eyes held the kind of look that came unbidden and naturally between two certain people. It had always been there between them—and remained still. She couldn't help the small smile that traced her own lips.

Then she nodded and stepped back. Her mother asked something about their luggage, and she answered automatically.

"I'll send someone up from the barn to unload your car," Jasper said, shifting his feet impatiently. "I want to show Aaron his surprise and the other new things around here."

Rachel heard the comments, but found her attention focused on Dallas and Aaron as they carefully loaded the colt and then shut the trailer doors. Nephew and uncle, two dark heads, two square backs and lean hips.

Dallas was heavier now, his build that of a fully mature man who worked hard with his body. His crisp poplin shirt stretched tight over his shoulders beneath the quilted vest that he wore. He was so much a physical man, and when he moved, it was as if with controlled power. His gentle strength was readily apparent when he squatted on his haunches to peer into Aaron's face and speak. He plucked the thin cigar from his lips, smiled, and his gray eyes sparkled in his deeply tanned face as he told Aaron to be thinking of a name for the horse.

Then Ace was giving Aaron a big hug. "I'm real glad you're here, partner."

Dallas straightened, and Rachel felt him look at her. She very carefully refrained from returning the gaze as she held out her hand for Aaron.

"You coming over later?" Ace asked.

Dallas disappeared around the trailer to get into the driver's side of the pickup.

Rachel nodded. "Yes—before dark."

Ace winked. "We'll be lookin' for you. Yancey and Quinn will be there. And we got a present for you, too, Rach," he said, surprising her by both the statement and affectionate tone. He waved as he opened the truck door and slid into the seat.

Rachel waved back. "We'll be there."

Aaron and her father went on ahead, talking excitedly. Now Aaron's mind was turned from the colt and ahead for what Grandpa J. was promising him.

Rachel linked arms with her mother and breathed deeply. "Oh, it's so good to be home."

Her mother squeezed her hand and smiled, then frowned slightly. "I'm sorry about your father and Ace. Ace simply couldn't wait, and when those two come within spitting distance of each other..."

"Never mind, Mama," Rachel said as they started up the quarry-tiled walk. "Ace looked well."

"He's had some blood pressure problems, and his eyes are giving him trouble."

Rachel nodded. "Quinn mentioned a bit of that when I last spoke to her. Dallas seems the same," she said, turning the conversation to what was really on her mind. Just a natural curiosity, she thought.

"Yes..." her mother answered slowly. Rachel felt her keen appraisal. "He almost married this past fall."

"Almost?" She didn't meet her mother's gaze. Her heartbeat quickened even as she told herself to quit being silly. Dallas was thirty-seven now; he should have married long ago.

Her mother nodded. "Uhmm...to Megan Howard. Maybe you know who she is. Her name was Watson. She graduated a year ahead of you, I believe, and married Tom Howard, but he was killed only a year later in a car wreck. Dallas has been dating her for about two years—still is, I understand."

"But they didn't get married?"

"No." Her mother held the door open. "Megan's grandfather or grandmother—something like that—died a week before the wedding, so it was postponed. I don't know what happened about their marriage, but they still date." She smiled. "You ramble a bit through the house, and I'll go have Willow prepare our coffee."

"Sugar!" Rachel called after her mother. "I'm putting a teaspoon of sugar in now." Her mother returned with a cluck of disapproval.

Rachel walked to the far end of the large hallway that ran the length of the house and gazed out the high, arched windows at the rear across the expanse of lawn. It was brown now, but in summer resembled green carpet. In the distance she saw her father and Aaron at the kennels. A puppy, of course. Aaron bent on his knees and laughed as it licked his face.

Sweet memories of laughing moments like that with her father swirled in her head. Puppies, horses, wide open spaces for a boy to run and play, as she had, were what Aaron had been missing. And the comfort, warmth and intimate stability of the family circle. She must see that he had these things. And how she craved them, as well.

Chapter Two

Rachel walked slowly back up the hallway and into the living room, touching and taking in the familiar. It was the house she'd grown up in. The walls were hung with paintings and handicrafts by several celebrated Indian artists—her mother among them. The colors and textures of the furnishings were of the earth—tans, browns and blues, leathers and woven woolens.

There was the mahogany and upholstered spring rocker-recliner that her great-grandmother had purchased by saving soap wrappers. And a Winchester '73 rifle that had belonged to her grandfather hung upon the wall. And set in amongst the rocks of the ornate fireplace were small, exquisitely formed, rust-colored rose rocks.

The rocks—sandstone formed naturally by wind, heat and rain into the shape of a blooming rose—were unique to this part of the country. These particular ones were a family heirloom, passed down from generation to generation for almost a hundred years. Back in the 1930s, when he'd built this home, her grandfather had felt making the rose rocks part of the fireplace was the most secure way of preserving them.

Rachel paused to run her fingers over one, just as she used to do at least once a day when she'd lived in this house. They were to her a symbol of the continuance of life—and a romantic symbol of everlasting love, for each one had been given to Maggie Cordell, Rachel's own great-great-grandmother, by her husband on every anniversary for fifty-eight years. Over those years Maggie had saved them; not one had been lost, even to this day.

Touching them now, Rachel felt the magical allure she'd experienced since childhood. And she realized she'd come home as much for herself as for her son. She'd felt something left behind, undone. Almost as if it was time to begin again weaving the threads of her life. Something that could only be done here.

"Your stones." Her mother's voice startled her, and Rachel turned to see her standing in the archway to the dining room. Beside her was a lovely, slender young woman who held a silver tray and smiled shyly.

"This is Willow," her mother said. "She's our housekeeper and general lifesaver now that Lindy has decided to work only half days. Willow, this is our daughter."

Rachel smiled at the girl, who she guessed was of Plains Indian extraction. "Hello, Willow. We're about to make your job at least two times harder."

The young woman's smile widened, and she stumbled out a polite "Nice to meet you," then carried the tray on out to the sun room.

Rachel's mother stepped to Rachel's side, saying, "You've loved those stones since your daddy told you their history—embellishing a lot, I might add. You were barely three years old, and I never could understand how you could remember the story at that age, much less comprehend it. And you worried the life out of me because you insisted on climbing up to touch each one."

"You wore my bottom out for it a number of times, as I remember," Rachel said. They clasped hands and sauntered through to the sun room. "And Daddy wouldn't be Daddy if he didn't exaggerate."

In the sun room Mira's artistic talent was again displayed on the painted clay tiles scattered among the plain of the covered patio. The scenes were Indian—horses, pottery, mother and child. Such artwork had begun for Mira as a hobby and developed into a fine craft, which she marketed in a number of stores in the Southwest besides their own. Mira was also known for her exquisite needle and beadwork, talents she'd passed along to Rachel, who was gradually becoming known for her arts in her own right.

"I emptied yours and Aaron's rooms of everything except the beds," her mother said, pouring coffee from the silver pot. "That way you two can arrange your furniture any way you want when it arrives. We'll put the beds out in the storage barn then—and anything else you need to store."

Her mother's face held quiet joy. At forty-nine, she could have been any age from thirty-five on up. Hers was an ageless beauty of peace and love that came from inside and manifested itself on her classic features.

Rachel touched her arm. "Thanks, Mom. I sold most of the furniture but do have quite a few boxes coming of things I simply couldn't part with. Things like the tiles you gave me and my glass-front bookcases. And my dining table." Her mother smiled. She'd been there when Rachel had found the antique oak table at an obscure shop in Tucson.

"But, Mom..." Rachel searched for the words. "Aaron and I may be better off if we get a place of our own quite soon, rather than waiting the six months I'd originally planned on."

"And not live here?" The shadows that crossed her mother's features plucked at Rachel's heart.

"I did mention that possibility before, Mama." Rachel looked down into her cup and then back up at Mira. "One of the reasons I left here before was because of the continual fighting between Daddy and Ace. Mine and Aaron's presence just seems to fan the flames. I don't want it to be that way again. Aaron doesn't need to be the pawn in a tug-of-war.''

Her mother nodded. ''I know, dear.'' She regarded Rachel a long moment. ''But do you really think where you live is going to change that?''

''No,'' Rachel answered after a moment. ''I guess not.''

''What members of a family do is put up with each other's faults and weaknesses—because we *are* family.'' Her mother spoke gently. ''Have faith in Aaron to understand Ace and Jasper and to adapt. He hasn't done so badly thus far.''

''He hasn't been around them constantly.''

''And he won't be now. He'll also be with you and me, his aunt and uncles, school, friends. Don't worry over him, Rachel. Few things in this world are perfect, and yet we humans not only survive, we usually do quite well. Aaron must learn to function in this world of diverse characters.'' She chuckled. ''And if he can learn to deal with his grandfathers, he can deal with anything life has in store.''

Rachel smiled, too. ''That's why I do want him around them. They each can teach him so much. He needs them. He needs the family.''

''And what do you need, Rachel?''

''I need all of you, too,'' she answered quietly.

''Well, we need you both. We've missed you so.'' Her mother's eyes misted, but only for an instant before she blinked and spoke more briskly. ''Your father has announced to all and sundry that his daughter will be working at the main store. And your being here will help take a load off of him, Rachel. Oran runs the store quite competently, but your father still feels the need to oversee. I think he drives Oran round the bend. It's simply because this store here was the family's first, the one *he* worked in and is so close to that he feels he must keep a hand in. Not like the Phoenix store—out of sight, out of mind. He hardly even looks at the balance sheets for it, simply hands them over to Oran. With you here at the main store, maybe he will let up—or at least quit bothering Oran.''

"And bother me, right?" Rachel said with a chuckle.

"Most probably."

"How does Oran feel about me coming to the store?"

"I think he's relieved. He's been handling the art and gift department himself since Jolene quit, and not only is it extra work, it's simply not his forte. I've helped him out on the buying in order to keep stocked. If he's in the least apprehensive about the boss's daughter working under him, so to speak, he hasn't let on." She gave a dry laugh at the idea. "I expect you and Oran will work together fine."

There came the muffled sound of her father's and Aaron's voices, and the two of them rounded the corner of the house. Aaron, laughing and jumping with his puppy, sprinted forward when he saw them.

He opened the glass door and burst into the room. "Look, Mom! He's a heeler—for herding. Grandpa says I can teach him all kinds of things and that he can sleep in my room."

Rachel gazed at the mottled gray, white and tan dog and thought it had to be one of the ugliest she'd ever seen, except for the animal's bright and loving brown eyes. She raised an eyebrow. "Is he housebroken?"

Her father coughed. "Sort of—I've worked with him some."

"He has a ways to go," her mother said dryly.

"I'll clean up after him, Grandma. I will."

"Of course you will, sweetheart." Mira smiled. "Now, let's go into the kitchen and find him a treat."

Rachel and her father were left alone. He bent to kiss her, and she held his hand to her cheek for a moment, before he took the chair beside her.

"I'm sorry, kiddo, about the fracas with Ace before." He leaned forward, arms on his thighs and big hands rubbing together. "But the man has little decent care for others and just gets under my skin worse than a prickly pear. He couldn't wait! He had to come bargin' in, like he was Lord Almighty!''

"Daddy, did you *have* to fight with him?''

Her father's jaw tightened. "I lost my temper. I admit it, and I'm properly ashamed for such violent behavior, to be sure. But I had reason.''

"Reason enough to show such behavior in front of your grandson?''

"He wasn't here when it happened—not when it started, anyway. And I didn't do it on purpose, Rach.''

Rachel regarded him a long second. "Because of Aaron, you and Ace are bound to be thrown together on occasion, vile though the thought may seem. But Aaron will be having school functions he'll want you both to attend and other such things.'' She paused, then said slowly, "I'm not going to ask you to change your feelings, Daddy. I know that happening is as probable as snow in July. But I am going to ask you to do whatever it takes to have peace between you and Ace—at least *appear* peaceful when in front of Aaron.''

"It's not all me, daughter,'' Jasper interrupted. "Ace won't let there be peace. Never has. He's got to have it all his way all the time.''

"I know about Ace, Daddy,'' Rachel said sharply. "I lived in the same house with him for five years.''

Her father looked at her—a look that more condemned than anything else.

She shoved the tendency for self-pity aside. "Daddy,'' she said more softly. "I know Ace is abrasive. But I also know that you can charm the stripes off a snake. If you want to. That's why I'm appealing to you. Because, of the two of you—your red hair aside—you have the more level head. Think of Aaron for a minute. What will it be like if his two grandfathers, the two most important men in his life right now, show blatant hate toward one another? That's why I'm saying that I don't give a cow chip what Ace says or does. I want you to be big enough to overlook it—or at least limit your response to a private meeting with him.''

With a nod her father again rubbed his hands together. "I know what you're saying, daughter.'' He met her gaze. "I know how hard we made it on you and Coy, and if I could change those times I would.'' He took a deep breath and looked away at the tile. "I'll do the best I can.'' His gaze came up. "By that I mean I'll bite my tongue and swallow my pride. But there is a limit, Rachel.'' He stabbed the air with his index finger. "And you knew the situation when you married Coy. I ain't going to suffer Ace Cordell to run all over me—and Aaron wouldn't have a grandfather he could be proud of if I did.''

Rachel knew there was nothing more she could say, nor time to say it, as Aaron and her mother appeared, proudly proclaiming the puppy's name would be Wheeler.

"I like that," Jasper bellowed. "Yep, I think that's as grand a name as you could come up with.'' Giving a wink, he took Rachel's hand into his own.

The sun was far to the west when Rachel and Aaron pulled beneath the arched iron entry that proclaimed the Cordell ranch. For Aaron it was the first time he'd seen the ranch since he was barely five years old. The house and outbuildings could be seen far down the driveway. Winter-brown pasture rolled away in all directions on either side. In the distance to the west was a line of trees.

"Is that the creek?'' Aaron asked, pointing toward the trees. "The one that starts from the spring on Grandpa J.'s ranch?'' He didn't say "our ranch,'' and Rachel wondered if he'd ever be able to fully associate himself with either one of the ranches, split as he was between the two.

She nodded. "Yes, that's Spring Creek. It's been here longer than either of your grandfathers, and will probably be here long after we're all gone.''

"That's what Grandpa J. said once.''

"Oh, he did. What else did he tell you?''

"That it'd watered buffalo and Indians and that there'd been a lot of fighting over it—range war, he said." His voice echoed with the magic of a boy's imagination.

"Uhmm... I imagine your Grandpa J. knows—and makes up a lot, too." She chuckled, and Aaron did, too.

"Hey! Isn't that Uncle Dallas over there?"

"Where?" Rachel slowed.

"Over there... riding."

"Yes... I believe so." Rachel brought the car to a full halt. Dallas waved and rode toward them. Aaron was out of the car in an instant and racing toward the white pipe fencing. Rachel followed more slowly. She heard Dallas call Aaron cowboy and ask what his present had been from his Grandpa Jasper.

"A blue heeler puppy," Aaron answered proudly just as Rachel joined him at the fence.

She gazed up at Dallas, so tall on a huge black horse. He wore a denim jacket lined with sheepskin, and his dark hat sat low across his forehead.

"Sounds like you made out okay for one day, cowboy," Dallas said. He grinned and leaned an arm across the saddle horn.

"Yeah, guess I did."

Dallas pushed his hat back and turned his crystal-gray eyes to Rachel. Neither of them spoke immediately. Rachel thought of what her mother had said about his dating Megan Howard, how they were practically married. Then her gaze fell to his lips, and she recalled, just for an instant, the swift kiss they'd shared once. And only that once. Yet she'd never forgotten it.

"Good to see you made it," he said. His drawl was pronounced, his deep voice smooth as a river flowing over fine silt.

"Of course. Haven't been gone so long I've forgotten the way."

He continued to stare at her.

She inclined her head, indicating his horse. "Shadow is looking fine."

"She's gettin' around pretty good for an old woman—turned twenty this year."

"She's twenty years old?" Aaron's eyes nearly popped from his head.

"Oh, a horse lives a long time." Dallas grinned at Rachel. "And, like women . . . they tend to get better, not older."

Again his eyes rested on her, as if he was trying to find something. Uncomfortable with his scrutiny, she averted her gaze and stepped back.

"We'd better head on up to the house."

He nodded and straightened, gathering the reins. "Dad and the others are waiting up there. I just came out to check a couple of heifers. About time for them to deliver. I'll be up in a few minutes."

"See ya, Uncle Dallas," Aaron called, and waved.

Dallas touched the brim of his hat and turned to ride back to the cattle.

Rachel drove up to the house and stopped the car in front of the large clapboard house that verged on being a mansion. Only then did she realize she'd been gripping the steering wheel until her knuckles shone white.

Emotions whirled within her, reaction from seeing both Dallas and the ranch that she hadn't visited since leaving over five years ago. The first thing she noticed was that the barn Coy had been helping build when he'd been killed was gone. The urgent yells of that day echoed in her ears. Dallas had come running as best he could, bearing Coy draped across his arms, unconscious, blood oozing from his temple. A two-by-ten board they'd been using in making joists for the second floor had fallen and smacked Coy in the head. The doctors had said he'd died almost instantly.

A smooth pasture stretched where the barn frame had been, appearing as if it'd never known a building made by man's hands.

Circling the car, she tossed an arm over Aaron's shoulders and forced a smile when what she wished in that split second was to be at her own home, in bed, the covers over her head. "This was where you were born."

The absurd emotion of that second passed, thank heaven. She stared with him at the house. It'd been built in the thirties and added on to several times since. A wide porch circled three sides. It held only chairs now but in summer was draped with ferns and other potted plants. Both Coy and Aaron had been born in the house, due to the odd circumstances of each of them deciding to enter the world early and on very stormy nights.

"I'm the only kid I know born in a house instead of a hospital," Aaron said.

"Believe me—it wasn't by choice."

The door opened, and a lovely young woman with dark brown hair swinging against her shoulders stepped out onto the porch. "Well, hi!"

"Hello, Quinn."

In an instant Quinn came bounding down the steps and hugged both Rachel and Aaron at once. Then she drew back and, still smiling broadly, took Aaron by the shoulders. "I'm your aunt Quinn, but don't you dare call me aunt. My heavens, but you're tall. Course, most Cordells are. And handsome, too. Bet the girls are all over you at school."

Aaron blushed and scrubbed the ground with the toe of his tennis shoe. "A few."

Quinn raised her eyes to Rachel. "You look fabulous. Phoenix must have agreed with you."

"It did, very much," Rachel said, sharing Quinn's pleasant, warm gaze. "But we're glad to be home. And you look great, too. Hardly a little girl anymore."

"Tell that to Daddy. I'm the baby of the family," she said laughingly to Aaron. "Always will be. Come on in, you two. Stella's made sangria and sweet cakes, and the men will be here any minute."

With Aaron and Quinn going hand in hand before her, Rachel mounted the stairs. Again memory pricked. She and Coy had been married nearly a year before she'd ever stepped foot on the Cordell ranch. Following red-hot passion and going against family and a heritage of a hundred years, they'd eloped. That first year Coy had worked at a variety of jobs before deciding to come home to live and to work for his father. The prodigal son, he'd termed himself, cocksure that Ace would accept him back.

Ace had stood in the doorway they now prepared to enter, filling it, hands on his hips, scowling rather like the wrath of God and scaring Rachel breathless. Coy had given that charming grin of his and said simply, "Hello, Dad. I'd like you to meet my wife." And Ace had taken Coy back into the family, just as Coy had predicted.

Ace Cordell loved each of his children, but there had been a special bond between him and Coy. Because of this bond, Ace had accepted Rachel, and over time Rachel's fear of her father-in-law had been muted by respect and affection. And he'd grown to love her, too, as much as he was able.

"Stella!" Quinn called. "Rachel and Aaron are here."

Immediately the woman who'd been the Cordell housekeeper for twenty years appeared from the kitchen down the hall.

"Good to see you, Miss Rachel. And my goodness, what a fine son! You're as handsome as every other Cordell around here." She gave a very red-faced Aaron a swift hug to her ample bosom, then turned to embrace Rachel.

"I'm glad to see you, too, Stella."

"Yancey's upstairs taking a shower," Quinn said, leading the way through the entry hall and into the long room that ran the length of the house, "and Dallas is out checking his cows. I'm not certain where Daddy got off to, but he told me to hold the fort."

"We ran into Dallas," Rachel said, glancing around the room. "He said he'll be up shortly."

It was an informal living space with fireplace, comfortable leather sofas and chairs, television and stereo, gun racks, bookcases and a long dining table at the far end. Perhaps at first glance it would appear a hodgepodge of things thrown together. But the discerning eye would notice that the dining table and matching chairs were made of solid mahogany, the sofas and recliner were fine-grain leather, the lamps true brass and crystal, the bookcases rich cherry wood, the two large Indian rugs woven of angora goat hair. Indeed everything in the room was of the finest quality available. The polished pine flooring had come from the original homestead, and antique photographs of family members and an Indian territory that only remained in memory graced the walls. The room breathed of substance and heritage—it breathed the essence of the Cordells.

Stella urged two small sweet cakes on Aaron and promised to bring another plate of them before she left for the evening.

"Hasn't changed much," Quinn commented, indicating both Stella and the room, then cutting her eyes to Rachel. "Come here, Aaron, and I'll introduce you to your family." She tugged him over to the wall of photos.

Suddenly pictures flashed through Rachel's mind. Memories of gay laughter and warm moments shared in the room. Then quickly followed the horrible scene of Coy hitting her, knocking her against the bookshelves, then of Coy and Dallas fighting and people pushing into the room to see. The two brothers had smashed one of Ace's prized Indian figurines. It had taken both Ace and Yancey to pull them apart, and oh, Lord, the accusations Coy had spewed from his mouth. Along with the memory came the sensation of a concrete block resting on her chest.

"Hey, Rachel!"

The call brought her pivoting around to see Yancey striding across the hall and into the room toward her. A wide grin on his handsome face, he reached to give her a hard hug. She felt him flinch and draw back, muttering, "Damn!"

Then he grinned. "Sorry, got a couple of cracked ribs I keep forgetting about."

"Oh, Yancey, I'm sorry."

He shrugged and kept on grinning. Rachel grinned back. She'd always liked Yancey Cordell. He was the most easygoing person she'd ever known; she'd never seen him truly angry. And he stood taller and was bigger boned than his father and brother, and every bit as rakishly handsome.

"It's his own fault," Quinn commented. "He refuses to admit he's getting a bit old to be riding hot-blooded bulls and wild broncs."

Yancey shrugged. "By damn, you're beautiful, Rach."

"Thank you. You always were one to spoil me." He and Dallas had both treated her like a queen.

Seeing her son's fascinated eyes resting upon his uncle, Rachel said, "Aaron, this is your uncle Yancey—Bareback Bronc Champion for three years running and All-Round Cowboy for two."

"And ladies' man extraordinaire," Quinn quipped.

Yancey's gaze flew to Aaron. His dark eyes widened with teasing surprise. "This is Aaron? Hot damn! This big kid is the little—" he made a motion with his hands "—that I used to give piggyback rides to."

"Boys do grow," Rachel said dryly.

Eyes dancing, Yancey extended his hand, saying, "Well, I'm glad to see you, Aaron."

Proudly Aaron shook his uncle's hand.

"Got a good grip, son. Maybe I could teach you about riding broncs."

"Oh, no, you don't," Quinn said as she handed Rachel a glass of sangria. "You're not going to get *my* nephew's brains knocked out. One addle-brain in the family is enough."

Yancey cast her a playfully withering glance and sauntered over to the table to pour himself a glass of sangria and snatch up a cake. "Sis," he said, his mouth full, "you've got to take that tuxedo back again."

"What? Again?" Quinn's face appeared to drop to her toes.

Yancey nodded. "I just tried it on, and the slacks would probably do, but I need at least another size larger in the coat."

"This one's the biggest available. And I've checked every store in the city."

"Well, what can I say? This one still doesn't fit."

"Then you're just going to have to take time for a fitting to have your suit made like everyone else."

"If you can get that what's-his-name out here to fit me sometime in the next week, I'll be still for it. Otherwise I'm leaving and won't be back for three weeks."

"Okay...okay. We'll figure out something. It'd be easier if you could have managed to be around for fittings when everyone else got theirs last fall."

"It'd be easier if I could wear my best blue jeans. Tried one of these orange cakes, kid? They're pretty good."

"Maybe you could just not show up," Quinn said ultrasweetly, "and help us out all the way around."

"That idea has merit," he quipped, handing Aaron another tiny sweet cake and taking one for himself.

Quinn frowned, and Rachel chuckled. Yancey hated to dress up for anything, fled it as he would a dose of castor oil. "Show up for what?" she asked.

Quinn flashed a smile. "For his stint as best man. Dallas and Megan Howard are getting married March twentieth."

Rachel had the oddest sensation of wondering whether she'd heard right and knowing she had at the same time. She found she couldn't do other than stare at the younger woman. An icy chill streaked down her spine, and then heat slipped up her throat to her face. "Oh?" she managed, hoping her expression shone with friendly interest.

"Yes." Quinn nodded. "It's great that you and Aaron can be here this time. This is their second try. They were supposed to get married last fall, but Megan's grandmother died, so they postponed. Then Megan got involved with decorating this big, new office-hotel complex up in Kansas City and couldn't get time for a wedding. She's almost finished there now and can take a break—but now the seasons have changed, so the clothes must, too. At least according to Megan.'' She spoke laughingly and with apparent fondness for her future sister-in-law.

"Well...that's really nice,'' Rachel said, finding the words strange. Yancey gazed at her above the rim of his glass with a thoughtful, disconcerting expression.

The sound of footsteps and Ace's voice drew all their eyes to the sliding glass door behind Yancey. Ace slid back the door with force and called out for Aaron. "Where's that boy?''

Then he was in the room and hugging his grandson and greeting Rachel. Her gaze strayed over Ace's shoulder, and she watched Dallas step quietly into the room through the same doorway. She saw him blinking as he adjusted to the dimmer light. The sides of his hair were slicked back and damp, and she remembered how the men always washed up at the sink in the barn. Then his eyes found hers and held for a moment. Her heart hammered. *So, you're getting married.*

Dallas had poured himself a glass of sangria and taken one sip when it was decided they'd all have to trail out to see Aaron's colt and the stable where he was kept. Nothing else would do, of course. Rachel walked ahead between Ace and Quinn, while Yancey lifted Aaron atop his shoulders, grimacing with pain but doing it nonetheless.

Walking alongside them, Dallas remained quiet while the others jabbered excitedly. Aaron had a hundred questions at once. "Is my horse in that stable? How tall are you, Uncle Yancey? How many horses do you have here?'' He reminded Dallas painfully of his father. Aaron's features reflected Coy's, his voice and open manner the same as Coy's at that age.

Dallas found himself thinking of the times he and Coy had sneaked down to Spring Creek, to a small pool where the water gathered and warmed, where they hunted frogs, daddy longlegs, spiders, any creeping thing. "I got one! I got one!" Coy would cry over and over. "Come see!" Dallas was glad for these good memories; they seemed to balance out what had happened between him and Coy in the end.

His gaze strayed to Rachel, and he saw Ace take her arm. "Added on to the stables and cow barn," his father said, pointing and indicating the massive, deceptively placid-looking Black Angus bull. "Dallas sold some of his breeding stock over in Spain the past spring, and there's the daddy who's doing it all."

She turned her head just enough to glance at him, her coffee-brown eyes meeting his for a fraction of a second. It was long enough to make Dallas remember how they'd looked at each other once, years ago.

He tried to keep his eyes off of her but couldn't seem to do it. Any man would have trouble doing it, he told himself, and wondered about her life back in Phoenix. Had she had a man there? Surely she couldn't have remained alone all these years. Absurd jealousy pricked.

They got Aaron's colt from his stall. Yancey showed the boy the fine points of walking the animal, about how the safest place to be was right next to the horse, even bumping up against him, and how Aaron must be careful to make no fast moves to startle him. Horses were skittish of just about everything.

Leaving Aaron and Yancey still fooling with the horse in the last glow of the late-winter light, the four of them walked back toward the house.

"You two go on up," Ace said to him and Quinn. "I want to show Rachel something."

Dallas looked at his father, seeing his flashing black eyes. He knew what the old man was about. Ace Cordell never thought twice about maneuvering people to get what he wanted—and what he wanted was Aaron to live and grow up on the Cordell ranch. He wanted to mold Aaron, just as he'd tried to do to all of his children. But Dallas didn't think Rachel was going to go for it.

"I thought you talked to him," Quinn said at his elbow as they walked back to the house.

"I did," he answered. "Should have saved my breath."

"Maybe she'll do it. It would sure make Daddy happy."

Dallas just shrugged and absently rested a hand on the back of his sister's neck. Rachel was a full-grown woman, he told himself as he watched her walk away with his father. Not the innocent young girl she'd been those years she'd lived here with Coy. She'd been on her own for five years, building a career, raising a son. It followed that she could handle his father. He hoped.

He realized Quinn was saying something to him. "What?"

"We have to get Yancey a fitting for his suit after all. And Megan's mother has decided she wants an ice sculpture at the reception." Her blue eyes regarded him anxiously. "I think this affair is getting much bigger than you wanted."

It was a hell of a thing to admit to himself he'd forgotten all about his coming wedding. He forced a grin. "Don't worry about it, Sis. We'll all have a good time—even Yancey once the girls get a load of him in that suit. You are making certain there'll be plenty of single women, aren't you?"

"I'm trying my best. Got eight so far." She grinned in return. "Oh, yes—I took the liberty earlier of inviting Rachel and Aaron."

"Good...thanks..." He didn't understand the feelings squirming around inside him. "Pour me a glass of whiskey—not that punch stuff," he said to Quinn. "I need to make a quick call to Megan. Thanks, Sis."

He used the telephone in the hall, glancing out the window to see Rachel and his father pass in front of the house as he waited for an answer. His gaze lingered on Rachel's smooth, graceful stride.

Megan's voice came across the line.

"Oh, darling, I'm glad you called," she said. "I meant to call you earlier, but Mother and I just got so involved here." Her voice dropped an octave. "We'll be working for hours more, I'm afraid. I'm sorry."

He'd been going to drive in and spend the night; they hadn't had a night alone in nearly two weeks because of Megan's heavy work schedule. Yet somehow her news didn't affect him.

"Okay," he said. "I need to be here early in the morning anyway. We've got a buyer for one of our bulls coming down from Montana."

After a couple of minutes he hung up. Quinn brought him his drink and he sipped it, thinking rather guiltily that he should feel more disappointed.

Rachel walked along beside Ace down a graveled lane running serenely between two grassy paddocks, with walkways leading to the bunkhouse and a number of guest cottages. Three hands sat in chairs on the dark bunkhouse porch, and one called a lazy greeting, then returned to their quiet conversation.

"I'm sure glad you and Aaron have come home," Ace said.

She looked up at him and smiled. "Me, too." She dared to slip her arm through his and was rewarded by his warm grin. With the sinking of the sun, it was growing quite cool, and she was glad for her heavy sweater.

"Despite it all—you being a Tyson and me being who I am—we've done okay, haven't we, Rach? I've tried to be as fair to you as my own."

She squeezed his arm. "I know, Ace."

"I know you think I spoil Aaron . . . and I guess I do. But he's my only grandson. Coy's son," he said with a sigh and tone that sliced into her heart. "My other sons sure don't seem to be in any hurry to be giving me any more grand-children." He frowned. "Least ways, Yancey *says* he ain't got any. I wonder how that boy can do so much womanizing and not get at least one foal somewhere."

"Oh, I think Yancey is more talk than action, Ace," Rachel said with a chuckle.

"Uh...maybe. Anyways, I know maybe I'm spoiling Aaron a mite, but I'm also trying to give him responsibility right along with it. He'll learn a lot by lookin' after that colt."

"I know he will." She took a breath. "And he'll learn a lot from you, too, Ace. The right things, I hope. If you're willing to try to keep your temper and not be scrapping with my father over little or nothing things. Aaron does *not* need to see you and my dad going at it like you hate each other's guts."

"We do hate each other, Rachel," Ace replied firmly. "It hasn't got nothin' to do with anyone else, so I don't mean you no disrespect."

"Oh, Ace." She stopped, biting back the irritation. "Okay. I've talked to my father, and he's agreed to do all he can to remain peaceable when he meets you. Now, I'm asking you to do the same—and I'm asking you to refrain from making disparaging comments about my father when around Aaron, too. This thing between you and Daddy won't do anything but confuse Aaron. It's hard enough for him growing up without a father. He needs both of you to fill the gap."

Ace nodded and looked into the distance. Then he turned his dark and unreadable gaze toward her. "Me and Jasper are who we are. We can't present a false picture to the boy. But I'll do my best to keep the peace, if Jasper will."

Rachel nodded. She'd gotten all she was going to get from either man.

Ace stopped; his boots crunched on the gravel in the quiet evening air. "I said I had a present for you."

He dug into the pocket of his denims and pulled out something. Taking Rachel's hand, he pressed a shiny, brass key into her palm.

She gazed at it for a second. "What is this?"

Ace took her elbow and turned her a fraction, then pointed to the house at the end of the lane. "That cottage there. It's for you and Aaron. All your own."

Chapter Three

Rachel looked from the key to the white house shaded by a tall cottonwood. It had a long front porch, shutters, and was edged with boxwood shrubs—the perfect refined southern cottage from a country painting. It struck her how little Ace knew her. The house wasn't her style. A silly thing to think, but seemingly very important in that moment.

"I told you when we talked of this before that I would be staying with my parents—at least for the first months."

Why? Why did he do this when he knew she didn't want it?

The key burned into her palm, and anger flared in her chest. Ace Cordell pushed and pushed until he succeeded in getting his way. But he wouldn't—couldn't—have it this time.

"I know, Rach. I know you've missed them. This is for after you've spent a few weeks at the Golden Rose. I know you wouldn't want to move back into the house with us, though heaven knows there's plenty of room. But this house would be yours and Co... Aaron's.''

She caught that he'd almost said hers and Coy's. She stared into his deeply tanned face, and her anger mingled with pity. Coy had been his favored, beloved son. He couldn't let go of him even after all these years. And she'd been Coy's wife—a living link with him.

Slowly she shook her head.

"It was Hull Womac's cottage," Ace said, as if ignoring her, "Dallas's right-hand man. But Hull left, and the new hand to take his place is a single fella and stays with the others in the bunkhouse. I had the cottage fixed up with everything, Rachel—microwave oven, dishwasher. Come look at it."

As if he could buy her.

"No, Ace."

"Aaron is Coy's son." He gestured, and the big silver-and-turquoise ring on his hand caught the waning light. "My son's son. My firstborn grandson. He should be raised here, where I was—where his father was."

"Aaron *is* your grandson," she said. "But he's also my father's and mother's grandson. And there are a few things that you and my father seem to forget. One is my mother. While you two are always captivating Aaron with your obsessive attention, she spends her time soothing ruffled egos and gets little time with *her* grandson. I'm going to see that she has a few months to indulge herself and get to know Aaron. Another is me, Ace." She jabbed at her chest. "Aaron is *my* son—and a person in his own right, too."

"I'm not denying any of that. I'm simply trying to give the boy the best he has coming."

"You're simply trying to buy him and make him over into another Coy. Didn't Coy have enough problems, Ace? Why try to pass them on to Aaron?"

Ace stared down at her. Feeling his intense hatred in that moment, she withered inside. Ace could be so very ugly when denied his way.

"Coy had a right to his suspicions about you and Dallas," he said. "Can you deny that?"

His words hit her like a wet cloth across the cheek. She raised her chin and determined not to feel shame. "He had no right. No. He brought that up out of guilt of his own carousing and carrying on with other women. You know it, and I know it, and now it's said, so don't ever bring it up again. Aaron is Coy's son, and I don't ever want him questioning that."

Ace looked off into the distance of Spring Creek. His jawline tightened. "I know Aaron is Coy's son. There is no doubt in my mind about that. And that is why I want him raised here." He returned his black eyes to her. "Think about it, Rachel. The house would give you the freedom you need. I wouldn't impose on you—however you chose to live. I just want Aaron near."

"No." She shook her head, sad he couldn't understand that what he wanted was not only impossible but so terribly wrong—for all of them. What a blow to a man used to making the world revolve the way he wanted. Shaking inwardly, she pressed the key into his hand and turned to walk swiftly toward the main house.

Tears stung her eyes. Why did she have to feel so damn responsible for everyone's happiness? Especially Ace's. He was a demanding, arrogant man who gave and refused love as it suited him. Why did she care about his feelings at all?

Perhaps because he seemed so lonely within himself. She pitied him. And she'd always been weaker than he, swayed by the force of his powerful personality—a pattern she couldn't afford now.

What he wanted, she simply couldn't do. It wouldn't be to Aaron's good to live here, so close under Ace's dominant influence. And she couldn't bear to live here again, she thought as she gazed up at the house where lights shone dimly from inside. Ace's influence and memories of Coy would reach out to strangle her. And Dallas would be married, bringing his wife here to live, as was the Cordell tradition.

She stopped at the car to get a tissue and was leaning against the fender, blowing her nose when the front door of the house opened. Startled, she glanced up to see Dallas step quietly from the house. He closed the door softly behind him and came down the stairs toward her. She recognized then the sound of his footsteps. There'd been a time when, in this very house, she'd hear him walking along the upstairs hallway, would know it was him by the relaxed and soft cadence of his steps.

He stopped close in front of her, stared down at her. She stared up at him. His pale gray eyes were dark in the dim light.

"You weren't thrilled with Ace's present," he said.

"Hardly." She gave a hoarse chuckle and looked away to the tissue in her hand. The way she plucked at it with her slim fingers tore at his heart.

"Dad's a big boy. He'll get over it."

"I know." She sighed. "He just keeps on hammering away at whatever he wants, and it's wearing on a person." She looked up at him then. "He mentioned this a month ago on the telephone when I told him Aaron and I were moving back. I told him then that we wouldn't live here. I even wrote it in a letter. But he acts as if I've never said a word."

"It's what makes him so successful. He never gives up on what he wants."

"No matter what it does to other people?"

Dallas nodded. "It isn't that he wants to hurt anyone. I don't think he thinks of that at all. He truly believes he's right in whatever he goes after." He paused, then said, "He can't seem to let go of Coy."

"I know," she said in a hoarse voice. She gazed at the ground and shook her head. "I can't do it, Dallas." She lifted her anxious gaze to him. "It wouldn't be good for Aaron, nor fair to my parents—nor to me, either. And especially Mom. She should have some time with Aaron.

Ace and Daddy are always stealing the show with him. It's time Mom had him to herself a bit. That's the main reason I'm staying at the Golden Rose instead of getting our own place right off. For Mom."

"Hey, I'm not disputing the fact with you, Rach."

The nearby pole lamp came on. Her face was exceedingly pale and drawn in its light. Her black lashes were so long, they appeared to brush her cheek. The urge to draw her to him, to comfort her and feel her rub that cheek against his chest swept him. He remained standing where he was, arms hanging at his sides, knowing the danger in following that urge. She was his brother's wife; he was promised to Megan.

"He's not right in this," she said, as if having to defend herself. He guessed she'd had a reason to feel that way for a long time around this place.

"No, he's not." He shifted to lean his hip against the car. "Just remember that—and what you want—and you'll win out."

Again she gave a hoarse chuckle. "Has anyone ever won out against Ace Cordell?"

"Yes. A lot of people. It's just that Dad never lets on that he's ever lost."

She smiled then, and it radiated to him. They stared a long time at each other. He didn't know what she was thinking, but he was remembering the way she used to laugh at little things—blowing leaves, a big-eyed calf, Tom and Jerry cartoons. And he remembered the sweetness of her kiss that one time, too. It wasn't so much the kiss, which had been a fleeting thing, just the touching of their lips. But what he recalled vividly was the way she'd lifted her face to him, slowly, in total innocence, simply following the natural force that drew them together in that moment.

"You've grown up," he said.

She nodded. "I've had help from a growing boy."

"You have a great deal to be proud of in Aaron."

"I think so. What I like best about Aaron is that he's a nice person. Not goody-goody or perfect—just nice."

He nodded, stuffed his fingers in his tight pockets and looked downward. Rachel scanned his profile, touched on his temple where small hairs curved over his ear, his smooth cheeks, the dark hairs that curled against his shirt collar. He was a ruggedly handsome man. And he was nice, too.

"I hear congratulations are in order," she said. It was a reminder to herself, as well.

He raised an eyebrow. "Yeah..." He seemed uncomfortable.

"I'm very happy for you, Dallas. She must be someone special for you to abandon bachelorhood after all these years."

He gave a dry chuckle. "I hope I haven't waited too long—you know, old dog and new tricks and all." Then, much in the manner of Aaron, he rubbed the toe of his black boot across the ground. "She is—Megan—she's pretty special."

"Ace must be very happy."

"Oh, he is that. He's been after me for years, wanting to increase his grandchild stock, you know."

They both paused, and finally Rachel said, "Quinn mentioned something about Megan being an interior decorator. Her own business?" It was something to say, a polite question to fill the gap.

He nodded. "Hers and her mother's. They're getting contracts from as far away as St. Louis and Las Vegas now."

Again an awkward silence swept them. Rachel would have liked to ask questions like, Do you truly love her? Do you talk of having children with her? But of course those were absurd questions never to be asked.

Instead she said, "I'd better get Aaron home. We've both had a long day." Suddenly she felt bone weary.

* * *

An hour later Rachel kissed Aaron good-night and walked slowly down the hall to her own room. She was again taking up the spacious bedroom she'd had as a child.

She closed the door with a sense of relief and stood looking at the lone bed with the lamp suspended above the headboard. At last she was alone and could rest. She leisurely peeled off her clothes and tossed them across one of her opened suitcases. After donning a lacy flannel gown, she sat cross-legged on the bed to brush her hair.

She intended to sleep until noon tomorrow, something she hadn't done in probably eight years—or longer. Normally she loved mornings, was fond of getting up and watching the sun rise. Oh, how Coy had hated this habit. He hadn't liked to get up in the morning and had preferred she remain in bed with him.

She'd been easily swayed to Coy's wants, she thought as she raked the brush through her long strands of hair in slow, relaxing strokes. He'd had, like his father, a way of getting people to do what he wanted. Or had she simply been weaker than he? She'd never been certain about this. Over the years she'd come to realize that she had within her the urge to please. Some people condemned this trait as a weakness, but as she'd grown to know herself, Rachel had decided that wanting to please others was a good thing, even a strong trait—if done for the right reasons.

Dallas filled her thoughts. He'd always liked mornings. There'd never been a time that she'd risen and not found him already up and having been out at morning chores. He loved ranching—loved the earth, the animals, the constant battling to wring from nature all she would give and to give back to her, as well. Rachel had often thought that the reason he'd never married was that he was already married to the Cordell Ranch.

She thought of the first time she'd laid eyes upon Dallas Cordell. He'd been standing in the bright sun in the park-

ing lot of the T and B Grocery, his hair blowing in the high
breeze, the most engaging grin on his face.

"So, this is the girl who turned my brother's head," he'd
said, his eyes sparkling with amusement, his voice uncom-
monly deep and smooth. "Welcome, Rachel Tyson Cordell. I wish I'd been at your wedding—glad we finally get to
meet." He'd taken both of her hands into his.

And with that very first contact, she'd experienced the
sense that he was someone she'd known forever.

That had been twelve years ago, years that seemed now
like a lifetime. And back then Coy and Dallas had been very
close. They'd had the same mother, Ace's first wife, who
had died when Coy was only three, Dallas seven. As a result the boys had grown up with a special bond. Dallas had
been plainly delighted when Coy returned to live and work
the ranch, the three of them, Ace, Dallas and Coy together.

But gradually, over that first year, dissension had set in
between the brothers. Coy had grown restless. Perhaps,
Rachel suspected then and now, he hadn't been ready to
marry as early as they had. He'd been a person given to
passionate impulses, only to find he'd made a mistake or
simply grown bored with his choice. He'd both shirked the
responsibility of the ranch, going away for days at a time,
and then railed at Dallas and Ace for controlling the whole
show, as he put it, and not allowing him enough command.
Ace had voluntarily stepped aside and given the ranch to
both brothers to run, but the problem wasn't solved. Coy
had then turned his full resentment on Dallas.

He'd felt trapped, she knew. Trapped at the ranch,
trapped by her, and then strangled when she'd borne him a
child. And yet he'd refused any suggestion of divorce or
moving away from the ranch.

He'd turned to drinking, and the reports that filtered back
to her of his romantic escapades had cut her self-worth in
half. For many years after his death she'd wondered what
had been wrong with her that her husband could not be
content.

Whenever she remembered those hard years, a lump would gather in her throat. The pain of humiliation and loneliness had been an almost physical thing. She'd pledged herself to Coy before God—and against her father's wishes. To up and leave him would seem like a complete failure. And she couldn't bear the thought of taking Aaron away from his father and grandfather. She'd tried to hold on, had told herself that things would get better.

She'd desperately needed a friend in her loneliness, and Dallas had offered her that. It had come so naturally to them. His smiles and gentle teasing had been a salve to her heart after her husband's cruel frowns and cutting remarks. At times, Lord forgive her, she'd felt that she'd married the wrong brother, that it should have been she and Dallas who'd joined their lives.

She'd leaned on Dallas too much. She'd turned to him with her love, which her husband had thrown back in her face.

The brothers' verbal arguments broke out into physical fights, one in particular over her. She couldn't remember now what had made Coy angry the afternoon he'd smacked her across the face in the living room, sending her sprawling back across the couch. It wasn't the first time he'd hit her—but it was the first time he'd ever done it in front of anyone. A number of people, for it had been during one of the many barbecues Ace used to like to throw. That fateful day nearly seventy guests had been at the ranch.

Dallas had sprung at Coy, grabbed him by the shirt and thrown him up against the bookcases. "Don't you ever hit her again!"

"She's my wife, brother! Or have you forgotten that?" Coy sneered, his face only inches from Dallas's. He'd been perfectly aware of the people squeezing their heads through the door to witness the conflict. "You may dally with her out in the barn or while you two are out ridin' on your precious pasture, but by law she's my wife, and I can do what I like!"

What happened next came to memory now only as dis-torted shadows. There'd been punching, glass breaking in the doors to the bookcases, and obscene shouts, and then Ace and Yancey and another man pulling the two brothers apart at last, while Rachel could do nothing more than watch the scene and listen in shame and horror.

Ace turned on her with his black eyes silently accusing. "Get yourself upstairs!" he ordered, degrading her fur-ther.

As she mounted the stairs with leaden feet, she heard Dallas say, "You ever hit her again and I'll kill you!"

Two weeks later Coy had died while working alone with Dallas. There'd been wild gossip and cruel suspicions by a number of people. Rachel had known none of the wild talk was true; Dallas would never have hurt Coy in such a way. And innocently or not, she'd been so much a part of all that had happened. She'd simply had to get away and try to sort out the emotional trauma that threatened to drown her.

And she'd had to get away from her desire for Dallas, for any relationship between them was impossible.

But the magnetic pull between them had not lessened. Not in all the five years.

A cold tingling traveled up her spine at the thought, and she realized she'd been sitting quite still for some time. A voice within answered, cautioning that it was not so—it couldn't be so. That she was imagining such feelings.

But she *knew* it was so.

She dropped the hairbrush to the floor and got up to turn out the light.

There was nothing to be done about it, she thought as she slipped beneath the covers. It was simply a fact, just as it had been years ago. She didn't know whether the attraction between herself and Dallas would have ever developed if she and Coy had had a good marriage. That was something she would never know.

She'd considered Dallas in her decision to return. She'd wanted to see him and find out if any feeling remained be-tween them. She hadn't thought any further than that—

certainly not about what she would do if feelings did remain.

Do? Why there was nothing to do.

Dallas was Coy's brother and a Cordell. She had been not only Coy's wife, but a Tyson. And Dallas was to be married in a matter of weeks. So there. That was the situation. He had his life to live—she had hers.

That she and Dallas were bound to meet often was a certainty, and Rachel was perfectly prepared for this. Dallas was Aaron's uncle, a member of the family with whom her life was woven—nothing more, nothing less.

But what she hadn't been prepared for on this, her second visit to the Cordell ranch two days later, was to meet Megan Howard. And until that instant, she hadn't known that she did *not* want to meet her.

As she pulled the station wagon to a halt behind a gleaming white convertible Cadillac in the circular driveway, she saw Dallas and a beautiful woman she knew instantly had to be Megan descending the front steps.

"Hi, Uncle Dallas!" Aaron called as he eagerly leaped from the car and ran forward.

"Hi there, cowboy!"

The distinct pleasure that crossed Dallas's face touched her heart. How glad she was for her son to have such an uncle. Her gaze moved to the woman beside him, and she brought herself up short. *You have no right to coveting emotions, Rachel Cordell—nor to hurt.* And she wouldn't, couldn't ever let such emotions show.

"We're a bit earlier than we told Ace." She smiled at the woman holding on to Dallas's arm, then looked at Dallas, though focused her gaze on his nose, not his eyes.

"You can never be too early for Dad. He doesn't give an inch with age. He was up at five and has already been riding," Dallas replied dryly. "He thinks if you sleep until seven, you're a loafer. He said something about going to work Aaron's colt a few minutes ago."

"Really?" Aaron swung around. "Mom?" He already had a sneaker poised to go.

"Yes . . . go ahead." She watched her son sprint off toward the horse barn like a jackrabbit, and then she turned to politely greet the woman holding on to Dallas's arm. Though she didn't meet his gaze, she could feel it upon her—as she'd always been able to do.

"He most certainly is a Cordell," the woman said with a chuckle. "All they think of is cows, horses and ranching. Even Quinn, at times. You must be Rachel. I'm Megan." Her voice was friendly and melodious, her smile bright. She extended a very white and lovely hand toward Rachel. The slim gold bracelets on her wrists tinkled faintly as they shook hands.

"Very glad to meet you." Rachel returned her smile; it would be impossible not to. "And yes, that was my son, Aaron, who couldn't wait for polite introductions. My congratulations to you on your upcoming marriage."

She had to look upward to where Megan and Dallas remained standing on the second stair. Megan was a beautiful woman—pale blond, naturally, if Rachel were to bet, and natural curls, too. Her eyes were sky-blue, her makeup as perfect as a model's. Everything about Megan Howard said class, elegance, perfection. She was indeed special. A rock-hard knot formed in Rachel's stomach.

"Thank you. I know Ace and all the family are thrilled that you and Aaron will be able to attend." Megan flashed that bright, beautiful smile again.

"We wouldn't miss it," Rachel replied politely, then glanced at Dallas, meeting his eyes fully before remembering to concentrate on his nose.

"You and Aaron about settled in over at the Golden Rose?" As Dallas spoke, he took in Rachel's shiny black hair caught in a leather band at the neck and left to cascade over her shoulder near to her waist. Again she wore a soft, full-flowing sweater, tight, revealing denims and tall moccasins.

"Yes," she said, nodding. At last her gaze strayed to meet his. It was unreadable. "It wasn't hard with so many helping hands." A bare smile tipped her lips, and he shared it.

"I'm sorry to cut this short, darling," Megan said, tugging on his elbow, recalling his attention, "but I mustn't be late for the luncheon."

Dallas sent Rachel a look of apology as he descended the final step. "Good to see you, Rachel. Stella has fresh coffee made, if you'd like to go in and visit. I know she'd love it."

"Yes . . . I'd enjoy that, too."

"Nice to have met you, Rachel," Megan said while slipping gracefully into the car seat, Dallas holding the door. "I'm sure we'll see more of each other."

"Yes . . . I'm sure we will."

Dallas slammed the door. Rachel automatically returned Megan's smile and wave, then turned to mount the stairs. She felt Dallas's gaze upon her but refused to look at him. She, Rachel Cordell, did not gaze longingly at other women's men.

She heard the car tires crunch on the gravel as she entered the house, and took a deep breath. Why in the world did she feel such pain? Such stupid, unreasonable pain? It wasn't like she and Dallas had ever had a relationship. They'd had nothing more than friendship. And kindness. Dallas had shared with her his kindness. That was all; anything more had been only a whisper in her heart—and that had been many years ago. Why did she feel she was losing him now?

"Stella," she called, and headed for the kitchen, intent on putting aside the foolish thoughts.

Stella extended a hearty and bustling welcome, insisting Rachel sit at the table and talk while she continued to put the finishing touches on elaborate cookies she was making for the wedding.

However Rachel did much more listening than talking. Stella was about the fastest southern talker that Rachel had

ever heard. In the space of a few minutes she learned that
Ace was "feeling his oats once more" after a bad night—he
had those often these days—that Yancey had given the tai-
lor fits—deliberately and all for fun—and that Quinn was
at the moment off in the city checking on why the invita-
tions for the wedding weren't ready and searching for
someone to do Wanda Jean, Megan's mother, an ice sculpture in the shape of a spewing fountain.

"Neither Miss Megan nor her mother have time to deal
with such things as this wedding, so it's our Quinn's doin',"
Stella said with obvious disapproval. Her place in the family was not that of a quiet servant, but more one of a dow-
ager aunt, and she assumed the role unabashedly.

She pointed the knife with pink icing on its tip at Rachel.
"And then I get roped into it all—like these cookies. Our
Quinn just had to have my specially decorated almond delights—and for several hundred people." She clucked her
tongue. "Our Quinn wants to do this, mind you—but that
doesn't mean that the rest of us do."

"And you can't deny Quinn," Rachel observed, amused.
Stella had come to the house when Quinn was a pre-
schooler and treated her like a precious granddaughter.

"I'm learning to, mind you." Stella raised both eyebrows and bobbed her head. "She wanted me to bake the
bride and groom a cake, and I refused. I don't care if I can
do it better than anyone else—won the celebration cake division at the state fair now four years runnin'—but I'm not
all that eager for this wedding, and I'm not agonna bake a
cake for it."

To Rachel's immense surprise, Stella again waved the
knife. "I don't care for Megan Howard—and don't look so
shocked." She pursed her lips. "I've held my peace, mostly
because maybe it's not my business. But that woman is not
for our Dallas. You met her outside now, didn't you? What
did you think?"

"Well...she seemed a very nice person. She's—"

"She smiled at you, didn't she?" Stella interrupted, making a smile seem criminal.

"Yes. And she has a lovely smile."

"She sure has. She uses that smile to get what she wants. She *knows* how to get what she wants." She beat the bowl of pale green icing with a vengeance.

"Stella, what you're implying makes Dallas sound stupid," Rachel said. Stella's head snapped upward. "You know he's no fool. He wouldn't care for the woman if she weren't a fine, caring person."

"Uhmph. Well, I know..." she conceded. "No, Dallas is no fool." Again she pointed the knife, this time with green icing. "And there's those who've tried him over the years. A man with his looks and money has plenty of women chasing after him, mind you. It's just that he deserves better than Miss Megan. She doesn't care for him enough. Doesn't care for what he's interested in. She's all wrapped up in her career." She gave the word "career" the same connotation she had "smile." "She puts her life and career above Dallas's, and that ain't the way a person loves another."

"Dallas is a man to know what he wants," Rachel said firmly. This she was certain of; Dallas had always known where he was in life, had known who he was and what he wanted.

"Uhmm...maybe." Stella whipped a spoon into the white icing. "Or maybe he's just given up on getting what he wants and is settling on second best."

She didn't look up from the bowl, and Rachel wondered exactly what she meant, but didn't ask. She'd just as soon let the discussion of Dallas's love life drop.

"Can I help you put those cookies in the box?" she asked.

"You sure can, honey. I've got fifteen dozen already in the freezer. This batch ought to do it." She squeezed Rachel's hand. "It's sure good to have our Rachel and Aaron back again." She winked. "Do you think our Aaron could stay the night tonight? It'd make ol' Ace awfully happy.''

"Oh, I suppose so, Stella," she said, snatching at the idea. She felt the ridiculous need to make up to Ace somehow for disappointing him the other night. "If you let me be the one to tell Ace—and receive his joy." She winked and lifted one of Stella's almond delights into her mouth. "I'll go find the two of them now."

Dallas pressed the accelerator and guided the Cadillac out onto the interstate heading into Oklahoma City. Traffic was unusually heavy for some reason, and he kept to the slower right lane.

"Can you go a bit faster, sweetheart?" Megan said. "I really can't afford to be late for this luncheon."

"They won't condemn you for five minutes, Meg."

"It's the impression. These people have a lot of firms lining up for the job of re-dressing their hotels. They can pick and choose—and I want our firm to be in the running." She smoothed at her white wool skirt. "I want us to get this job."

"I thought you had enough to keep you busy for the next year." Dallas watched the side mirror for a break in the traffic.

"If Mama and I get this account, we'll expand. The Webster Hotels will mean we've made it—and good." She shot him a smile, an avid gleam lighting her blue eyes.

He returned his gaze to the road and felt a sour spot in his stomach. Megan had ambition, and there was nothing wrong with that. She was capable, talented.

But even as he repeated these things to himself, he felt irritation. He was a man, with a man's need to feel important to his woman. Sometimes he got the distinct feeling that if she had to choose between her decorating business and him, the business would win. He imagined most women at this late date would be dwelling on their approaching wedding, be all wrapped up in the plans. But Megan's thoughts were riveted on this Webster Hotel job—not with tying her life to his or their first night as man and wife.

It was a distinct blow to the ego, he thought, chiding himself. He was a bit old for such. And it wasn't like they hadn't been sleeping together in the past year and a half. Their wedding night would present no romantic surprises. The fact laid heavy on him. He'd rather like a romantic wedding night.

He was sounding like a little kid! He *was* important to her. Just as she was important to him. He'd felt a kinship with her from the moment they'd first met two years ago. Megan was easy for him to be with, rarely put any demands on him. She enjoyed his company; he enjoyed hers. They liked the same music and disliked the same television shows and movies. She laughed easily and often and was wonderful in bed, though they'd never been what he'd term hot and heavy there. They were just comfortable together. She was a good friend, and he loved her.

A jangling sounded deep inside him when he thought of this. He *did* love her, didn't he? Damn, what a time to be questioning that! The jitters, his friend, Clyde Jennings, had said. Clyde had promised that even the rock-steady Dallas Cordell would get the jitters.

Well, if this was the jitters, he sure as hell didn't care for them.

He saw his chance and eased the Cadillac out into the faster lane. They'd make the luncheon at the Skirvin in time, he thought. That would please Megan. She probably had the jitters, too, because she'd definitely been a bit irritable herself lately.

He ran a finger around his starched collar and wished he was back at the ranch.

Rachel was there.

She'd looked pale and too thin, but beautiful still. He wondered whether he'd ever cease to be struck by her long, gleaming hair. He liked long hair on a woman. It was a turn-on to run his hands through, to take a brush to.

He'd done that once with Rachel. One night when he'd found her on the back porch brushing her hair. She'd been pregnant with Aaron then, and he'd had no right to the feelings he'd begun to have for her. Four strokes he'd made through her hair before handing her back the brush.

They needed to talk, he thought. Maybe they'd never said anything all those years ago, but he knew she'd understood his feelings. No, they'd never talked about it, because that would have been an even greater sin against Coy—and everyone else. So she'd left, and Dallas had always wondered whether she'd run away because of him. And now he felt the strain between them and knew it wasn't easy on her. They needed to get things said and put behind them.

"You're awfully quiet," Megan said. "A penny for your thoughts."

Dallas chuckled and kept his eyes on the road. "About our wedding." It was close enough. He pulled a cigar from his coat pocket. "Have you decided where you want to go on our honeymoon—St. Thomas or Cancun? Or have you thought of another choice?"

"Quinn's checking on the dates for getting us into a good hotel at both of those places and Cozumel, too. There's a wonderful resort on St. Thomas, but I'm afraid I should have looked into it much earlier. I've just been so busy. Wherever Quinn can get a first-class hotel is where we'll go. How long do you think you can stay away?"

"Two weeks, probably."

"No more than that for me, darling. Especially if we get this Webster Hotels job. We'll go into high gear then."

High gear? What was she in now?

Stop it! Stop behaving like an adolescent.

Yet something within him shouted that he'd bypassed adolescence somewhere along the way and wanted it now.

"Rachel is quite a beautiful woman," Megan said. "And her Aaron is a darling. Looks quite like the rest of the Cordell men."

"Coy looked a lot like that when he was that age."

"Is it hard on Ace—seeing a reflection of Coy?"

Dallas shrugged. "I think so. But even without Aaron, he won't forget Coy." No, his father wouldn't forget—nor forgive.

"He apparently doesn't realize that Rachel is not his daughter-in-law anymore, either. Not really. I wonder what he'll do when she decides to marry again." Dallas glanced over sharply and met her gaze. "She is a beautiful young woman," Megan pointed out. "I'm surprised she's still single. She must have loved your brother very much."

"She did." Dallas knew this. And more than love for Coy, Rachel was a woman who didn't take commitment lightly. She'd remained with his brother long after many a woman would have cut out.

He took the exit for downtown and silently cursed the congested road. Wasn't it only a few short years ago that the city had seem so deserted? Now it was beginning to get the increased traffic of most cities.

"Oh, look!" Megan pointed excitedly. "There's Mother up ahead of us. And we're not going to be late. Oh, thank you, sweetheart, for bringing me." She touched his arm and winked. "You're so handsome. The people of the Webster Hotels will see I have great taste by the man I'm with."

She laughed lightly. Gazing into her beautiful face, Dallas wondered why he felt lower than a sinkhole.

Chapter Four

Dallas was in Hoving, at the bank with Yancey, talking with Clyde Jennings, when he saw Rachel and Aaron through the plate-glass window. They were walking along the sidewalk on the other side of Main Street and entered Bennie's, the local pizza and hamburger place and favored after-school hangout for kids.

With only a moment's hesitation, Dallas excused himself from the conversation, telling Yancey he'd meet him later down at Royce Motors, where Yancey needed to go for a truck part. He strode across the wide street, telling himself he didn't need to be doing what he was doing.

He was only going to talk to her—that was all! There was nothing wrong with having a friendly conversation with an old friend and member of the family.

The bell on the old wooden-and-glass door jingled as he opened it. Rachel was sitting in one of the padded red booths along the wall; she glanced up, and a slow smile traced her lips.

"Hello," he said as he approached.

"Hi, Uncle Dallas!" Aaron squirmed over. "Sit down with us."

"Hi, Dallas." Rachel's voice was soft and warmly inviting.

"I don't think I've been in here in ten years," he said, slipping beside Aaron.

"Mom said this was where she and Dad used to hang out," Aaron said. "Did you, too?"

"I sure did. Used to play pool on those tables back there."

"Those same ones?"

"One of them is the same."

Aaron chuckled. "Pool tables must live a long time—like horses."

Dallas gave him a playful slug in the arm. Over soft drinks they talked of the school, and Aaron told of going to meet his teacher and seeing his classroom. He appeared greatly impressed with the three computers in class. After a bit Dallas gave Aaron five dollars to go off into the back room to play video games.

"Five dollars!" Aaron exclaimed. "All right!" And he scampered away.

He should be ashamed of such bribery, he thought, but he wasn't. Gazing across into Rachel's deep, dark eyes, he couldn't be anything other than glad for the few minutes of semiprivacy. There was no one in either of the adjoining booths; Gayle up at the counter was eyeing them curiously, but couldn't hear them speaking.

"Seems he's going to like the school here," Dallas said.

Rachel nodded and sought to still the nervous quivering in her stomach. "His teacher's young and very much in tune with her students. I think it helps that she's quite pretty." Dallas's slow smile brought a flush of joy to her heart.

"Does he do okay—in school?"

"Yes . . . A's and B's mostly. He doesn't like the confinement, though. He'd rather be outside, active."

"A normal boy."

Her quivering stomach relaxed as the self-conscious tension between them seemed to ebb. No one was staring at them, she told herself as Dallas asked about Aaron's likes and dislikes and she answered. She didn't even know anyone in Bennie's anymore. Somehow the subject changed, and Rachel found herself talking about Phoenix, of its beauty and heat and growing population.

"Was the move hard for you?" Dallas asked, his voice characteristically deep and soft.

"A bit," she answered slowly, sensing an intimacy swirl between them. "We had friends, a comfortable house, a grocery store where I could easily find the toothpicks and matches. But I wanted to come home."

He stared steadily at her. "Did you leave anyone behind?"

"No..." She glanced down at her glass. "No one." She kept her voice light. "There's not much time for socializing between work and raising a son alone."

Asking her whether there'd been a man in her life wasn't that intimate or earthshaking, she told herself as she lifted her glass to her lips. It was a natural question, a friendly one. Then she found herself staring into his luminous gray eyes again.

"I missed you when you went away," he said in a low, vibrant tone.

For several seconds she couldn't speak. She knew what she wanted to say but struggled with saying it.

"I missed you, too," she said at last, and felt a great weight lifted from her chest. It was the closest she'd ever come to telling him how she'd felt about him.

Their gazes held, and watching the smile inch across his lips brought a grin up and out from her heart.

"Rachel."

Her father's voice boomed out, jerking her attention to the doorway. He was frowning as he lumbered forward. He gave Dallas a terse nod. "Afternoon," he said, then turned his gaze back to Rachel. "I'm finished at the feed store and got your mother's prescription. Are you and Aaron ready to go?'' He shifted his gaze to the back, glancing around for Aaron.

"Aaron's playing video games, Daddy. Why don't you sit with us and wait for him?"

She knew very well her father was miffed at finding her sitting with Dallas. And he wouldn't care to be sitting at the same table with one of the Cordell boys, as he always referred to them. But Rachel decided it was time she quit humoring her father's ridiculous prejudices.

His gaze flickered from her to Dallas, then back again. His disapproving frown deepened. "I'll just go back and have Aaron show me about these video game things. Holler when you're ready to leave."

As he walked away, embarrassment burned within Rachel. She stared at the glass in front of her and fingered the beads of moisture on it. She felt Dallas's gaze, and after a moment raised her eyes.

He gave a dry grin.

"I guess trying to change their minds is like trying to spit into the wind," she said, referring to both of their fathers. "I'm sorry—Dad was terribly rude. He's not really like that, Dallas. He's good and kind—"

"You don't owe me an explanation, Rach. I've grown up with it, too."

She smiled wanly, knowing it was true.

"I'd better say goodbye now, before Jasper grinds his teeth to dust." He rose. "Yancey's waiting for me, anyway. Be seein' you and Aaron."

"Yes," she said, almost in a whisper. Then added, on impulse, "Thanks for stopping, Dallas. It's nice to see a friendly face."

"You bet." He touched the brim of his hat and turned away.

She watched his tall, lean form disappear out the door and called to mind that his wedding was only weeks away. Minutes later her father joined her.

"You and Dallas seem mighty friendly these days," he said.

"I should hope so," she replied quickly. "He's Aaron's uncle—and a friend."

She met his gaze, and he stared at her for long seconds before saying, "He's getting married."

"I know—and I'm very happy for him."

Another stare, then he said, "Aaron's a real ace on those machines. Maybe I'll get one of those for the house. I kinda like them."

Yancey was at the parts counter of Royce Motors, flirting with Ginny Royce, when Dallas entered. For a few minutes Dallas enjoyed watching Yancey enjoy himself, then they left. Yancey was driving, and Dallas leaned his head back and closed his eyes as his brother stepped heavily on the accelerator and sent him pressing into the soft leather of the Lincoln's seat cushions.

Whatever it was—an energy, an awareness, a vibration—something he couldn't put into words still remained strongly between himself and Rachel. It was the sort of awareness especial to certain males and females, the whys and wherefores never fully understood or explained by anyone on earth. It simply happened.

It was nothing new to him, of course. At thirty-seven he'd experienced it more times than he could count, ever since the fourth grade, when he began to truly appreciate the opposite sex. It had happened at school, at bars, at social functions, sometimes fleetingly with a stranger on the street. He had it with Megan.

But not nearly so strongly as with Rachel.

With Rachel it was as if he heard her heartbeat—and she heard his.

Was it because she was forbidden fruit? Was that all it was? He hated the thought for the cheapness it invoked.

He thought of how he wanted to see her again, of places he could see her—the Tyson store, when she came to bring

Aaron to the ranch, chance meetings like today's. Immediately he censured himself for such thoughts. They were dangerous, stupid. *Stupid!*

What was wrong with him? He'd never thought of himself as the kind of man who would have such thoughts. He was engaged, for heaven's sake!

It came to him then that Yancey was speaking to him. "...take it up to Sterns and have them take care of it."

"What?"

"The front end..." Yancey inclined his head toward the hood of the Lincoln. "It needs alignment."

"Yeah...we'll get to it next week."

Yancey glanced at him, then back at the road. After another long silence he said, "I'm cutting out of here tomorrow, but I'll keep in touch—and I'll be sure to be back here for the wedding."

Dallas looked over at him. "You could consider sticking around, little brother. Dad doesn't say much, but he hasn't been feeling very good lately. His blood pressure's up."

Yancey shook his head and gave a small, hoarse laugh. "I doubt if Dad notices whether I'm here or not—unless he has a horse he's havin' trouble handling."

Dallas was surprised by his brother's words and bitter tone. "Dad notices when you're gone—which is most of the time, I might add."

"Look...I'm not the oldest son—or Coy, who was his favorite, something we all know. And I'm not the youngest daughter. I'm the foal Ace had by a woman who was supposed to be a quick affair."

This was all too true, circumstances that had scarred Yancey but that he'd seemed to learn to accept, at least most of the time. He and Dallas had talked about it, in bits and pieces through the years. Dallas guessed he'd thought that his brother had outgrown the hurt but saw now that Yancey had simply succeeded in hiding it. He looked for words to help his younger brother.

"Ace is proud of you, Yancey. He shows everyone your trophies and news clippings. He just isn't the best at letting a person know his feelings."

Yancey gave his characteristic shrug, the one that said to hell with it. "He does okay in letting people know his feelings—especially when he's mad." He raised an eyebrow. "I know you're closing in on forty and all that..." He was changing the subject he found uncomfortably personal, and Dallas let it go, too.

"Thanks a lot, little brother. I got three years to go, yet."

"Close enough. But no reason to feel like you gotta get married, *big* brother. You sure you've given this thing enough thought?"

Dallas shook his head with dry amusement. It was no secret between them that Yancey wasn't exactly taken with Megan—or Megan with Yancey. "I think two years would be considered enough time for thinking in anyone's book. And it's me marrying Megan, Yance, not you."

"Well...that's so, but I still think it's not too late to re-think everything. Things have changed. Rachel's home now. Maybe you should do some more considering."

Anger stiffened his spine. "What Coy said years back wasn't true."

"I know that, Dal." Yancey glanced at him quickly, then returned his gaze to the road. "We all know that and have never thought any different. But I also know you and Rachel always did get along well—and she's a mighty pretty woman. Another mare entering the pasture, you know, and you should check out all the ones available before choosing." He grinned his best Yancey grin.

Dallas had to smile in return. Everything with Yancey was put in horse terms. "I'll agree to that, little brother. But I wouldn't say Rachel's exactly available. I can't quite see myself courting my brother's wife."

"His widow," Yancey corrected quietly. "Rachel is a widow. And last I heard, widows were highly available."

Dallas didn't reply. Yancey's statement seemed to burn into his mind for a brief moment, then flicker away, as if not daring to remain.

On Monday of the following week, Aaron started school. Normally a bus would pick him up at the end of the drive-way, but for his first day his grandmother would take him. It had been Rachel's idea for her mother to drive Aaron, and her mother had been so dearly surprised and delighted. But gazing at her son now, Rachel was suffering an attack of separation anxiety.

"You're sure you have everything?" She inclined her head toward his bag. "Paper, pencils...that erasable pen..."

Aaron nodded with impatience. "Yeah, Mom. I packed it all last night—and you checked it then. Remember?"

"You know the phone numbers if you need anything?"

"Yes."

"Rachel," her mother said, "would you like to come along?"

"No...no." She smiled and leaned over to hug her mother. "You two better get going or you'll be late."

"We've been ready, Mom. You're the one holding us up."

"Then get along."

"We'll go for a good ride when you get home, Aaron." Her father winked.

"See ya, Grandad. Willow." Aaron flashed them all a smile, then wrapped an arm around her waist for a quick hug.

Rachel stood in the front door with her father and called goodbye to them. She felt distinctly forlorn. She was send-ing her son off to be in the care all day long of people she knew very little. She wanted to cry.

"You should've let me go along with them," her father said.

That made Rachel smile. "Oh, Daddy. Let Mom have some time with Aaron by herself."

He rested a big hand at the back of her neck. "I know—I hog the show." He grinned at her. "Join me in a second cup of coffee?"

She cocked her head. "What I'd really like is to take a ride before I head into the city. It's been so long since I've been able to do that. And this morning is perfect for it."

He cast her a look of total understanding. "I'll call out to the barn and have Nick saddle up Cara, the mare Aaron's been riding. She'll be easy for you."

Standing on tiptoe, Rachel quickly kissed her father's cheek, then left him smiling broadly.

She'd had the idea to ride upon waking and had dressed for it in denims, two warm sweaters and boots. It would be the first time she'd been completely alone since returning home.

It was somewhat surprising to be able to mount and ride off on the mare with ease. Though she and Aaron had been riding a number of times at a stable out in Phoenix, she was definitely rusty. In a matter of minutes she had Cara loping away from the confines of the buildings and paddocks and out into the clear pasture. Cara rode easily, just as her father had promised.

The sun was a gold ball in the east, the morning air refreshing. She concentrated on the beauty around her and tried not to think of Aaron. Children went to school every day. She'd met his teacher and liked her. The school was highly rated in the state. It was absolutely idiotic to cry, and yet tears streamed down her face. Mother worries—she'd have them all her life, she thought with a sob and a chuckle.

And there was something else, too. Someone else lingering on her mind and weighing heavily on her heart. Dallas. As she gazed at the blackjack oaks and bluestem grass waving in the morning breeze, she had to think of him.

She blinked and wiped away the tears. This was his world, and no doubt he was right now out there somewhere beneath the same sun that she was. She'd turned Cara south toward the Cordell ranch even before she'd realized doing it. And she admitted a longing in her heart. Perhaps she would see him, fantastic and outlandish idea that it was.

Rachel Cordell, she admonished herself, you've hit thirty and are going round the bend. She took a deep breath and focused for a moment on the rhythm of the loping horse. The last week had been such a strain. She was tired, and her emotions were battered. Things would settle down now.

She couldn't deny to herself any longer that one very important reason for returning home had been to see Dallas again. She'd had to find out if the feelings she'd held for him had been true, or simply an escape from her troubled marriage. She now knew those feelings had been very true. She'd found that answer the moment her gaze had met his.

But what did it matter? It was silly, foolish, impossible. She was his sister-in-law. And a Tyson. And he had found a woman to love, to be his wife. As it should be.

Still she rode southeast until she reached the fence separating the two ranches. She could go no farther and reined the hard-breathing mare to a stop.

At least fifty black cows ranged the grassy rolling hills in the near distance. Rachel ran an absent gaze over them, giving herself time to catch her breath just as the horse was. Then suddenly she saw a rider approaching, having come from a copse of trees over where Spring Creek flowed.

Dallas? Whoever it was had obviously spotted her, was coming over to speak to her. Of course it couldn't be Dallas. The chances for that were too slim. Yet this was his ranch, and he did favor checking his stock on horseback every morning.

Oh, my Lord. It was Dallas! Oh, my sweet heaven . . .

Her heart pounded as he neared; she recognized his form and the way he sat his black horse. His dark hat was set low and tight on his head. She couldn't see his eyes in the shadow of the brim, but she felt their gaze. She waited, telling herself it would be rude to turn away. Anticipation and anxiety warred within her spirit.

"Good morning!" He called out to her while still fifty feet away.

"Good morning." She answered his smile with one of her own.

He reined his horse to a stop just on the other side of the fence, swept his hat from his head and raked his fingers through his thick, burnished brown hair. A lock of it fell across his forehead. His eyes reflected the pale blue of the morning sky and sparkled with pleasure.

Oh, I'm glad to see you, too, Dallas.

"So, how's the big morning going?" he asked. "Aaron's first day at school, isn't it? And supposedly his mother's first full day at work."

"Mom took Aaron to school. I halfway wanted to— halfway didn't. It's a lot like when he started kindergarten. I feel sort of lost."

His eyes were warm and studying as he casually leaned forward on his saddle horn. Birds twittered loudly from the nearby cottonwood; the cool breeze caressed her face. They were totally, utterly alone. A longing to pour out her fears and doubts swept her, but she pushed it firmly away.

"This your first chance to ride?" He noted the guarded expression that crossed her face and disliked it. They'd felt things and thought things and hidden things since they'd first known each other. He was damn tired of it.

She nodded, and a secret smile touched her lips. "It's one of the privileges of being the owner's daughter. I can make my own hours, and no one can say anything about it—at least to my face."

Her light chuckle was good to hear. Then her dark eyes widened when he moved to dismount.

"You got a few extra minutes, Rach? I'd like to talk."

The surprise on her face he'd expected. But there was something else there, for only an instant. Something that resembled pleasure, before it was carefully hidden.

She nodded. "A few more minutes won't matter one way or the other." Leather creaked as she swung gracefully to the ground.

He left his horse and squeezed carefully through the barbed wire of the fence, then stood facing her. As he discreetly looked at her gentle swells and curves beneath her bulky sweater and slim-fitting denims, he wondered how to begin and even exactly what it was he needed to say.

Dallas's blue-gray eyes were intent upon hers. How much she wanted to press a hand to the sharp plain of his cheek, but instead held tight to the mare's reins. It was touching to see him, a strong man, fearless against a two-thousand-pound bull, now tongue-tied, things dammed up in his heart and unable to pour out. She wanted to help him, to speak to him, too. But much of what she'd like to say was forbidden to her. Her desires could only bring him hurt—could hurt all the family.

She tethered the horse to the fence post, more because of wanting to do something with her hands than anything else. Again she lifted her gaze to his.

He cleared his throat. "I almost called you out in Phoenix, more than once," he said, and shifted his stance. "Then I thought it was probably better if I left you alone. But I've wanted you to know, Rach, I'm sorry... about what happened with Coy. I tried that day. I tried like hell to catch that board." His last sentence came out a ragged whisper, and pain etched his features.

"Oh, Dallas, I know that. I don't blame you." *Had he been carrying such a burden all these years?* "I've never blamed you. It was an accident." She laid her hand upon his arm and wished to erase the agony written on his face.

They'd all been in shock for days after Coy's death. She recalled how Dallas had appeared a dead man walking around. She'd wanted to speak to him, but there'd never been a private moment. And after what Coy had accused them both of, she'd felt it better to keep her distance. She didn't want to make things worse between him and Ace or to incite wild talk. And she'd thought then that Dallas preferred and needed his solitude.

He nodded and rubbed his forehead. "An accident. A damn, stupid accident. And like most of them, it could have been avoided." He vehemently stabbed his chest. "*I* should have known better, Rach. I shouldn't have allowed Coy to be helping with the work that day. I knew he'd been drinking. Hell, his hands shook so much he kept dropping nails and smashed his finger near to a pulp with the hammer before he felt it. I was just so damn mad at him. Mad at what he was doing to himself, to Dad, to his son... and to you."

"It wasn't your fault. If there's any blame to be laid, it's on Coy himself." The horror of that day slashed fresh into her chest. She dropped her voice. "It's taken a while, but I've come to understand a few things. We're all imperfect creatures in an imperfect world, and we all do the best we can. And when it comes down to it, I think Coy was doing the best he could. He certainly didn't set out to hurt any of us—or himself."

She looked down to the grass, watching it wave around his ankle.

Dallas shook his head as he remembered his brother. He stared at Rachel's shining black hair and saw Coy's. His brother had been a handsome man. Dallas had loved him so much. And though painful, it was also a relief to talk to someone else who'd loved him, too. Quinn and Yancey had loved Coy perhaps, but not like Dallas had—or Ace. And he couldn't talk to Ace.

"No," he said. "Coy wasn't one to wish harm to anyone—except when he started that drinking." He shook his head and clenched his hands. "When I saw him hit you that day, all I could think about was punching his face in. I was so mad. Mad because he hit you, Rach, yes, but the truth of it was that I was furious with him for screwin' up the relationship he and I had. It'd been so good—and then he'd gone and changed. My little brother had turned into someone I didn't know or even like. And he'd left me—gone away somehow, somewhere." Even now he felt the abandonment.

"He still loved you, Dallas. You were his brother."

He looked out across the land with clouded eyes. "I keep asking myself if there was some way I could have helped him."

"I know," she said simply. "I do, too. But I'd done everything I knew. I'd tried to stand by him, and maybe that had been wrong. But there's no way to go back and undo—for any of us."

"When he was a kid, he used to tag after me, and every time he got a scrape, I was there to put a bandage on it." He thought back with pensive amusement. "Once I carried him piggyback for almost a mile because he'd gotten this big, two-inch thorn in his foot and blood oozed out around it. He hated the sight of blood."

"He sure did. He fainted in the delivery room when Aaron was born." Their eyes met, and for an instant they shared the warm memories.

"I try to remember the good times with him." He thought for a moment and then chuckled. "Like that day he brought you home and told Dad he'd come home to stay—with his wife, the former Rachel Tyson. I thought for a minute there Dad was going to strangle on his tongue. Coy had a hell of a lot of nerve and style when he set his mind to it." It was good to recall times before the changes came upon his brother.

"I shook so bad that day, I could hardly walk." She chuckled, too. "Coy held my hand and didn't let go."

"He loved you, Rach." He thought about the way she must have felt, knowing about the other women his brother had romanced—and in the end hadn't tried to hide. *Coy, what in the world happened to you?*

She looked away at the pasture and didn't speak. A sad, wistful expression played upon her face.

Dallas laid his hand upon her shoulder and lifted her chin with his thumb. He felt her heartbeat beneath his palm. She smelled of sweet flowers...roses...and warm sunshine. Her face was creamy white, her eyes brown as buckeye seeds and filled with concern. The urge to protect her, look after her swelled within him once again—as it had those years ago.

"Did you go away because of me?" he asked. "Because of what was happening between us? What Coy accused us of?"

She gazed at him a long moment before answering. "That was a big reason." She let out a long breath. Dallas's heart squeezed. "We . . . I had been turning toward you. I wanted to even more after Coy died. We couldn't do that, and I didn't want *anyone* to think what Coy had said was true. I didn't want yours or Aaron's names tainted—or to hurt the family. And I just had to get away." She pinched her eyes closed, then opened them. "Ace and Daddy were suffocating me. I just had to get away to get myself straightened out."

He wondered whether she cared for him still. But there was no asking such a question. He didn't think he could handle knowing either way.

"Dad wanted to take Aaron from you," he said.

"Yes," she whispered, and stared at his shirt. He knew Jasper and Mira hadn't known, and had wondered how she'd managed to bear the burden of such a threat alone.

"He went to his lawyer and prepared to file suit." Her eyes flew upward to meet his. "Yancey and I tried to change his mind when we found out. We even threatened to leave the ranch." He chuckled dryly and looked away at the wide stretch of blue sky, remembering. "I think he would have let us go—but when Quinn threatened the same thing, he backed down."

"Oh, thank you, Dallas." Her hand came up to rest on his wrist. Tears glistened in her dark eyes.

"Were you happy these last years, Rach?" He searched her face with his eyes and stroked the soft skin of her neck with his thumb.

She gave a small smile. "Reasonably so. Selfish though it sounds, I liked having Aaron all to myself. I could pour my love into him—and his love seemed to make up for what a mess I'd made with Coy." Anguish clutched her fine, delicate features. "I loved Coy so much, Dallas. Once."

"I know."

He stared at her, and a wanting engulfed him. He stood there with her, alone, feeling her leaning toward him, though she didn't move at all.

And then, his gaze straying to her lips, he bent and kissed her. It was an action without conscious thought. He wanted to give comfort and receive it—to simply make contact with her.

His lips brushed hers lightly, warmly, sweetly. Then he lifted his head a bare two inches, and she gazed into his eyes made crystal by the bright sunlight. The breeze tugged at his hair and caressed her cheek.

"Thanks for talking about him with me, Rach." He dropped his hand.

Rachel knew she should step backward but felt held in place by emotions swirling inside her. She nodded. "Thanks for all you've done for me, Dal. You were a friend when I so desperately needed one. And you were one for Coy, too."

Gratitude? Was that all she felt? No . . .

She did step backward then. "I have to be getting back."

He nodded and moved toward the fence. He untied her reins and handed them to her, then held the mare while she mounted.

"Dallas . . . I wish you happiness."

He smiled tenderly, and his luminous gray eyes rested on hers. "Wasn't it Lincoln who said a man is about as happy as he makes up his mind to be?" Then he stepped away to squeeze back through the fence.

With a jerk of the reins, Rachel turned the mare and urged her into a canter in the one direction from which she'd come. She didn't really see, for her mind lingered on the man she'd left behind.

A man who could never be hers. He couldn't even truly be a friend. People and circumstances wouldn't allow it.

Chapter Five

Dallas's sweet kiss seemed to echo on her lips. To haunt and taunt her. Fleeting—a kiss of hello and goodbye to a friend.

Accept it, she told herself. It was reality, could not be changed. It was best. And as it should be. Dallas had someone to love; he was happy. She was happy for him. It would do no good to wish for what might have been if things were different. Things *weren't* different.

So lost in her thoughts and efforts to deal with her heartache, Rachel didn't see her father until he galloped up beside her and called to her.

"Rachel!"

Startled, she took in everything at once—her location some distance from the fence and in a low pasture, her father's big buckskin gelding breathing hard and champing at the bit, her father's expression of fury as he cut in front of her and forced her to rein in hard. The mare responded, then pranced skittishly.

Staring at her father, she instantly knew he'd witnessed her meeting with Dallas.

"Did you plan it?" he asked cryptically. "Was he out here waiting for you all the time?"

How could he think such a thing? "Were you spying on me?"

"Anyone within a radius of a quarter mile could have seen you kissing your own brother-in-law!"

"If you were so curious, you should have come closer to see it better. Maybe then you'd have seen it was far from a clandestine, passionate kiss."

"Don't talk to your father in such a fashion!"

"Then don't talk to your daughter in such a fashion!"

They glared at each other for long seconds.

"I came out to give you company on your ride home," her father said in a dry, haughty tone. "I see you didn't require my company."

"I *happened* to run into Dallas. He was checking on his stock." She turned her head so he wouldn't see her trembling lips. Why did she have to explain such to her own father? Why did he want her to feel that speaking with Dallas was something shameful? Was he ashamed of her?

The kiss. He'd seen the kiss. Her heart sank with disappointment that anyone had witnessed their private moment. A moment only their own—and one her father would misinterpret.

"I'm not blind, daughter. I wasn't blind five years ago, either. I've seen the way you two look at each other—and so's your mother." His gravelly voice rang with angry condemnation, and Rachel thought they probably could have heard him in China.

She drew herself up straight and met his fiery eyes. "We've done nothing to be ashamed of. Never. I can't deny that I care for Dallas. He's been a very good friend to me. But I have never done anything *wrong*!"

He stared at her a moment, then let out a long breath. His shoulder slumped. "Ah, Rachel. I know that, damn it!" He rubbed his chin. "I just . . . I just don't want somethin' happenin' to run you off again," he said, contrite worry lacing his voice. "You were a good wife to Coy—a no-good son of a bitch."

"Daddy, don't talk that way about him!" Anger sputtered like sparks from a fresh-lit fuse. "He was my husband, Aaron's father."

"So he was—but you had enough unhappiness with that Coy Cordell to last a lifetime. Don't you think I saw the bruises long before Dallas saw him a hittin' on ya? I saw them, by God! And I wanted to kill that husband of yours. I heard the shameful stories about him, too. You think it wasn't hard for me to face people at the club—or even church with your mother? And I hold Ace to blame for not taking that young hellion into hand. He was either stupid or blind when it came to Coy. Why in the hell you stayed with him, I'll never know. You should have come home. You hear me? You should have come home!"

His voice rang out over the hills again, and Rachel saw the relief it was to him to finally speak what he'd held inside for five long years. And it was hard for a man like him to hold his tongue, but he'd done it because he'd been afraid of hurting her.

She saw the love within his anger. "Daddy," she said softly, "you always taught me to stick to my commitments. I'd pledged my life to Coy. I . . . I might have left him if things had kept on the way they were, but I had to keep trying for a while longer." She sent him a pointed look. "And you never would let go of telling me how wrong I'd been. I couldn't stand hearing that over and over." Softer, she added, "And I loved him, Daddy."

"I know you did, daughter," he said with a sigh. "I know. And a damn Cordell at that." He stretched his legs tight in the stirrups. "What about Dallas? Do you love him, too?" Again the condemnation.

She stared at him, battling the truth in her heart. *She couldn't love him.*

"There's nothing for me and Dallas, Daddy. He's Aaron's uncle and a special friend to me. He always will be."

He gazed at her and shook his head. "I don't want you to be gettin' hurt again, Rach. God in heaven knows I don't want that. I admit, I respect Dallas. Guess he's the best of the lot, but still, he's a Cordell—and Coy's brother, for God's sake." Again his eyes blazed. "And those Cordells never bring anything but trouble. I wish we could be well shut of them."

"Well, we can't. Like it or not, our families are joined. As much by yours and Ace's hate as by my son."

She squeezed her legs against the mare and clucked her into motion, heading home. Her father came up beside her and moved ahead.

"Get that old girl to movin', Rach."

He laughed and sent his horse into a full gallop. Rachel followed immediately. But even the elation of riding across the land, the wind blowing her hair, couldn't take away the heaviness on her spirit.

Dallas found himself drifting off all morning long. After riding back to the barn, he found himself there but couldn't remember the ride in between. He went to the infirmary and stood there a good five minutes before he remembered he'd come to prepare the cattle injection gun for Pete.

While gazing at the daily ledger on the computer screen, he found memories haunting him, as did thoughts of Rachel. He kept seeing the wisps of her dark hair blowing across her pale face. He felt a bit guilty for kissing her—even though it'd hardly been a lover's kiss. He hoped she hadn't misinterpreted it. He hadn't meant to insult her. Lord, he didn't know what he'd meant.

He lunched with his father, who noticed his preoccupation. "Thinkin' about this marrying business, son?" The old man seemed amused.

"There's a lot to do before I can leave," Dallas said.

His father nodded and gazed at him. "Whatever don't get done, me and Yancey'll handle. He'll stay around this ranch a bit if I have to hobble him." He raised an eyebrow. "Have you convinced Megan to come live here at the house after your honeymoon?"

"She can't be that far away from her office during the week, Dad. She'd spend half her time driving back and forth. She'll be here on the weekends."

"You sure as hell can't be off into that town house of hers very often and still run this ranch. Her in the city, you out here. How the hell are you two goin' t' give me any grandkids that way?"

The old man meant it exactly as it sounded. His main concern was for a grandchild, not for Dallas's marriage. Dallas knew his father well, and usually didn't let such things bother him, but this time the comment grated on his nerves.

"Sorry, but I hadn't thought of getting married for the sole purpose of giving you a grandchild," he said dryly.

"Well, you been sleepin' with Megan for two years now— why in the hell get married if not to have kids?"

"Why did *you* get married—three times?"

"Humph...that's the way it was done in my day. Couldn't just be sleepin' with a woman—at least not for long and not get called to account for it. And I wanted my children." He stuck out his chin. "And I want grandchildren, too. Nothin' wrong with that. Coy knew the importance of family and children. Brought his wife here to live like he should."

From out of the blue came Coy's name. This was something usual with the old man, too. And as always, Dallas felt his father's faint accusation. His father had never said it, and Dallas tried to tell himself it was all his imagination, but he sensed the old man blamed him for Coy's death, as well as for losing his grandson Aaron. He stared at his iced tea and fingered the beads of moisture on the glass.

"Megan is wantin' children, ain't she?" his father asked.

Dallas glanced up. "I think that's mine and Megan's business, Dad."

His father stared at him a long second. "Guess you're right. My home. You're my son. But ain't none of it my business." He pushed his chair back, got up and strode out of the room. His boots echoed on the hardwood flooring.

Dallas took his glass of tea and walked to the open window to look out at the backyard. His gaze fell on the rope swing suspended from the big, old elm. All of them had played on it as kids—Aaron often played there now. His stomach knotted.

Megan wanted children, later. They both had agreed they had time. He hadn't really cared one way or the other until he'd seen Aaron. Something about seeing his brother's son had brought on a longing for a child of his own. And the fact was that he wasn't getting any younger.

He thought about his father's question: just why was he getting married?

The reasons came to mind—he wanted to share his life with a woman, with Megan, because he loved her. That he wanted the roots of his own family, and because he was damn tired of being alone. All were viable reasons.

And yet somehow the doubts were settling upon him again. He wondered whether he truly loved Megan—and felt too damn confused to know *what* he felt.

During the following weeks Rachel's work at the store helped to provide a distraction for her mind and heart and brought a much-welcomed sense of continuity and stability into her life. Monday through Friday she got to the store before ten, had lunch at one, if she had one at all, and left around seven.

She took complete charge of the store's gift and art department, just as she had in their store in Phoenix. The woman who'd managed it previously had left abruptly without notice, and in the months since, the head manager of both stores had been trying to handle the job. Oran looked on Rachel as a godsend who saved him from drowning in something for which he had little understanding. His world was one of figures, debits and credits and stock on hand—not colors and textures and artistic appeal.

A number of mornings Rachel took a ride after getting Aaron off to school on the bus, though she did not again venture anywhere near Cordell land. And every morning she met her father's suspicious gaze. It was this gaze as much as anything else that sent her on the ride. It annoyed her no end that he treated her like a child, one about to err at any moment.

She thought about looking for her own place, but was far too busy putting in nine to ten hours a day down at the store. And it brought her such pleasure to see her mother and Aaron finally getting a great deal of time together.

Each of them—her mother, father, Ace and herself—showed Aaron the land and surrounding area. From her mother and father he learned the history of the tribe and family. From Ace he learned a mixture of the then and now of Cordell Ranch and family enterprises, Ace taking him for an afternoon into the oil company's offices. Of course, then her father had to take him into the store for an entire evening.

When there was time, Rachel showed him pieces of her childhood and once took him to see Coy's grave, as she had promised. It surprised her that she felt so little heartache. She'd succeeded in putting the past where it belonged, she realized with a sense of relief and gratefulness.

Rachel told herself firmly that there was no point to thinking of Dallas, something that would have been much easier if she didn't keep running into him—on those times she took Aaron over to the Cordell ranch, at Brewer's Quick-Stop grocery, and once she met him at the gas station—she pulling in, he pulling out. Or the fateful afternoon when she'd taken off early in order to see Aaron play in his first basketball game after school.

She'd joined her mother and father and Dave Powers, who also had a boy on the team. Dave had been a year ahead of her in school. She'd dated him a number of times before settling on Coy as the love of her life. Dave was divorced, he told her now, and had custody of his only son. He looked very much as he had while in school, still slender and handsome, a few gray hairs among his pale brown ones, and tiny lines—which added character rather than age—shooting out from his green eyes.

"Dave's built a big trucking business," her father put into their conversation in a not very subtle attempt at matchmaking. "You got three yards now, don't you, Dave? I heard you just opened one up out in Los Angeles."

"Sacramento," Dave said. He sent Rachel a knowing grin, and she smiled in return. "So, you're here to stay?"

She nodded. Out of the corner of her eye she caught sight of Ace and Dallas entering, and immediately put a tight lid on the tug to her heart. She'd known he could be coming, she reminded herself; she herself had told Ace of the game.

Both men nodded to her, then took seats several aisles away. Beside her, her father made some comment under his breath and shifted in his seat. She cast him a warning glance.

"I didn't say anything," he protested with wide-eyed innocence.

"Your thoughts might get you into trouble," she cautioned, half teasing.

Then the game started, and everyone's attention was turned toward the shiny basketball court. Repeatedly her father's voice rose above the others, though for him it wasn't a shout, as he called cheers and complaints. Several times Rachel saw Ace lean forward and frown in their direction. She saw because she was looking at Dallas.

"Daddy..." She laid a cautioning hand on her father's arm. "Lower your voice. The referee doesn't appreciate your views."

He lowered his voice. Rachel's gaze strayed to find Dallas turned, gazing at her. His expression was unreadable.

Yet she felt the energy between them, the knowing as their gazes met. And again and again, despite her supreme effort not to, she found her gaze straying to his dark head. And again and again his eyes were waiting.

He didn't like her sitting beside Dave. Didn't like her talking to him. She knew this as if he'd spoken aloud. Well, he was getting married, she told him silently. He had no right to like or dislike anything she did.

She was with Dave getting cold drinks for the boys before the concession stand closed after the game when the fight broke out between Ace and Jasper. Dave had just asked her to join him for dinner when the commotion around the corner, in the gymnasium lobby, drew their attention. She heard the crowd murmuring and saw people pressing in one direction. And then a boy cried, "It's Aaron's grandpas."

Leaving Dave with the drinks, Rachel ran forward and pushed through the crowd. Seeing her father's flushed face contorted with rage, his thick burnished curls tumbling to his forehead, sent her heart plummeting to her toes. Where was Aaron? She searched frantically, as a mother lion anxious to protect her young.

"You're lyin' and you know it, Ace Cordell!" her father bellowed. Her mother pressing against his chest was the only reason her father wasn't swinging.

"You're calling the kettle black is what you're doin', Jasper Tyson!" Ace retorted in a harsh, low voice. "Either that or you're goin' senile. Anybody round here in those days can tell you the truth of it—*I* shot the winning basket in our game with Lindsay back then. *I* was the star player for both years."

Dallas had hold of Ace's arm and took his father's hat from someone who'd picked it up from the floor. He smacked the hat into the old man's chest, forcing him to take it and unball his fists. His gaze strayed downward to find Aaron staring with wild dismay. The boy's eyes moved swiftly from one grandfather to the other, not knowing where to settle. Dallas restrained the urge to strangle both men for what they'd inflicted on the boy.

"Dad . . ." He tugged at his father's arm and spoke low. "This isn't the time." *Life for the Cordells was never dull.* The thought came angrily, compounded by the memory of Rachel sitting with Dave Powers.

He had his father out in the parking lot, and the old man was grumbling, "I got just as much right to Aaron as that old gasbag Jasper," when Rachel called to them.

"Ace!" Her expression was thunderous. She strode forward and flicked her long hair back from her shoulder. "Did you see Aaron's face?" she demanded. "Are you proud of yourself?"

"Why don't you ask Jasper?" Ace shot back. "He started it!"

"You called him a liar," she said. "Right in front of Aaron."

"Let it go, Rachel," Dallas said then, forcing the words through tight lips. He was damn mad and not quite certain as to why. "Jasper swung first, like he always does."

Rachel looked suddenly as if he'd slapped her, but while he registered the reaction, he didn't feel anything other than frustrated and angry.

"Dad was explaining to Aaron the story behind one of those old photographs of a game hangin' on the wall when Jasper butted in, taking objection to certain facts. Now because of this you won't let Aaron come home with Dad like he was supposed to. I don't call that fair by any stretch of the imagination—nor all that good for Aaron. It shows you're taking sides, just as much as anyone else."

Fire leaped into her eyes, and she drew her shoulders up straight. "*I* didn't choose for him. Aaron made that decision on his own. He doesn't care to go with either of his grandfathers. He's coming with me and Dave to dinner." Her words sliced into his gut. She looked to Ace. "I will have him call you this evening, Ace, so you can smooth things over with him. For now he needs distance. You and my father have totally embarrassed him.'' Her eyes narrowed. ''Think about that.''

She pivoted and stalked away—to Dave Powers, who waited on the gymnasium steps.

A second later Dallas turned on his heel and stalked to his pickup. ''Comin'?'' he growled at his father. Ace's shocked expression registered in the back of his mind, but he was too preoccupied with the strange anger twisting around inside to pay it any attention.

By the time Rachel returned home with Aaron that evening, much of her worry over the effect the episode would have on her son had abated. It seemed that, while embarrassing, the fight between his grandfathers was also a source of pride. A number of boys envied Aaron for having two grandfathers who could swing a good punch and didn't mind doing it.

However, while she was happy for her son over this turn of events, it complicated her efforts to impress upon Aaron the wrongdoing of physical violence. Their family had always been Quaker, for heaven's sake—even Jasper, though his actions in this vein belied it.

Her father poked his head into her room just as she was slipping into bed.

''I'm awfully sorry about this afternoon, daughter,'' he said. He gazed at her with rumpled eyebrows, making the puppy face that always tugged at her heart.

She patted the bed beside her. ''It's Aaron you need to apologize to,'' she said as he sat down.

He nodded his curly head. ''I did.'' He cast a lopsided grin. ''He thinks it's all right for the old man to have a good punch.''

''Daddy...'' she warned.

''I know. My bent toward fighting has always been a trying thing to the Lord—and your mother.'' His grin showed little regret. ''Did you and Dave have a good time?''

''Me and Dave and Aaron and Davie,'' she clarified.

"Okay—but you like Dave, don't you?"

She shrugged. "He's nice, Daddy."

"Will you see him again?"

She shook her head. "We didn't really click."

"You should get out more."

"I will. Don't push."

He nodded, then kissed her forehead before leaving.

She lay in the darkness and stretched her arm out across the wide expanse of bed. Dallas was probably with Megan, she thought with irritation. *Imagine him being jealous of her with Dave.* It'd probably been her imagination. He had no reason to care what she did.

He'd had no right to speak to her like he had, either.

Lord, she ached—an ache that possessed her bones. She was lonesome. Lonesome for Dallas—but no...that was fruitless, better put aside. But how did she do it? *How did she do it?*

Rachel ran into Dallas a number of times in the following days when she took and picked up Aaron from the Cordell ranch. And she had the distinct impression that he took pains not to hang around to speak to her. She was just as glad; she was uncomfortable with the meetings, as well.

Which made it a total surprise when she looked up one morning to see him standing in the doorway of her office.

"Hello," he said in that deep, gravelly voice.

"Hello..."

His crystal-gray eyes met hers and held; his lips spread slowly into that sweet, familiar half grin.

Her heart answered and sent a smile bubbling up and out. "Come in. I would ask you to sit..." She stood and indicated the couch and chair, which were piled high with boxes, files and assorted vases, tiles, weavings and paintings. "But as you can see, everything's already taken."

"Appears that you're entrenched." He ambled forward, twirling his Stetson in his hands. His pale blue, western-cut sport coat brought out the steely color of his eyes.

His denims held a sharp crease, and his dark boots were spit-shined—his pair for visiting the city. "Hope I'm not interrupting too much."

"Oh, no...no." She smiled and slipped her hands into the hidden pockets of her skirt. How she'd always loved the distinctive cadence of his voice! "These are new arrivals, and I like to look them over before we put them out. It's routine."

Her mind flitted to the tenseness of their last meeting, and she wondered whether he thought of it, too.

The telephone rang, and she reached to answer it. It was catalog shipping, tracing the whereabouts of three hand-painted vases ordered by a customer. Rachel could hardly keep her mind on checking inventory sheets for the vases rather than watching Dallas. When she'd hung up, he was standing before a painting propped up on the couch—a distinctive oil depicting a young Apache brave on his first solitary hunt.

He raised an eyebrow. "Blue Nightingale," he said, waving his hat at the picture.

"Yes." She nodded. "He's very talented and beginning to be in demand. His style reminds me much of Remington."

"I went to school with Blue," he drawled, giving a wide smile. "His name then was Frank, and he drew all over my notebooks. Should have saved some of them."

She shared his chuckle. "There's no doubt that you could have sold them for a *very* good price."

His eyes were so clear, so warm on her. How she loved looking into them—*but she shouldn't*. She looked away to her desk.

Dallas caught the change. Her eager warmth fled and was replaced by sharp caution—much as used to happen when Coy would enter the room with her. It hurt, and he didn't want to bring hurt into her world. And he didn't like for her to shut him out.

"Aaron says you're all settled in over at the Golden Rose, and he seems to be pretty satisfied with school—except for having to sit on the bench most of every basketball game."

"Yes."

She smiled, and he saw the memory of that fateful game in her eyes. She didn't speak of it; he wouldn't, either.

"He didn't play basketball back in Phoenix, so he has a lot of work to do to catch up with the other boys in his class. It helps that he's a bit ahead academically."

"I dragged out our old basketball goal and promised to get it put up. I also told him he could paint it himself and pay for a new net." He enjoyed her twinkling eyes.

"Good idea."

He pulled a panatela from the package in his breast pocket and slipped it between his lips, casting about in his mind for words to explain why he'd come. His subject was personal and one that seemed to have a big Forbidden sign hung over it—at least for the two of them. Yet she should know. And it was a good excuse to see her. Damn it! It shouldn't be like this between them—two people who liked each other so much.

The telephone rang again, and for an instant Dallas was glad. She sent him a wry smile and placed an ashtray near him on her desk, then stretched to lift the receiver. Her movements were smooth, and he enjoyed watching her. Her sleek, dark hair fell over her shoulder and across her breast. The fluid fabric of her gray skirt lay against her legs, and he didn't feel one iota of guilt in studying the shape of those legs from the thighs downward.

"I'll call you back in a few minutes," she said to the person on the phone, and quickly hung up.

"You're in great demand."

"I'm thinking of asking for a raise tonight at dinner—another advantage in living with the boss."

They shared a chuckle, and then Rachel waited for him to speak.

He pulled the thin cigar from his mouth. "I thought I'd better let you know that Aaron is asking questions about Coy," he said.

Her dark eyes clouded. "I've never hidden anything from him about his father. What sort of questions is he asking?"

"I heard him asking Pete—you remember him? He's been with us about twenty years, off and on, because he has his own little spread south of ours about thirty-five miles." When she nodded, he continued, "He was asking Pete about Coy's accident."

"Oh." She blinked and gave a nod as she looked away.

"I guess he didn't want to speak to Dad or any of us— probably thought it would upset us." He watched her carefully, trying to gauge the depth of her feelings. "He wanted to know where the barn was that his father had been building when he'd been killed, how big it'd been. Pete's pretty good with kids, has three of his own and handled it easy enough. But I made a point to catch Aaron alone later and talked with him some about Coy. I wanted him to know he could talk with any of us about his father whenever he wanted."

She laid a hand lightly on his arm, then removed it. "I've tried to tell him everything I could about Coy." Her gaze became hard. "But I've never told him about the trouble between Coy and me. I don't want him to hear of it. He wouldn't understand—it would only cause him mass confusion. I have told him how his father died, but he probably sensed how hard it was for me to talk about. I admit I've only done it once, and that was long ago. I guess seeing the very place sent his mind to questioning. No doubt he has some memory of that day and the ones following. It's natural for him to be curious."

"You haven't told him anything about Coy's problems?"

"No. Those were mine and Coy's problems, not Aaron's."

He thought about this and he gazed at her. "Those weren't all yours and Coy's problems, Rach. Most of it was Coy himself—getting into escapades that people haven't forgotten. Maybe Aaron wasn't likely to hear of it out in Phoenix—but living here, chances are that sooner or later he's going to. And it would be best if it came from you." He watched the stubborn gleam slip into her eyes.

"No," Rachel said, shaking her head and feeling her whole body rejecting the idea. "A boy needs to feel his father is the greatest man on earth. Especially a boy without that father. I want Aaron to have this."

"He needs to see his father as a whole, living, breathing man, not a god. A person can't relate to a perfect god."

"I haven't presented Coy as a god," she retorted, annoyed for some reason she didn't understand.

Slowly Dallas nodded and tucked the cigar back into his mouth. "It's up to you. I'm sorry for butting in."

"Oh, you didn't butt in." She gazed into his eyes. "Aaron is your nephew, and I've always respected your opinion. I just don't happen to agree with it this time." Her tone softened. "But thanks for caring, Dal." The familiar form of his name slipped from her lips as naturally and warmly as a south wind in summertime. And she saw it touch him as it had her before he looked away.

"Sure," he said, stepping toward the door. He carefully set his hat upon his head and paused to gaze at her. "You seein' much of Dave Powers these days?"

The question caught her off guard. "No..." she said slowly at last.

"Well..." He shifted awkwardly. "He's a good guy."

"Yes, he is."

"I'll let you get back to all that work. Hadn't meant to keep you."

"I'll walk down with you." But at that moment Jenny, the clerk of the arts and gifts department, appeared at her door and looked uncertainly from her to Dallas.

"That's okay." Dallas's lips quirked. "Been coming to Tyson's for my jeans and hats and suits since I was about knee-high to a grasshopper. I can find my way." He walked rapidly away along the business offices' balcony.

"I'm sorry for interrupting, Mrs. Cordell," Jenny said.

"You were going to call me Rachel, remember?" She grinned at the younger woman, who'd been greatly impressed with Rachel being one of *the* Tysons.

Jenny smiled back, and her gaze strayed over the handrail and down to the floor below, where Dallas was striding toward the front doors. Tall and broad shouldered, he wasn't a figure easily missed even amid all the colorful racks of clothes and milling customers.

"Well, what is it?" Rachel asked, repressing a smile. The Cordell men usually received such attention—even Ace at his age.

"Oh, there's a lady downstairs who loves the calf-length, beaded moccasins..." Jenny looked doubtful. "But she has such big feet that she can't fit into any that we have. Can we special order her some?"

"Yes, but it will take at least six weeks and maybe longer. These moccasins are handmade, and I only have two suppliers." She raised an eyebrow. "How big are this woman's feet?"

Jenny's eyes widened, and she put a hand up to hide her grin. "I never saw such big feet in my entire life."

Rachel chuckled and stepped toward the stairs. "Well, let's go talk to her. Having such mammoth feet must be a great trial for her—and if she wants a pair of five-hundred-dollar hand-beaded moccasins, we're going to help her get them."

That evening Rachel had cause to be confronted with Dallas's suggestion about telling Aaron more of the truth about his father.

"We were studying the Choctaw and Chickasaw tribes in class today," Aaron said. It was their quiet time before he went to bed. "I told Miss Haley some of the Chickasaw words Grandpa has been teaching me." He gave a small smile of pride.

"Bet she was impressed."

"Yeah…she wants me to tell the class more, maybe have Grandpa come talk to us." He carefully removed his chewing gum from his mouth and placed it in its special dish, then paused to stare at his reflection in the dresser mirror.

"I don't look very Indian. My eyes are gray—almost blue," he said, clearly dissatisfied.

"A lot of Chickasaws had blue eyes," she told him. "Even back in the 1800s—blue-eyed warriors, they were called. And a lot of Indians don't look like Indians are reported to look."

"Grandma does—and you do, sort of." He cocked his head, studying her.

"Grandpa J. is part Chickasaw," she pointed out. "He doesn't look it, at all. He took after his daddy, who was very fair."

"Is Papa Ace a lot Indian?"

She nodded. "Papa Ace is about three-quarters Choctaw-Chickasaw. Does he look it?"

Aaron chuckled. "Yep—especially when he's mad."

He got into bed, and Rachel pulled up the sheet, smoothing it over his chest. When she looked to his face, she found him staring at her and could almost feel him wondering about asking a question.

"Did my dad drink a lot?"

That wasn't a question she'd expected.

"Why?"

"Mike Collins said he was a drunk. He said his dad told him, 'cause his dad used to be a friend of Dad's."

His gaze demanded an answer, and Rachel wondered what in the world to tell him. If she lied and he discovered she had, would he believe any of what she'd told him about his father?

"I think if Mike's father had been a true friend of your father's, he wouldn't now be calling him a drunk. What do you think?"

After a moment he nodded.

"Your dad drank, Aaron, yes," she said slowly, and forced herself to look him in the eyes. "He drank more than he should have, but I wouldn't call him a drunk." Coward, she condemned herself.

He nodded and looked away, as if he sensed her reluctance to speak of such things. Children knew so much by instinct.

"Aaron . . ." She placed her hand over his and prayed for wisdom. In the back of her mind she heard Dallas's voice advising the truth. "I've tried to tell you about your father, to help you know him. I guess I've tended to tell you only the good things, those things I like to remember and want you to remember."

She looked down at their hands pressed together, then back up at him. "Your dad drank too much sometimes. And he could get in some good fights, too. Fights he usually won, if that makes it better." She allowed a small smile. "You might hear a lot of things about your daddy, honey. He could be pretty wild. He had a quick temper sometimes, and he had his problems. He wasn't perfect. None of us are, sweetheart. But there's one thing I want you to know about your dad, and that is that he loved you, Aaron. He loved you very much."

It was why he stayed with me, she thought. He loved you. He truly loved his family and hated disappointing them.

"Okay, Mom." He nodded and gave her a comforting smile—her son of ten years wanting to comfort her.

"And, Aaron, you can talk to your uncle Dallas about your dad. He knew him just about better than anyone."

"Better than Papa Ace?"

"I think so. They were very close when they were younger." She adjusted the sheet, which didn't need it, then kissed him. "Good night, sweetheart. See you in the morning."

She turned out the light and walked slowly to her room. All these years she'd been doing as Dallas had said that very morning—presenting Coy as some sort of perfect god. And she thought that deep down she'd known this, but being a single parent was no easy task. It was hard to see all sides of the job, and there'd been no one to help her with her own troubled emotions. She knew that at first she'd simply been denying the truth about Coy. It'd only been in the later years that she'd been able to face and let go of the hurtful past.

Dallas. Again she was having to lean on him. Again, if not intimately close, he was still there for her, and for Aaron, when they needed him.

Dallas sat on the front porch, surrounded by comforting darkness. The pungent odor of his panatela filled his nostrils. He gazed out at the nearby paddock, where two horses pranced into the silver glow cast by the pole lamp. But in his mind he saw Rachel as she'd looked that morning. Her sleek, satiny hair falling over her shoulder, her big brown-black eyes that at times reflected every emotion of her heart, and at others seemed totally inscrutable, though nevertheless alluring.

He ground his teeth as he thought of her in the company of Dave Powers. He couldn't stand the thought of her with another man.

He'd been lying to himself for two long years.

Hell, he'd been lying to himself since the day Rachel had left the ranch.

He'd thought that Megan would fill the hole within him, but he knew now that she never could. He doubted seriously that any woman could. Except Rachel. Seeing her that morning had brought that fact to sharp focus, rather like getting an old mule's attention by smacking it between the eyes with a two-by-four, he thought with a bitter chuckle.

It went down hard. He hadn't made too many mistakes in his life. That wasn't bragging; that was fact. He'd been born with the superb trait of knowing exactly who he was, what he wanted in life and how to go about getting it. But it could also be said that when he did happen to make a mistake, it was a lulu.

He played his tongue over his thin cigar. There was only one thing to do, and that was break off with Megan. He couldn't marry her knowing in his heart that he loved another woman.

And if it meant spending the remainder of his life alone, he would do so, rather than settle for less than what he felt for Rachel.

Immediately his mind jumped ahead, imagining Megan's reaction when he told her. It wasn't a pretty picture. She was going to be hurt. But he rather felt it would be more her pride that suffered and not her heart. And it certainly would be better on them both to end it now, well before years of hurt could pile up.

He squeezed his eyes closed as regret washed over him. The old man wasn't going to like this. Not one bit. It seemed to Dallas that during most of his life he'd been a disappointment to his father. He hadn't married and, at the ripe age of thirty-seven, still hadn't brought home grandchildren to carry on the family traditions. And it wasn't at all to his credit that one of the reasons he'd decided to marry Megan was in hopes of finally pleasing the old man.

He wished his father would understand, but sitting there in the darkness, Dallas felt certain that all he could expect from his father was angry condemnation.

A mess, he thought, rising and tossing the end of his cigar down to the gravel driveway. He'd made one hell of a mess out of things, and now he'd have to do his best to set it right.

He would see Megan first thing in the morning.

Chapter Six

Dallas felt a mighty small man when he appeared at Megan's town house the following morning and groped around for the words to tell her that he couldn't marry her. Of all the fantasies he'd ever had in his life, this was not one of them.

He'd lain awake most of the night, and ever since rising that morning had been rehearsing what he would say. But when the actual moment came, the words he'd rehearsed didn't come out the way he'd intended. He proceeded to insert his size-eleven foot neatly into his mouth. And he cursed himself for ever getting into this predicament in the first place.

But rather than crying, as he'd braced himself for, she'd shouted the most amazing thing.

"What will everyone say?" She stared at him for a moment, her eyes like those of a spooked calf, then raked a hand through her blond curls and paced the living room, gesturing and screaming. "I've invited the governor, for

God's sake! His wife has been consulting with us about re-doing their vacation home. I've invited the head people from Webster Hotels! I've got guests coming down from Kansas City. And you are making me look like an idiot!''

"I'm sorry, Meg. It wasn't—"

"You're *sorry*? Oh, damn you, Dallas!" In the next instant she reached out, grasped up a nearby vase and flung it at him.

Dallas ducked. She had a good aim, for the vase whizzed over his head, missing him by a hairbreadth, and crashed into the wall behind him. He opened his mouth to try again to apologize, but suddenly a heavy crystal ashtray was flying through the air. It broke in two when it thudded against the wall.

"You can't do this to me! I've made plans!" Her words rang in his ears as he opened the door and slipped out.

She astonished him by following, clad only in her white silk robe and slippers, all the way out to his pickup at the curb. He wasn't at all proud of the instinct that propelled him along—pure disgust with her, with himself.

"I promise you, Dallas, I'll sue if you don't marry me." She stomped both high-heeled slippered feet. "I'll not call everyone and tell them that you *jilted* me. I won't!"

"*I'll* call everybody," he said, and paused in the opened door to his truck, gazing at her over its hood. "I'll tell everyone it was my fault, which it is."

"Don't you *dare*! Then everyone will think there's something wrong with me." She clenched her fists at her side.

"Then *you* call them and tell them you jilted me."

"Then everyone will think I'm a mean witch."

He stared at her, at a loss.

"Oh—you're one son of a bitch, Dallas Cordell!" She whirled and ran back to the town house, shouting over her shoulder. "I'll see you pay for this. Damn you to hell!"

He slipped into the seat, slammed the door and started the engine. It was cloudy, fifty-five degrees with a cutting north wind, but Dallas felt as if it was a hundred and ten.

He wasn't extremely proud of the immense relief he felt at being out of his marriage to Megan. In fact he felt as if he'd just narrowly escaped a scalping. She'd revealed a side of herself he hadn't known existed, which made him wonder what other things there were about her that he may not have known. But he couldn't blame her, he thought, because he hadn't known himself too well, either. As he drove away, he felt like one son of a bitch.

Doggedly determined to get it all dealt with as soon as possible, he drove straight to the Cordell Corporation offices, where he knew his father was spending the morning checking over the week's drilling operations.

For a few desperate moments he entertained the idea that maybe the old man would understand. As he rode up the elevator to the executive offices, he was filled with a longing to pour his heart out to his father. He needed the old man to understand, needed his reassurance and comfort. Yet reason told him that in all his life he'd never been able to talk to his father. Ace Cordell didn't listen—he gave orders.

"You're just nervous," his father said after Dallas had told him. "You'll feel fine once the 'I do's' are said. Go on back and apologize, and everything will be fine."

Dallas shook his head and gazed at his father across the wide expanse of oak desk. They both remained standing. "No, Dad. I just can't marry her. It won't work. It's been a mistake from the first, but I can't change that. What I can change is making a worse mistake by going ahead and marrying her."

"A bare week before the wedding is a little late to be deciding such a thing," his father said sternly.

"I think it's preferable to deciding it afterward."

"What are you goin' to do? Stay single all your life? Who are you goin' to pass your part of the ranch on to?"

"I don't have to answer to any of those questions. What I do know is that marriage to Megan would be totally wrong—for both of us."

"You settin' your eyes on Rachel?" His father's black eyes snapped with contempt.

Hot resentment rose in Dallas.

"Dad, it's true I care for Rachel," he said, straining to keep his voice even. "I always have, first like a sister and then it became something more. I'm through pretending otherwise. But Coy was her husband and my brother. I never forgot that. I don't forget that now."

He paused, staring at his father's coldly distant expression. "How I feel about Rachel has something to do with me not marrying Megan. It has to. Because I can't settle for less than feeling for my wife that something special I've had a taste of with Rachel. But I'm not setting my sights on anyone. I'm just trying to straighten out one hell of a mistake."

He waited, giving his father a chance to offer the support and comfort he so desperately needed.

"You have an obligation to this family not to embarrass us, as well as to marry and raise heirs," the old man said sharply.

"I have a bigger obligation to myself, Dad."

They stared at each other, and Dallas wondered whether his father had ever understood him—would ever accept him.

"You're a man grown," the old man said. "You'll do as you wish."

When his father did nothing more than turn his back and stare out the wide expanse of plate-glass window, pain shot through him. It was the old man's way.

Regret setting heavily on his shoulders, Dallas turned and quietly left.

Rachel heard the news about the wedding being called off from Quinn.

"Dal spent a good part of the afternoon calling people himself, Rach. It took hours. He let me help him some, but insisted calling over fifty of the people we'd invited. And he kept saying it was a mutual agreement between them to call off the wedding. I mean, why did he have to give any explanation at all? It wasn't anyone's business," she said with scorn. "And I happen to know it was Dal who called things off, because Dad is livid with him for doing it."

Then her voice cracked. "I'm so worried about Dallas, Rach. He . . . well, he's always been the strong one around here, and he looks like the wrath of God has fallen on his shoulders. He told Stella not to make him any dinner and rode out about an hour ago—and now storms are building."

"Dallas knows how to handle being out in a storm, Quinn," Rachel said with a confidence she didn't feel. Dallas was hurting—and she hurt for him. "How's Ace's blood pressure?"

"Somewhere around roof level. Oh, Lord, he's in a snit. He doesn't say a lot, which speaks volumes. He had a headache earlier and for once listened when I told him he should lie down. Stella coaxed him along with a back massage."

"Is he taking his medicine?"

"Stella and I have been making certain of that." Quinn paused, then said, "You know, Rachel, I never knew how much I relied on Dallas until he isn't here. I know he's around somewhere and will come home, but it's like he's left us . . . You know what I mean?" Her voice shook.

"Yes . . ." she said softly. "It's going to be all right, Quinn. Everyone just needs time, that's all."

She bid Quinn goodbye and stood with her hand resting on the receiver. She gazed out the window at the sun setting behind dark, purple clouds. Then she squeezed her eyes closed.

Are you all right, Dallas? Where are you? You're hurting—I can feel it.

"What is it, sweetheart?" Her mother entered the hallway. Her father and Aaron followed, stopping their teasing and laughter when they saw her.

"It's Dallas—he and Megan have called off their wedding."

Aaron stared at her with wide, curious eyes, and she had no desire to say more in front of him.

"Oh, that's too bad," her mother said. The concern in her eyes was for Rachel.

"For good?" her father asked.

"It appears so."

"Stella's goin' to be mad," Aaron pronounced. "She made all those cookies."

"Come on, son," Jasper coaxed, "and we'll catch *The Andy Griffith Show* before you have to get a bath."

Rachel followed the others into the family room to watch television, but her mind was far away.

Dallas wasn't going to marry Megan. What had happened? He'd called it off. Why?

She scolded herself for the joy and excitement that nibbled at her heart. Oh, Lord, forgive her, but she was so glad!

Yet Dallas was hurting, and she didn't want that.

Her mind chased around in circles with the thoughts and emotions. When the thunder started, she jumped. Shortly after came the rain—and a shiver down her spine; she felt suddenly chilled. She knew Dallas was out in the rain. She didn't know how she knew, only that she did.

She'd just finished tucking Aaron into bed when the telephone rang. Her father answered on the kitchen extension and after a few minutes called her to the phone.

"It's Yancey," he said, handing over the receiver. He didn't leave, but went over to leisurely pour himself a cup of coffee.

"Yancey? When did you get in?"

"About twenty minutes ago. Broke my hand second time out, so figured I might as well come on home." A slight chuckle traced his voice. "Quinn told me about everything, and she's about to bite her nails down to nothin'. I just asked your dad if Dallas happened to have come over there. I knew it was a long shot, but we're getting pretty worried.

It's been raining hard now over an hour, and the wind's picking up."

"Here?" She glanced to her father. "Why...he hasn't returned, then?"

"No. I'm fixin' to go looking for him. Just thought I'd try calling a few close places first. Called down to Clyde Jennings, but he hasn't seen him, either."

"Did he ride Shadow?" Alarm stiffened her shoulders.

"Yeah...I don't think there's much to worry about. That mare's a good one, and Dallas knows the land."

"You might try the old rock springhouse down on Spring Creek," Rachel said. "The one that sets right near our fence line. You probably won't be able to see it until you're right on it because of the trees. At least there used to be trees."

"There's still trees there," her father put in.

"Dad says there's still trees, Yance."

"I know the place," Yancey said. "Haven't seen it in years, but I'll just follow the creek up your way."

"Is Stella still there...to be with Quinn?" she asked.

"Yeah. She's staying the night."

"And your father—how's he doing?"

"He's okay, but mad as hell. He refuses to take any more calls from friends asking about Dal and Megan. He even ripped the hall telephone cord out of the wall."

Rachel sighed. "Yancey...be careful."

"Hey, I'm a tough bronc rider, remember? And I'll take one of the fellas from the bunkhouse with me."

"Good. Please call me when you find him." Lower, she added, "No matter what time."

"Sure, Rach."

She replaced the receiver and turned to see both parents staring at her. Her mother passed over a cup of coffee.

"What happened?" her father asked, his voice like that of a drill sergeant.

"I don't know exactly." Rachel wrapped her hands around the cup. Chills continued to race down her spine. "According to Quinn, Dallas broke off with Megan. Undoubtedly he and Ace had words over it. Dallas rode off late this afternoon and hasn't returned."

"Oh, dear," her mother said. "How's Ace?"

"Furious, and no doubt his blood pressure is sky-high. But he's taking his medicine and seems okay so far."

"Why'd Dallas call it quits?" her father asked, his gaze sharp.

"Only Dallas knows that, Daddy." She returned his gaze.

A gust of wind rattled the window, drawing her eyes. Rain lashed the night-black glass.

Rachel set her cup on the counter and moved toward the mudroom off the kitchen. "I'm going to look for him."

Her father stepped quickly and placed a restraining hand on her arm. "He's a man grown, Rachel. He don't need you or anybody runnin' out, mollycoddlin' him. Like as not, he wouldn't appreciate it."

"He *needs* someone now, Daddy. I can feel it. You know that even a good horse could get upset in this storm. Throw him off." Though it wasn't his body but his state of mind she was worrying over.

"It'd take more than a spooked horse to throw Dallas out of the saddle. You want to go for yourself."

"Oh, Daddy..." Yes, she wanted to go for herself. She couldn't stand worrying about him.

"Rachel," her mother said softly, drawing her gaze. "You don't know the land anymore and are out of practice with handling a horse in this situation. Even if you took the Jeep, you'd probably get stranded out there, and we'd all have to come find you. I know it's the harder thing to do, but you must think of everyone and stay here. You've told Yancey where to look and now you must wait." Her gaze was kind and comforting.

After a moment Rachel nodded. "You're right."

"Have some more coffee, daughter. And a couple of cookies." Her father freshened her cup. He always thought food cured every ill.

With a nod Rachel reached for her cup of coffee. What her father had said was true, she told herself. It wasn't likely that Shadow would spook and throw Dallas out of the saddle. Most probably he'd taken shelter to wait out the storm—and to be alone, away from Ace. Again she thought of how it wasn't a physical hurt she worried over, but an emotional one.

But she didn't have a part in his life. A million walls stood between them. She was his friend, but only to a certain point and no closer. No matter how much she wished to comfort him, to help shoulder his burden right now, she couldn't do it. It was forbidden.

Shadow sloshed through a puddle as Dallas rode slowly through the opened gate into the barnyard. The wind smacked cold rain into his face, and the calf across his lap wiggled and let out a weak cry. The calf was wet, further soaking Dallas's pants. His slicker protected his shirt, but rain had blown up beneath to his waist and part of his sleeves, too. He was cold and wished for a pot of steaming coffee laced with whiskey.

When he lifted his head and peered out beneath the streaming brim of his hat, he saw Yancey illuminated by a single light where he stood in the stable barn. His horse was beside him, saddled and ready to ride. A couple of steps closer and Dallas recognized Bob Taylor right behind him.

"Damn you, Dallas! Where you been?"

Dallas rode Shadow into the shelter of the stable. Yancey's arms were already raised to take the calf. "Hello to you, too, little brother."

"Me and Pete were fixin' to come lookin' for you—and we weren't lookin' forward to it."

"I appreciate the gesture, Yance," Dallas said as he dismounted. He shook water from his hat and slicker and tossed them over a nearby stool. "I didn't mean to cause you any worry, but I couldn't leave that calf. I was heading back ahead of the rain when I found this heifer in trouble. Lost her, but I was able to save the babe. I was right glad for the rain to wash him off then.''

"I'll take care of your mare for you, Dal,'' Bob said, taking the reins.

"Thanks.'' Dallas patted her neck. "Go along, girl,'' he crooned softly, then turned and looked at his brother as the horse was led away. "When'd you get in?''

"This evening.''

"What happened to your hand?'' Dallas peeled off his wet leather gloves. He was very tired and oddly glad to see his brother.

"Bronc stepped on it.''

Dallas stifled a grin. "That calf's drippin' on your boots.''

"Damn you, Dallas.'' Yancey plunked the calf back into Dallas's arms. The look in his eyes was one of fond relief. "I'll put my horse up and be with you in a few minutes.'' He paused. "You'd better call up to the house and tell them you're alive and well. And I promised to call Rachel—she's pretty worried, too. Do you want to call her?'' He raised an eyebrow.

"I'll call her,'' Dallas answered quietly.

He carried the calf into the empty stall next to the tack room, then hurried to get a blanket to wrap him in and fresh hay for the floor.

Using the telephone in the front office, he called up to the house and told Quinn he was fine. After hanging up, he paused to wipe his hands down his damp denims. He dialed Rachel's number from memory. Some emotion he couldn't name washed over him when he heard her voice come across the line.

"It's Dallas,'' he said.

"Oh, Dal.'' She touched the receiver, wanting to touch him. "You're all right, then?''

"Fine, Rach. I found a heifer calving when I was out. She was early and had trouble. I stayed to get the calf and bring him home.''

So like him. Dallas didn't lose calves; birth was something special to him.

"Did Yancey find you?"

"I caught him and Bob before they left, so they stayed dry, if highly irritated at me." He chuckled.

Silence hummed over the line as she pictured his face and gave thanks that he was safe.

"Thanks for calling," she said at last.

"Rach...I've broken off with Meg."

"I know."

"I want to talk to you."

Her heart leaped into her throat.

No...they couldn't think along such lines. It was forbidden.

"There's no need," she said, wondering what she meant. She simply didn't know what to say.

"I'll call you tomorrow," he said. "Good night."

"Good night," she answered faintly, and slowly replaced the receiver.

Dallas was no longer engaged, she thought. He was free—she was free. But were they really?

No. No person lived without responsibilities to others. It was the price of being part of the human race, of enjoying the love of family and friends. She had her son and her family to think of. And, mutually, she and Dallas had his family to consider.

Still, he wanted to talk to her.

Dallas sat with Yancey on the soft hay in the shadowy stall made cozy by a heat lamp. The calf had been fed and slept peacefully beneath his blanket.

Dallas had pulled off his boots and was toasting his wet feet beneath the heat lamp. His pants felt steamy, and his panatela tasted damp. He and Yancey shared a bottle of good Jack Daniel's sour-mash whiskey they'd found in the desk in the office.

"You sure have surprised me, big brother," Yancey said, passing over the bottle. "It's me that's supposed to get this family in an uproar—or Coy—not you. Yep, ol' Dallas Cordell has always been Mr. Reliable himself."

"I never set out to be so reliable," Dallas said. He took a healthy draw from the bottle, then jabbed his cigar back into the corner of his mouth. "I was just being me. I'm still just bein' me, but I guess Dad can't see it."

"He sees it." Yancey spoke quietly and gazed at Dallas intently. "He's powerfully upset, mostly because he sees himself in you like he's never done before. And he was worried about you."

"I figured you all knew *I* knew what I was doing." Dallas was quite surprised at everyone's concern. "I've been out in the rain before."

"You haven't ever just thrown over your fiancée before." Yancey's eyes twinkled. "How'd she take it?"

"She broke a vase and an ashtray against the wall—she was aiming at my head." Dallas chuckled and handed back the bottle. He was amazed at what had happened to him that day—and he wondered why he was feeling so full of himself. In fact he was feeling a certain life that had escaped him for longer than he could remember.

"No kiddin'?" The fact seemed to tickle Yancey. "Maybe she has more fire than I'd given her credit for. I thought only cold, hard cash ran through her veins."

Dallas shook his head. "I know Megan liked my money, Yance. But it wasn't all that. She's made it into the high-dollar business now and doesn't really need my money. What she did like was our 'old and established' family name." He gestured with the bottle. "Don't sell Megan short. She was offering me her love and devotion, all she had to spare. She'd struggled hard when Tom died—he left bills that took her five years to pay. But pay them she did. She just never wanted to be poor again—and for that none of us can blame her."

"Okay...then why did you break off with her?"

"I don't love her enough. And wanting me for name and security isn't enough for her, either. She'll see that, eventually. I finally realized what I want—and if I can't have it, it isn't goin' to hurt any more staying single." He took his cigar from his mouth and twirled it between his fingers. "I don't want to end up having three wives like Dad did. When I marry, I want it to be for keeps."

Yancey reached for the bottle and took a healthy drink. Pausing, he said, "I wish I knew what I want. I'd like to find a woman—*one* woman. But I just haven't found one I thought I could live the rest of my life with. I get bored. You know, big brother, I ain't never been in love. Not in all my life."

"You will be," Dallas said. "It may just take time. And you may not like it when it happens, 'cause it sure as hell screws you up inside like a knotted rope." He watched Yancey take several gulps from the bottle. "We aren't goin' to feel too good tomorrow."

"Yeah, but it warms us tonight."

They shared a chuckle.

"So, what now, big brother?" Yancey asked, his gaze sharp.

"I'm going to see Rachel," Dallas said without hesitation. "I'm going to talk to her."

"Do you love her, Dal?"

He sucked in a heavy breath and let it out slowly. "Yes." He puffed on his cigar and stared for a moment at the scarred and dented stall wall. From the distant radio came an old Jerry Lee Lewis tune. He looked again at his brother.

"I've loved her almost from the first time I saw her. But Coy was my brother, and I never stepped over the line. But as you pointed out several weeks ago—Rachel is now a widow. That line no longer exists. And I think it's finally time I told her how I feel."

Yancey lifted the whiskey bottle as a toast. "I wish you the best, big brother. And I envy you."

Lines, Dallas thought as he watched the upward-twirling smoke of his panatela. There were a million of them still—his father and Jasper, Aaron, wicked tongues of gossips that could hurt deeply those people he cared for. And Rachel. He had no way of knowing how she felt about him.

She cared for him; this he knew. But how much? And would she be willing to face all the risks it would take for them to make a life together? He could only ask. He couldn't blame her if she didn't want to; it would not be easy for them. They both stood to lose an awful lot—perhaps she more than he.

Chapter Seven

Dallas got up early and worked away his hangover on morning chores—work he didn't usually do anymore, such as haying and graining the cattle and cleaning stalls. These chores were normally done by ranch hands, but this morning Dallas needed the strenuous exertion.

He kept thinking of Rachel, wondering what she would say when he told her. Only a few short weeks ago he'd thought that he couldn't handle knowing how she felt about him. Now he had to know.

Things could backfire. He'd given his family one hell of a good jolt already. If he took up any kind of relationship with Rachel, it was liable to ignite another world war between both families.

There was no sense in jumping ahead, he told himself. He wouldn't "set his sights," as his father had said. He'd deal with it one step at a time.

He made a point to have breakfast with his father, even though he knew it wasn't going to be pleasant. The old man was bound to be fuming for days to come over things not going the way he'd planned. But Dallas figured he might as well begin trying to smooth things over as much as he could.

Yancey and the old man were already at the table when Dallas entered the dining room. As usual Quinn was still in bed.

"You boys are gettin' round mighty good for having come in two sheets to the wind at one o'clock this mornin'," his father commented. As always he was dressed in a starched white shirt, buttoned to the neck, with a premium turquoise-stone string tie. Forearms resting on the table edge, he flashed his gaze from Yancey over to Dallas.

"Stella pumped me full of vitamins along with coffee this mornin'," Yancey said. He definitely looked a little pale. His breakfast consisted of toast and coffee.

The old man grunted and focused his attention on his plate, heaped high with his normal eggs, sausage, biscuits and gravy, fried potatoes and hot peppers.

Dallas filled a plate from the silver serving dishes on the buffet, then took his regular place to the right of his father. Quickly he studied the old man. Concern and irritation churned within him. He couldn't live his life by worrying every minute whether what he did or said was going to cause his father to have a stroke or heart attack. But could he live with himself if he *did* bring on an attack?

After several minutes of tense silence, Dallas said, "I'm going into the city later, Dad. Is there anything you need?"

His father's black eyes came up slowly and rested on him. They were sharp and cold. "I'm goin' in later, myself—to see Megan and Wanda and apologize for my son's inexcusable behavior."

Dallas met the old man's gaze. "I'm sure they'd appreciate that," he answered quietly.

During the next ten minutes the only sounds were those of quiet breathing and silver pinging against china. Yancey did ask Dallas about the calf, and Dallas answered. Then both of them fell back into their own thoughts. Finished, their father pushed back his chair.

"You plannin' on staying around for a few days?" the old man said to Yancey as he rose.

"Thought I might," Yancey answered.

Their father nodded. "Mira's bringing Aaron over this afternoon after school. I'd like to start him on liftin' his colts hooves and learnin' the moves for showing. You could help out—if you can stir yourself enough to be bothered."

A wry grin tugged at Yancey's lips. "I live for it, Dad."

The old man paused and rested a hand on his belt. His eyes flashed from Yancey over to Dallas. "You asked me if I needed anything. Well, what I do need," he said, raising his right eyebrow, "is for both of my sons to remember the respect I *thought* I taught them—and to remember who they are and that they have an obligation to this family to marry and plant some seeds that can bear the Cordell name. I'd like to hear grandchildren in this house before I die." With that said, he stalked from the room.

Yancey sat back and chuckled loudly. "Boy, he ain't goin' to give an inch, Dal."

Dallas looked across at his brother and had to chuckle, too, though it echoed sadly within him. Hell, they were all Cordells—big, proud and stubborn. It ran in their blood.

The bright midmorning sun slanting in the big window behind her made Rachel squint at the papers on her desk. She twirled her chair around and closed the light-filtering drapes, then paused, catching her father's voice in Oran's office next door.

Jasper Tyson, she decided, had been born with a voice that echoed from mountaintops. He wasn't angry or upset—he was just talking, and no doubt the customers could clearly hear him downstairs. The next instant her father's voice became a muffled boom as Oran closed his office door.

Rachel's telephone rang.

Her pulse quickened as she recognized Dallas's low-voiced hello. "How are you this bright, shining morning?" he asked.

"Fine . . . and you?"

"Fine."

The line buzzed for long seconds in which Rachel pictured his steely gray eyes and the way his brows furrowed above them when he was deeply considering something, as she sensed him doing now.

"Can you have lunch with me?" he asked, sending her heartbeat racing.

"Yes," she answered with almost no hesitation. After all, there was nothing wrong with having lunch with him. He needed to talk; she would listen.

"I'll pick you up at noon."

Her father's muffled voice came again from Oran's office. "No . . ." she said, "let me meet you." Why did she feel she had to hide what she was doing, for goodness' sake?

"Murphy's?"

Oh, she loved Murphy's! "Yes. I'll see you then."

"At noon." His voice vibrated with amused pleasure and reluctance to say goodbye.

"Yes, at noon," she answered, stifling a chuckle.

"I'll be wearing a blue shirt with a gray cord coat."

"Light gray or dark gray?"

"Medium."

She laughed aloud then. "I hope I don't miss you."

"Oh, I don't think you can miss me—I'll be the *handsome* guy in the gray coat. Do you want to meet me inside or out on the porch—or in the parking lot?"

Just as she opened her mouth to answer, a knock drew her gaze to the doorway. "I'll wait," her father said in a loud whisper, smiling and holding up a finger.

"Inside." She lowered her voice and focused on her desktop.

"See you then," Dallas said, losing the amused tone.

"Yes—see you then."

She replaced the receiver and lifted her gaze to find her father smiling at her. "Can we have lunch today? Your mother has stood me up in favor of taking advantage of this beautiful day to do some painting."

"Oh, Daddy, I'm sorry, but I've made a lunch date." She cursed her dry mouth.

He pulled an elaborate frown. "Then how about tomorrow? I'll drive in just especially for it."

"Okay... I'd love it."

"You get back to work, now," he cautioned with mock severity, then strode away.

Rachel listened as he spoke to people in the offices. He would wander around the store for a long time, talking to all the employees, many he'd known his entire life. He loved to do that and often even worked a cash register. He was likely to remain well into the lunch hour or later, if it suited him— which was why Rachel hadn't wanted Dallas to pick her up.

You shouldn't be doing something you feel you have to hide, she scolded herself. But it wasn't shame; it was just that she didn't want to stir up trouble.

She glanced to the digital clock on her desk. Five past eleven—only forty minutes until she would leave to go meet Dallas. She took up a pencil, tapped it against her cheek and returned her attention to the shipping invoice for ten hand-loomed wool blankets from the Navaho Nation. But the numbers before her faded, Dallas's face taking their place.

Again her gaze strayed to the clock, which now read seven past eleven. A foolish happiness and impatience fluttered in her stomach. She was very glad that she'd worn the ivory wool-knit dress with the brilliantly colored scarf tossed over her shoulder. It made her feel feminine and lovely. She hoped Dallas would think her so.

No! She brought herself up short. She should *not* be thinking such things. It was only borrowing trouble.

When she pulled into the parking lot of Murphy's, she saw Dallas leaning against the porch post. The breeze ruffled his hair and tugged at the ends of his ribbon tie. He smiled and waved, walking forward to meet her as she pulled into a parking slot.

A decidedly sexual stirring started in her belly as she watched his sauntering stride and the way his firm thighs stretched his sharply creased denims. She pushed it away.

"Thought you were going to wait inside," she teased as she opened the car door and got out.

"There was a guy out here with a gray coat, and I thought you'd go off with him." He grinned and gazed pointedly at her. For an instant Rachel found herself staring at his luminous eyes. The stirrings made themselves known again. And this time there was no way she could push them aside.

She broke the gaze and stepped toward the restaurant. Suddenly she found herself shaking. Yesterday he'd broken off his marriage. That had been a change. But the facts between them hadn't changed. And here she stood, with him touching her, looking at her with more intimacy than he should. The feelings jumping and twisting within her scared the daylights out of her.

In an effort to maintain control, she stopped and turned to face him. "Dal, what is it you want to discuss? We can..." She paused, realizing the absurdity of suggesting they talk right there. "You don't have to take me to lunch just to talk."

"I want to take you to lunch, Rachel." His eyes darkened. "Please, just relax and let's enjoy a meal. Then we can talk."

"Okay," she said softly. Then she smiled. "I'd love one of Murphy's beef pies." The light that jumped into his eyes gave her heart wings.

The atmosphere of Murphy's was calm and serene, the decor rustic southwestern: clay tile floor, rugged oak tables inlaid with colorful Spanish tiles, slow-moving ceiling fans and tarnished antiques and old pictures of Indians from the various Nations filling the walls. The food was a mixture of Mexican and American Indian. Murphy himself was half-

Chickasaw, his spicy meat-pie recipe one that had been passed down through his family.

They sat at a table in the back corner beside the window. Dallas ordered steak *fajitas* and beer; Rachel ordered a meat pie and iced tea. She couldn't help studying Dallas, looking for telltale signs of his emotions. Was he heartbroken to have broken off with Megan? He didn't seem to be—and she felt terribly selfish because of the pleasure that tingled within her at this. Was it so wrong to be so glad to be there with him?

They talked of everything and nothing—of the calf Dallas had saved, of weather, of beef prices, of Rachel's bead-work, of Aaron's basketball team and the colt Ace had given him.

It was the first time for them—a time alone, without the disapproving observance of others. An opportunity to share the small facets that made up their lives. And for a short while Rachel was happier than she could remember being in such a long time. She forgot all about forbidden emotions and simply enjoyed Dallas's smile, his voice, the look in his eyes. She enjoyed, too, feeling every inch a woman.

Until he said, "You're beautiful."

The sunlight shafting through the window gave his eyes a spellbinding iridescence. His words and the whispered longings within her own body brought her back to reality.

She shook her head and looked away. "Dallas, don't—"

"You don't want me to say what I'm thinking?"

"We shouldn't be here like this. You know that."

"What's so wrong with having lunch with me, Rach?"

She met his gaze and stared at him a long moment, seeing the truth in his words yet feeling vaguely guilty all the same. She couldn't explain it.

He returned her look. Then, digging into his pocket, he slid back his chair and tossed several bills on the table. "Let's take a walk."

As he led the way along the sidewalk toward the beautifully cared-for lawn of a nearby church, he took her hand.

His was exceedingly warm. She felt his strength and clung to it. Just for these few precious moments she would hold his hand.

He didn't speak until he stopped in the shade of a tall elm. The old neighborhood street was quiet.

"Rachel . . ." He took a deep breath. "For the past five years I guess I haven't felt much of anything. The years I tried to forget you." His eyes held hers. "I'd deadened myself so much I almost married a woman simply because I thought I wasn't capable of being greatly stirred by anyone. And then I saw you again—and I began to know different. I love you."

She looked away to the ribbon tie at his neck, watching its tails flutter gently in the cool breeze. She struggled with the emotions doing fierce battle within her. His hand tightened around her own.

At last she lifted her gaze. "We've barely seen each other in five years—you broke off with Megan only yesterday. Perhaps you need more time to sort all this out to know what you're truly feeling."

He gently shook his head; his eyes bore into hers. "Do you?"

She touched her fingertips to his cheek and gazed into his crystal eyes. Her heart squeezed.

"If I tell you the truth—that I love you, too—will it change anything? Will it change the fact our fathers hate each other and would despise any relationship between us beyond a casual hello and goodbye? Or that I was your brother's wife—and that the suspicion he planted in everyone's minds will always linger?"

His eyes grew dark. "There's always been something special between us," he said. He looked up at the sky; his jawline tightened. "So many times I haven't had to speak to you to know what you were thinking or feeling. I could just look at you. Or I'd need someone to talk to, just to hear a voice so I didn't feel so alone, and there you'd come. Laughing and joking. I've never done that with any other woman. And when you went away, sometimes I thought I could *feel* you suffering. A hundred times I picked up the telephone to call you, to try to help you, but I told myself it might make things worse for you.'' He returned his piercing gaze to her. ''You make me feel things about life and myself that no other person ever has.''

He touched her cheek, and she gave in to leaning her face against his wide palm.

''Rachel . . .'' His voice came ragged. ''I'm a long time coming to this realization, but, honey, the past is just that— the past. You were my brother's wife, and I honored that. I would have cut off my right arm before I would've done anything against Coy. So I kept my love to myself.

''But now he's gone, and we're still alive. We have today, and it will be what we make of it. And I believe that Coy would say these same things to you, because that's the kind of man he was. He wouldn't begrudge you all the happiness you could find—with me or with anyone.''

Tenderness welled up in her. ''I know he wouldn't,'' she said in a hoarse whisper.

She searched his eyes for long seconds, then spoke gently the things that had to be said.

''But I'm still a Tyson. Neither my father nor Ace will ever accept us together, Dal. And I have Aaron to think of. He'll be caught in the midst of it all, and the talk—''

''We can't change what people say,'' he said, interrupting. ''But we don't have to let gossip and the wants of others dictate our lives. You don't *know* what Aaron would say. We can face that and deal with it together—and as far as I'm concerned, Aaron is the only person we need to think about in any of this.''

''Dallas . . . how will you separate yourself from your family?'' She studied his eyes and said firmly, ''I can't go to live at the ranch again. I don't want Aaron so close to Ace's influence—I can't stand to be, either. I cannot live in the same house as I did with Coy.''

''So . . . I'll get us a house.''

She shook her head. He wanted it to be so simple, but it wasn't. "The ranch is your world. How would you run things as well from somewhere else?"

"It's done all the time, Rach. People run two or three ranches hundreds of miles apart—states apart." He took her face roughly between his palms.

"I *love* you, Rachel. I want you to be my wife. I want to be your husband. I won't settle for less—not ever again."

The ragged longing in his eyes and voice tore at her heart. Tears blurred her vision even as she willed herself not to cry.

She shook her head and took hold of his wrists. "I thank you for that. You can't know how much that means to me." She could barely force the words past the painful lump in her throat. "But it can't be, Dallas. It can't. We don't live on an isolated island. There are so many other people to be considered. There's bound to be talk that could hurt our families terribly. And I don't want to hurt my father. I did that once—I won't disappoint him again." She sniffed and straightened her shoulders. "And I won't subject Aaron to the talk or the arguing or the confusion he's bound to have. I will never do anything to hurt him. He's had enough with the loss of his father."

She jerked away from his hands and shook her head. "I won't risk it, Dal. I won't!"

Hurt and anger mingled in his steely eyes.

"I won't push, Rachel," he said in a deep, low voice. "You must do as you feel best. But I damn well won't go away, either. Whether you like it or not, our lives are linked."

He stared at her, then reached out and took her arm to pull her against him. She was powerless to resist and, Lord help her, when his head came down, she lifted her lips to meet his. She would have this from him, a memory to carry in her heart.

His kiss was hot and hungry, not at all like the ones of gentle innocence they had shared before. He pressed her against the length of him and laid claim to her soul. When he finally raised his head, her own was spinning.

She'd kissed him in return, with equal passion. There was no denying it. And the bold light in his eyes told her he knew it.

She pushed from his chest, and he let her go.

"I'll be around, Rach," he promised, his voice ragged and deep.

She gazed at him for a moment longer before pivoting and walking rapidly away. The urge to turn and run back to throw herself into his arms was powerful, but thinking of her parents and son, she resisted.

At the corner the urge overpowered her, and she paused to glance over her shoulder. Dallas stood beneath the elm still, gazing at her. She felt that gaze as she hurried away across the street, tears streaming down her face.

"Papa Ace taught me how to lift up my colt's feet today," Aaron said that evening at the dinner table.

He was bubbling over with enthusiasm about the colt and their lessons because Ace had told Aaron that he could compete in the amateur halter class at a paint-horse show coming up in two months.

"Scout just has to win it," he mumbled around a mouthful of potatoes. "He's the prettiest horse I ever saw."

"Don't talk with your mouth full," Rachel cautioned, giving him a smile. *Dallas must understand—she had Aaron to consider.*

Her gaze strayed to her mother and then her father. *She couldn't for one moment entertain the idea of marrying Dallas.*

Being an only child to parents such as hers gave all three of them a special relationship—such as she had with Aaron. She'd always been open with both her parents, had always been able to go to them for advice and comfort. When she had taken up with Coy, it had put a horrible breach in that special relationship that had at last almost healed in these past five years. To marry Dallas would tear her relationship with her parents wide apart—maybe never to be healed again. Not only couldn't she bear that for herself or for them, but Aaron would be caught in it all, too.

But how would she bear living without Dallas?

"Where did you and your friend go for lunch, Rachel?" her father asked, jolting her out of her thoughts.

"Oh...to...to Murphy's." Her words stumbled out.

"Hey, I like that place. Mind if we go there for our lunch tomorrow?"

"No, that'd be fine." She'd forgotten about her lunch date with her father. *Oh, she didn't want to go to Murphy's.*

"Jasper, why don't you take Rachel to the new Embassy Gardens? I think she'd enjoy it." Her mother shifted her gaze to Rachel. "It's like eating in a beautiful greenhouse."

"Well...okay." Her father rubbed his stomach. "They have a pretty good cheesecake there." Her parents shared a smile.

After dinner Rachel sat in the darkened sun room with her mother, enjoying coffee, while Aaron and her father retired to watch a videotaped recording of *The Andy Griffith Show*, which had become their favorite television program.

"Is something wrong, sweetheart?" her mother asked softly.

"No," Rachel answered quickly with a shake of her head. "Why?" She averted her eyes to the delicate china cup and took a long sip.

"You hardly ate a thing...and I think I know my daughter well enough to know when something is bothering her."

Rachel forced herself to look at her mother. She gave a small smile. "I think I'm just tired—all the stress from the move catching up with me. And allergies that I didn't have out in Phoenix."

For a long moment they gazed at each other. Rachel knew her mother didn't believe her explanation, and she had a sudden impulse to confide in her mother. But she couldn't, of course. She didn't want to take a chance on hurting her mother—or asking her mother to play confidant, keeping it from her father. There'd been no secrets between the two in the thirty-odd years of marriage.

No, this was not something for which she could run to her mother for help. This she must handle alone.

Rising, she said, "I think I'll get into the hot tub for a while."

For a few more precious moments alone, Dallas gazed at the coral sunset and watched the last sliver of the orange sun slip beyond the horizon. The scent of the panatela clamped between his teeth mingled with that of the night air. He ached with longing for Rachel. It was as if now that he'd given voice to his feelings, his passion for her was bubbling up within him a hundred times stronger than before, never again to be stifled.

Patience. He had to have patience. Wisdom gained over his relatively short thirty-seven years told him that the last word hadn't been spoken yet between him and Rachel. Her mouth had given voice to practical considerations, ones that couldn't be ignored and with which he agreed. But her eyes and lips had spoken of yet deeper truths. She loved him as much as he did her. And he'd just have to give her time to come around.

But what if she didn't?

He would live his life as he did now. He'd rather remain alone for the rest of his life than settle for less than he could have with Rachel. Boy, would his father hate that—maybe even more than he'd hate him and Rachel together, he thought with a dry chuckle.

Tossing the butt of his cigar to the ground, he twisted his boot on it, then turned and walked between the stable and cow barn back toward the house. The sound of rapid foot-

PLAY THE

LUCKY CARNIVAL WHEEL

scratch-off game
and get as many as
SIX FREE GIFTS . . .

HOW TO PLAY:

1. With a coin, carefully scratch off the silver area at right. Then check your number against the chart below it to find out which gifts you're eligible to receive.

2. You'll receive brand-new Silhouette Special Edition® novels and possibly other gifts—ABSOLUTELY FREE! Send back this card and we'll promptly send you the free books and gifts you qualify for!

3. We're betting you'll want more of these heartwarming romances, so unless you tell us otherwise, every month we'll send you 6 more wonderful novels to read and enjoy. Always delivered right to your home. And always at a discount off the cover price!

4. Your satisfaction is guaranteed! You may return any shipment of books and cancel at any time. The Free Books and Gifts remain yours to keep!

NO COST! NO RISK!
NO OBLIGATION TO BUY!

More Good News For Members Only!

When you join the Silhouette Reader Service™, you'll receive 6 heartwarming romance novels each month delivered to your home. You'll also get additional free gifts from time to time as well as our members-only newsletter. It's your privileged look at upcoming books and profiles of our most popular authors!

If offer card is missing, write to: Harlequin Reader Service, 901 Fuhrmann Blvd., P.O. Box 1867, Buffalo, NY 14269-1867 steps drew his gaze. Quinn came hurrying toward him; her expression and movements betrayed agitation.

"I'm glad I found you," she said a bit breathlessly. She laid a hand on his arm to stop him. "I thought I'd better warn you—Daddy brought Megan home for dinner."

Dallas stood there, stunned and yet not so, either. He tried to be mad, but it was as if his longing for Rachel overshadowed everything else. If he couldn't have Rachel, then nothing else in life seemed to matter very much.

Quinn slipped her arm through his, and together they walked back to the house. "Dallas," she said as they mounted the back stairs, "is there anything I can do?"

He shook his head. "No, but thanks. And don't look so worried."

"You're not going to change your mind and marry her like Daddy wants, are you?"

He regarded her. "I thought you liked Megan."

"I liked her okay, but I like it better that you decided not to marry her." She raised her eyebrows questioningly.

He smiled dryly. "I haven't changed my mind."

"Then the yelling I can handle." She flashed him an encouraging smile.

But there was no yelling. Dallas greeted Megan and his father with polite warmth and all the charm he possessed, thoroughly confounding them. Both of them had obviously expected anger, if not rage at his father's highhandedness. Dallas told himself he should be ashamed for putting on a show. Several times he almost lost it by bursting out laughing at the expressions on Megan's and his father's faces. And Yancey's twinkling eyes and hidden grins didn't help.

Perhaps he'd missed his calling in life, he thought as he escorted Megan to her seat in the dining room and even held her chair. He probably could have been a very good gigolo.

Toward the end of dinner, which Stella served, at the same time managing to be in the room enough to hear just about every word spoken, Megan brought up the wedding.

"Quinn has taken care of canceling everything quite efficiently," Dallas said calmly. "She's even handled making certain all the guests were called."

Megan licked her lips, and the old man stared hard at him.

"Thank you, Quinn," Megan said quietly to his sister.

Dallas folded his napkin and laid it on the table. "Megan, if you wouldn't mind, I'd like to have a few words alone with you."

Her mouth quirked into a small smile. "I'd like that, too."

Dallas led the way to his father's study and closed the double doors. He would have rather gone outside beneath the stars, but he knew Megan wouldn't. He leaned against his father's carved desk; she sat gracefully in one of the leather chairs.

"I wanted to tell you again that I'm sorry, Megan. What I did was lousy—I shouldn't have let everything go so far. All I can say is that I didn't realize certain things before. We were suited great as long as neither of us required much from the other—you do your thing, and I do mine. But marriage requires giving of ourselves—which neither of us seemed to be able to do."

She looked hurt and slowly rose, arching her breasts at him in a coy movement. "It's I who should be apologizing. I behaved very ugly yesterday, Dallas. I'm not proud of it, and the truth is that I took great care all the time we've been seeing each other that you would never see that side of me. I have a terrible temper."

She pressed herself against his arm and gazed up at him beneath her long dark lashes.

"And I'm sorry, darling...so very sorry for the last months. I know I've taken you for granted." Her lips formed a pretty pout. "And because of that I've lost you." Her eyes grew moist, and she ran a hand over his arm. "Please, Dallas, can't you forgive enough to give me another chance? I've learned my lesson."

She parted her moist lips and sent him a heavy gaze. Dallas felt he was watching a master in deliberate seduction. Suddenly it seemed Megan was very much like his father—she didn't give up easily. He supposed he should be flattered. But he was more disgusted. Did she know him so little, have so little regard for him after two years?

He stepped away from her. "You had every right to want to bash my brains in, Megan—and you and I both know it. Don't back down on that stand simply because you think we can backtrack," he said firmly. "Because we can't. I haven't changed my mind. It won't work between us."

Her blue eyes blazed. "And you think it will work with your precious Rachel?"

"Don't bring her into this," he cautioned, warning in his tone.

"You used me for these years, and now you think you can just toss me aside since she's come back."

Dallas took a breath. He probably deserved all this, but he wasn't going to stand there and take it. There was no sense to recriminations.

"I said I was sorry." He paused, regarding her, seeing the fury tightening her petite body. She was like a bobcat poised to spring. "That's all I can offer you—or do you want money? I can give you a little bit of that. I don't actually have a lot of cash, Megan."

She gave a caustic laugh. "I don't need a *little bit* of your money." She lifted her chin; her blue eyes narrowed. "You'll regret it, Dallas. Oh, how I'll make certain you regret this."

He'd hurt her pride, he realized then quite clearly. And that was a hurt that went bone deep. He regarded her silently, forcing her to tell him what else she wanted to say without his having to ask.

"Your father and I lunched together today," she said, a whisper of a smile touching her lips. "And he's driving me back tonight. It may be late, so don't worry if he doesn't return until morning."

He snapped his head up and stared at her.

She gave a saucy smile. "I wouldn't want him driving so far alone so late at night—surely you wouldn't, either."

He stared at her, assessing what she was saying. Her expression told him very clearly—she was intending to pursue a relationship, serious or not, with the old man.

"Is this to get back at me, Megan?"

She looked deliberately thoughtful. "Your father and I happen to enjoy each other—we think a lot alike. He's attentive to a woman without desiring a lot in return, which younger men seem to. And he's wanting terribly to make up to me for the humiliation his son has inflicted." A bare, hard smile touched her carefully made-up lips. "If my having a relationship with your father should upset you, then all the better."

Dallas studied her. Her pale blue eyes glittered; her mouth quirked on the edge of a satisfied smile.

"You're not afraid I might tell him of your designs?" he asked, amused but hiding it.

"He wouldn't believe you. He's too mad at you to believe anything you say." Satisfaction echoed in her voice.

He gazed down at the rug, then lifted his eyes pointedly to hers. "I don't have to worry about my father," he said. "He's no fool. And he's known many a woman in his time. He gives only what he wishes—never any more. As a woman who can offer him only being his wife, you'll rate a poor second to his children or grandchildren."

Her self-assured smile faded. "Damn you, Dallas."

He stepped out toward the door. "You said that before. Shall we join the others?" He opened the door and waited politely for her to go first.

After a pointed glare in his direction, she lifted her chin and passed in front of him. He came behind and watched her sidle up to his father, turning on all the considerable charm she possessed. Yancey shot him a raised eyebrow and shared a grin. Then, over Megan's head, the old man shot him a speculative gaze. To Dallas's surprise he saw his father's lips turn upward with a mischievous grin.

Rachel did not see Dallas. For the next weeks she either had Ace pick Aaron up from school or had her mother drive him over to the Cordell Ranch. It was her only defense against herself.

Even so, the longing gnawed at her. More than once she cursed Dallas for ever admitting his love for her, because the knowing made it a thousand times harder to turn away. It was as if she stood behind a thick glass, able to view paradise but barred from ever entering into it.

Dallas loves me... Dallas is free... he's waiting.

He came to her with the bawling of a calf, the warmth of the sun on her cheek and the scent of tobacco. She saw him in the sunrise and the sunset. And she heard about him from Aaron.

"Uncle Dallas helped me with my jump shots today. Did you know he was a basketball all-star in high school, Mom?"

"Uncle Dallas let me bottle-feed that baby calf today."

"Uncle Dallas said hello, Mom."

She couldn't avoid him forever, of course. There came a day when she had to drive Aaron over to the Cordell Ranch, and when she pulled to a stop before the house, Dallas stepped out onto the porch. She knew he'd been waiting and was filled with pleasure—though she knew full well she shouldn't be.

He strode easily down the steps and over to greet them. He smiled first at Aaron, and then his gaze swung around to rest warmly on Rachel.

"Is Papa out with my colt, Uncle Dallas?"

"Yes..." Dallas said, jerking his attention back down to her son. "He's waiting for you."

"Okay! See ya, Mom." He gave her a quick, hard hug around the middle and then flew away toward the barns.

Rachel gazed down at the gravel, then at Dallas's boots, then his belt and lastly, his face. He'd grown more tanned, and his eyes seemed paler.

"You doin' all right?" he asked. His low tone vibrated within her.

"Yes, fine. And you?"

"Okay." He pinned her with those glistening pale eyes.

She turned toward the car. "Aaron's staying the night," she said. Reaching through the open window, she pulled out a vinyl duffel bag. "Here're his things."

He reached for the bag, and their hands brushed. The touch sent a tingling shooting up her arm. "I'll put it up in his room," he said.

She nodded and knew she could leave but dreaded it at the same time. "Aaron's been moved up to one of the starters for the last game of their basketball season. I'm grateful for the help you've given him."

He shrugged. "It hasn't taken much time. I just showed him the basics and then had him practice."

"So he said." She had to smile. "He said you *made* him practice."

A trace of a grin touched his lips, too. "The boy tends to have a bit of a lazy streak."

"And we all let him get away with it," she finished for him.

He inclined his head for an answer and continued to stare at her.

"Well...I'd best be going. I promised Mom we'd go shopping this evening."

She opened the car door and slipped behind the wheel. He closed the door after her, then rested his hand on the open window.

"You going to early church with your parents tomorrow?" he asked in a very low voice. His gaze was steady.

"Yes, I'd planned to." His eyes held her captive; her heart fluttered.

"I'll be out in the west pasture around eight tomorrow morning," he said. "The mornings are awfully pretty out there."

For one long second more, he held her gaze. Then he stepped back and straightened. With clumsy fingers, Rachel started the car and shifted into gear, driving away.

Eight tomorrow morning. The mornings are awfully pretty. His voice echoed in her mind.

As she stared at the gravel driveway before her, she thought of her life. It seemed in that moment exactly like that dry, gravel driveway, heading away into nowhere. And she was the only one who could change that.

Chapter Eight

Rachel held a cup of coffee between her hands and gazed out at the beautiful spring morning.

The house was quiet. Willow was away until evening, and Rachel's parents had left an hour earlier to enjoy a leisurely breakfast at Biscuit Hill Restaurant before church services. It was a tradition with them. Her father maintained he needed that time to get all his talking out before accompanying her mother to the conservative Quaker meetinghouse where much of their service was spent in silence—something he found hard to abide.

Her parents had raised her to have high standards in regards to respect, trust and honesty. In their eyes she had bent those standards when she'd run off and married Coy. She didn't want to let them down again.

Which was one reason why, at 7:40, she was still arguing heatedly with herself. She still hadn't decided to meet Dallas.

She hadn't lied to her parents, she thought. She'd simply said she wasn't accompanying them this morning. She'd given them no reason. They hadn't asked, though her mother had given her a very thoughtful look.

Abruptly she turned from the window, set her cup to the bedside table and lifted the telephone receiver, punching the numbers for the phone that rang in both the hands' cottages and the barn.

"Nick," she said when he answered after six long rings, "please saddle Cara for me."

She was a child no longer. She had to live by her own set of rules. She would go—and before all the doubts and practical reasons overwhelmed her again. Sometimes practicality got in the way of life.

In a flurry of motion she stripped from her gown and robe and pulled clothes from the dresser, jerking them on. She raked a brush through her hair, loosely braided and fastened it with a leather strip. Peering into the mirror, she dabbed blush to her cheeks and brushed a bit of powder on her face. She hopped out the door, tugging on her boots as she went.

The digital clock on the counter in the kitchen said seven-forty-five. She popped frozen homemade sausage biscuits into the microwave, then filled an insulated canteen with hot coffee. She wrapped the hot biscuits in foil and placed them along with linen napkins and tin cups into a string bag. At the last minute she added sugar—Dallas used to take a heaping teaspoon of sugar in his coffee.

It was two minutes past eight when she headed Cara into the southern breeze. The sun was high and warm but the air nippy as it was given to be on early spring mornings. She urged Cara into a full lope, reveling in the horse's rhythm and the fresh breeze that blew in her face. Dallas hadn't said which part of the Cordell west pasture. She could only guess, and headed for the area where she'd seen him that one time weeks ago.

Would he wait for her?

Oh, Lord, please let him wait.

Both she and Cara were breathing hard when they came up over a hill and saw the fence that marked the division between the ranches in the distance. Rachel strained to see as she pressed Cara onward. She saw only cattle.

For a moment she waited at the fence and gazed toward where she'd seen Dallas that day. When he didn't appear from the trees, she turned Cara and headed west, toward an area where trees thickened around the fence.

And then, as if from nowhere, Dallas appeared. He was on foot, hat pushed to the back of his head, panatela protruding from his lips. He stopped and leaned against a fence post beneath a giant hackberry tree. When she rode closer, she saw his smile, the brown hair fluttering across his forehead and the way his brown flannel shirt stretched across his shoulders. Behind him was a wagon—piled with hay!

"Good morning," he said quietly when she halted Cara.

"Good morning."

She stared down into twinkling gray-blue eyes filled with delight.

He lifted his arms. "Let me help you over to my side, ma'am," he said with an exaggerated drawl.

Joy flooded her, bubbling up in laughter. She felt so finely alive, and beautiful and womanly. And in love.

"You know the way to a man's heart," Dallas said, munching on one of the biscuits Rachel had brought.

He enjoyed looking at her. The sunshine filtered through the tree branches above to glisten upon her dark hair hanging over her breast. Her cheeks were rosy with life; her eyes sparkled. And he knew by the look in those fathomless coffee-brown eyes that she would be his before she left.

"Well, you don't do bad yourself, sir." She licked her lips with the tip of her tongue and smiled above what was left of a sweet honey bun he'd brought. It was one of several packaged sweets that he'd grabbed the evening before, remembering that she used to like them and counting on her coming this morning.

"Cold?" he asked.

She shook her head. "Not really."

They sat on two wool blankets atop the soft hay of the wagon—Dallas half lying. The shade was cooler than it would be out in the sun, but it was also much more private. Neither of them seemed to require conversation; it was enough just to be together. They sipped the coffee she had brought—it was much better than what he'd made.

He drank deeply, then glanced up to see Rachel studying him over the rim of her cup. "Aaron's not too happy with you," she said, her expression impassive.

"Oh?" He wondered what he'd done, but the knot of worry between his shoulder blades disappeared when she grinned.

"He says you *made* him muck his horse's stall, even after Ace said one of the hands could do it."

Dallas nodded. "Guilty."

"Well . . . he went out and mucked Cara's stall the other day without being told," she said quietly.

"He's a good kid."

"I think so. Even if he is pretty bullheaded, like all the rest of the men in his family."

He raised an eyebrow and smiled, finding himself lost in her shining hair and ivory skin. He watched her eyes stray to his chest, then slowly back up again. A gentle throb started in his loins.

"No less than the women," he drawled as he gazed at the feminine swells of her breasts. Then he looked upward to see whether he was getting the reaction he expected. He was— her face bore a delicate flush.

With a teasing grin, she leaned over and tickled his nose with a piece of straw.

"Come here..." he commanded in a low husky tone that sent a rush through Rachel. His eyes were heavy with desire.

She froze, her gaze fastened on his, her heartbeat echoing in her ears. Suddenly all the cautions popped at once into her mind and whirled around . . . and hot desire. She'd waited so long . . .

He reached out; his hand closed around her wrist. Gently he tugged her forward until she rested against his chest. She inhaled the alluring scents of him. With his gaze still holding hers, he pressed a hand to the back of her neck to pull her head toward him. Heat washed over her in the manner of water rippling over pebbles. His breath teased her cheeks a split second before his lips met hers.

Their kiss was sweet and warm, then turned hard and hot. His shoulder muscles rippled and hardened beneath her hands. His tongue sparred with hers, and she savored the taste of him—that of sweet coffee and tobacco. When at last he broke away, she gasped for breath and pressed her forehead against his cheek. Through blurred vision she saw his chest heaving.

She twisted and lay in the cushiony hay, gazing up at him as he loomed over her. Budding tree limbs and blue sky formed a background for his tanned face. She touched a finger to his cheek, then stroked downward to his chin.

How long she'd wanted to lie like this, to be in his arms and surrounded by his love. So many lonely nights she dreamed of him . . . imagined him . . .

Using one hand, he tugged her hair free of its braid, then combed his fingers through it. With feminine pleasure she watched him gaze with wonder at her hair as he spread it against the blanket and down over her shoulder.

"Don't ever cut it," he said fiercely. His eyes burned into hers, and again he stroked her tresses. Spreading out across the blanket and down upon her ivory skin, they resembled ripples of water beneath a bright moon at night.

"I want you," he whispered raggedly. And never had he known such wanting—nor such love. It was the culmination of years of longing bursting up from the secret places where he'd hidden it, denied it all these years.

"I want you, too." Her voice vibrated with desire.

He gazed into her deep, dark eyes, savoring the moment. There was no denying that she'd known exactly what would happen—and she'd still come to meet him.

For now, nothing else mattered. And she told him so with her eyes.

His hand moved to stroke her inner thigh, and pleasure sliced through him at the fire that lit her eyes. Automatically she moved her leg against his hand.

Slow...slow, he cautioned himself as the throbbing within him took off like a racing stallion.

As he stroked upward over her denim-clad leg and gently cupped her pubescence, she moaned, shattering whatever was left of his reserve. He pushed at her sweater, seeking the warm silkiness of her skin, having to have it next to his.

"Rachel..." he whispered. "Oh, Rachel..."

They made love with sweet abandonment, as two spirits soaring in the wind. And also as if they each knew this singular day and time would never come again.

There, surrounded by nature, which neither condoned nor condemned, they shed their clothes. Slowly at first. Dallas slipped her sweater over her head and caressed her heated skin. Even his calluses brought pleasure, as did his moist, eager lips. She unbuttoned his shirt. Their passion rose as their skin touched, and no longer were they content to move slowly.

The blanket was coarse against Rachel's back; Dallas's hands were tender on her breasts. His lips were warm and sweet and wet everywhere they pressed. Repeatedly he sought and tested and found the secret passion points of her body, pressing those points until Rachel thought she would die of the pleasure. His skin was smooth and hot, and his rock-hard muscles trembled against her with restrained desire.

His lips found and teased her tender nipples, and she cried out, arching against him. *Oh, Dallas...* She raked her fingers through his thick, silky hair. *My love...*

A throbbing ache opened wide within her. A sweet, hot ache that demanded fulfillment.

The fresh breeze caressed her skin, as did his hands and breath. Wondrous passion swept through her body, fraying every nerve, filling every cell. And then they came together, merging, demanding and giving in the mindless, glorious fashion of male and female. She was his; he was hers.

For a very precious ten minutes, no more, Rachel lay in the shelter of Dallas's strong arm, pressed against the length of him. He'd pulled one of the blankets atop them; beneath it the sweat of their naked bodies mingled. His thumb drew circles on her side; his heartbeat thudded in her ear. Neither of them spoke, as if the moment was too fragile to be broken by voices. At last they had made love.

Questions tried to force their way into her mind still wonderfully drugged by their lovemaking. She pushed them away; she didn't want to think, wanted to hold this moment as long as possible.

But still, as the minutes ticked by, the practical side of her nature made itself known. Where to from here? They'd shared their love, but the barriers remained between them. And she'd been so juvenile in not using any birth control.

She squeezed her eyes closed against tears. It had been so beautiful. She didn't want to spoil the moment with thinking—about anything!

Dallas stirred. "Guess we can't be layin' around here all day."

"You don't want to get caught with your boots off," she teased, finding her voice coming hoarse past the lump in her throat.

They both sat up. Cool air rushed over Rachel's body and seemed to go right through a hole in her heart.

The blanket fell around Dallas's hips, and Rachel modestly used part of it to cover her breasts. She found herself staring at his bare chest. His skin was a pale coppery color, smooth and stretched tight over full muscles.

Suddenly he extended his hands and cupped her cheeks. Her heavy hair fell over his arms and caressed her bare back. He brought his lips to hers in a slow, enticing kiss in which he nibbled and sucked on her lips until the ache of longing flamed again in her belly.

When he raised his head, she lifted her eyes to find a shadow dimmed the twinkle in his eyes.

"If you don't get dressed, those horses are going to have to stay tethered for another hour at least." He winked and handed over her sweater.

Rachel was grateful for his gathering up his clothes and disappearing around the side of the wagon to let her dress in privacy. Silly modesty, she thought, in the light of what they'd shared.

When she hopped to the ground, she found him leaning against the front wheel, smoking one of his favored thin cigars. He studied her, and she felt his unvoiced questions.

"You know the O'Connor place?" he asked.

She shook her head.

He looked away, as if what he was saying was hard for him. "It's south, prime land along the Washita." He faced her. "I bought five hundred acres of it when it went for sale at auction two years ago. And last week I bought the house from Ted O'Connor. It's a two-bedroom rock, nothing fancy, and it needs work."

His words took her breath. "Does your father know?" she asked.

"Yes."

"What would happen to Ace if he learned we wanted to marry? Don't you think about that?" she asked, lifting her chin and flinging her hair back over her shoulder.

His eyes flashed. "I do." He shifted his stance. "But I can't make decisions about my life by worrying about the effect those decisions will have on my father."

"I can't *not* think of it, Dallas. You know what store he puts in his sons bringing their wives home to live—it's the main reason he forgave Coy for marrying me in the first place."

"He forgave Coy because Coy was his favorite," Dallas said bluntly. "And also because having you at the ranch was a way to get at Jasper."

She searched her mind for words to explain her fears. "We will hurt them, Dallas. All of them. So very badly."

"You're putting them over *me*." His crystal eyes narrowed with anger.

"I'm trying to think of *everyone* that I love. You can try to say it doesn't matter, but it does." She recalled the bitter lessons of the past. "Believe me, it does. There's truth in the saying that a marriage is only as good as the in-laws."

He stared at her for long seconds in which an inexpressive, almost frightening mask came over his face. "Do you use any birth control?" he asked.

She froze. "No," she said with a shake of her head. Since Coy's death she hadn't had reason to.

He inclined his head. "I'll take precautions for the next time."

"Are you planning on this happening again?" He assumed a lot, she thought, feeling suddenly foolish and irritated and terribly degraded. And alone, for it was as if an invisible wall had sprung up to separate them.

His lips quirked, and that irritating manly know-it-all expression flitted across his face. "I think that'll be up to you," he said. "I'll be around and willing."

Rachel swung away, ashamed of the wanting that still coursed through her veins. Her pride wanted to say that she wouldn't come to him again, that she wouldn't live this way, but her heart couldn't make such a statement.

He seemed so cold, so angry all of a sudden—and she couldn't pretend she didn't understand. She, too, was angry. At him for his attitude, at herself for her weakness and at the situation they were caught in.

Well, perhaps she was confused and not quite proud of herself, but he didn't have to act so high-and-mighty, either. She retaliated in the only way possible, by striding away to the fence.

"You don't want to forget your canteen and bag," he called after her. "Someone may ask questions."

"We have plenty—no one will notice," she retorted over her shoulder.

But with quick strides he caught up with her and laid a hand on her shoulder. "I'll help you over the fence," he said, though his voice still held that odd coldness.

She was mounted on the mare when he took hold of the animal's bridle. "Rachel . . . it was the best for me."

She stared down into his iridescent eyes. Warmth pooled in her belly, then coursed through her body. Her heart leaped with sweet joy. She saw the questioning in his eyes. "For me, too."

His hand came to rest on her thigh and began to stroke downward. He pulled something from his pocket and held it up to her.

"I found this the other day and thought you might like it." His gray eyes were unreadable.

Slowly she reached out to take the object. Her heart leaped to her throat as she saw it was a rose rock, about the size of a quarter and exquisitely formed. She fingered its rough-edged petals and looked at it with vision blurred by tears.

"Thank you." Her voice came out a ragged whisper.

He shrugged and gave a bare grin, then turned away with a wave. In an instant he was back over the fence and walking away toward the wagon. Rachel clucked to Cara and urged her into a trot, the rose rock pressed into her palm.

Dallas allowed the horses to make their own slow pace. He leaned on his thighs, the reins held loosely in his hands.

He'd bit his tongue against saying the words bursting within him, he thought angrily. He'd wanted to tell Rachel again how he loved her, but if she didn't know it by what had just happened between them, then she'd never know it. He'd wanted to ask her again to marry him—but he'd said it once; to do so again would be like begging.

He wouldn't speak of any of those things, he thought firmly. He was pushing himself about as far as he would go. Seeing Rachel in secret didn't set well with him. Damn it! He didn't have anything to hide!

He caught the rustle of the hay in the wagon, and for an instant recalled that same sound when he'd pressed Rachel deeper into its softness. Her skin was like silk, and her scent had almost driven him crazy. It had been better between them than his best imaginings. And if God would give him anything he asked, he asked now that he be allowed to make love to Rachel many more times in this lifetime. If he couldn't he might as well join a monastery, because he'd been ruined for any other woman.

That night, as Rachel was tucking Aaron into bed, he showed her a pocketknife Dallas had given him. "He said it was Dad's when he was a kid," Aaron said.

Rachel gazed at the scarred pearl-handled knife with mixed emotions. Aaron was just ten, too young for such a thing, she thought. But it had belonged to his father—and no doubt had been a precious keepsake for Dallas.

"He said I'm not too young, Mom," Aaron said, as if reading her thoughts. "I'll be careful."

"I should hope. Put it here so you won't lose it," she said, opening the bedstand drawer. With typical mother thoughts, she hoped he'd forget about it for a few years.

She tucked the covers up around him and pretended to overlook Wheeler stealing up on the bed.

Later, in the privacy of her bedroom, she stared at her reflection in the mirror and wondered whether she knew the woman looking out at her. That morning she'd made love with Dallas. The fact echoed within her; the memory of his touch still heated her skin. She touched her lips, feeling again his kiss.

She'd burned for Dallas. And still did.

The weeks passed, and Rachel did what she'd never imagined she would—she became Dallas's lover. And rather than feeling constant shame, she felt wonderfully alive, as if she'd found the door to paradise.

One evening he waited for her after work and took her for a romantic dinner and then dancing, where their bodies pressed together and moved with the rhythm of the music. There was no time to be alone, so they savored the bit of time they did have. Another time she met him for a drive in the country. Driving and holding hands, laughing and talking, loving each other with their eyes. He took her one evening to the town house of a friend who was away on an extended trip, and there they made love, then had a picnic on the floor in front of the fireplace and made love again. Rachel had never known such passion—nor such love.

Then came the time Dallas showed her where he'd found her the rose rock. It was a rust-colored butte on the land he'd bought from O'Connor. The area hadn't changed since the days when the Plains Indians had undoubtedly used it as a lookout to the surrounding flatland.

"This was once Cordell land," Dallas said, gazing around with the expression of a man who reveres the land simply because it is. "Way back before the allotments and division of the Chickasaw territory."

"No Cordells filed on it for their allotments?" she asked, savoring looking at him.

He nodded. "Yes, they did. But over the years and with marriages, it passed out of Indian and Cordell hands." That had happened so much, Rachel knew.

"Will you show me the house?" she asked finally, because she had to, though she sensed he would refuse.

He gazed at her a long minute, then shook his head. He made no explanation. He didn't have to. There was a great understanding that existed between them without words. Rachel knew Dallas would only show her the house when she was prepared to live there with him.

He took her hand, and together they explored the butte, searching for and finding rose rocks. Rachel enjoyed looking at them, then left them where they were—where they belonged.

On a secluded shelf of the butte, sheltered from the cool spring wind and warmed by sunshine, Dallas made love to her. Wonderful, exquisite love. Leisurely, with deliberate tantalizing slowness, he explored her body with his hands, finding tender places she hadn't even known existed. She did the same with him, her passion sweeping aside her inhibitions. For the first time since that morning in the hay wagon, the words "I love you" burst from her lips. Thankfully, wonderfully, he answered in kind. And afterward he held her, naked beneath a wide blue sky. She listened to his heart and thought with wonder that she'd never known anything like the emotion spilling over from her heart.

Dallas was gentle, sexy, sometimes fiery, often stubborn and always strong. He was so *sure* of everything. He was all she could ever want. There would be no other man for her, ever.

And it became harder to deny the longing inside to be completely his. Though he did not speak again of marriage.

What was she going to do?

If she chose to join her life with Dallas's, she knew she would hurt her parents deeply. She could also very well lose all connection with them, and she took a chance of alienating Aaron, as well, or at the very least putting him in the impossible situation between her and Dallas and all three of his grandparents.

But how could she give up Dallas? Pain shot through her at the thought; she didn't think she could bear it.

With every passing day she balanced between fearing she would lose Dallas and the certainty that eventually their affair would be found out—and then everyone was going to lose, all the way around.

You're putting them above me. Dallas's accusation sprang into her thoughts. It was an uncomfortable memory.

Dallas was in a foul humor. This year's rains had been all but nonexistent, and spring was rapidly slipping away. There was a hard knot that persisted in his loins—and the only way to get rid of it was denied him.

He hadn't seen Rachel in a week. He'd had to go away for a couple of days, and then she'd been busy at the store and had social engagements with her parents.

One evening he'd attended a political barbecue with Clyde Jennings because he'd known Jasper would no doubt be there and had hoped Rachel would be with him. He'd spied her at a distance, dancing with some handsome dude—some jerk with blond hair that looked like it came from a bottle and boots that had come from Italy. He'd been about to greet her and the dude when Jasper had joined the couple and the three had gone off together.

He didn't call her; she didn't call him. Apparently she didn't have a problem with that, he fumed as he made an inventory of the veterinarian supplies in the cabinet in the barn. He'd lost count of the needles twice, so he gave up and just listed an approximate number.

He'd told her he wouldn't press, he reminded himself as he turned to look for mineral blocks. She had to have time to come around—and he'd thought she was. Each time they made love, it was harder to let her go away from him, and he'd sensed it was the same for her.

Had he been wrong?

She was determined to put everyone else's happiness and welfare above his own. That ought to tell him how much she loved him.

A noise caught his attention, and he turned to see Aaron in the doorway. The boy stood there, clothes splattered with white splotches and both tennis shoes untied.

"I finished," he said. His big gray eyes were very solemn.

"What did you do with the brush?"

"I washed it and hung it back up." Dallas nodded and turned back to the cabinets. "How's your basketball goal look now?" He knew Aaron was a bit angry with him for making him paint the pole for his basketball goal.

"Pretty good," Aaron said. His lighter voice again drew Dallas's gaze.

"Feel better about it, do you?" he asked, and shared a smile with the boy. His heart squeezed as it often did when he looked at Aaron and saw the resemblance to both Coy and Rachel.

"Yeah..." Aaron came into the room. Casting a curious glance at the open cabinets, he leaned against the counter. Dallas ascertained that they had only a few mineral blocks and no salt blocks, and noted it on the feed-store shopping list.

"Your mom coming for you tonight?" Dallas asked, trying to act nonchalant.

"No...she's working late. Quinn's taking me home."

Dallas nodded, disappointed. *He damn well wouldn't call her.*

"Uncle Dallas..."

"Yes..." Dallas looked up when the boy didn't continue.

Aaron swallowed. "Our basketball team is having this father-son dinner on Friday to celebrate the end of the season—sort of." He scuffed his dirty sneaker on the cement floor. "Do you think you could go with me?"

It took Dallas a minute to answer, wondering whether he should ask Rachel first. The old man and Jasper weren't going to be too happy about this.

"Well, sure, Aaron. I'd be glad to."

The boy's face lit up like a neon sign in the desert. "I'm sorry I waited so late to ask...but, well, I figured on asking Papa Ace or Grandpa J., but whichever one I asked would make the other one mad." He scuffed his sneaker again. "None of the other kids are bringing their grandpa—and you're more like a dad. You make me do things." The vulnerable look on his face cut straight through to Dallas's heart.

"Thanks... I think." They shared a chuckle.

Then the boy's eyebrows knotted. "Will you tell Papa?" he asked hesitantly.

"Sure... no problem."

"Thanks! I'd better get washed up before I get in Quinn's car or she'll skin me."

As Dallas watched Aaron scamper off, a new hope kindled within him. Aaron was his nephew, his brother's son. Dallas had as much responsibility for Aaron's future as either grandfather did. He'd never looked at it quite like that before—and he didn't think Rachel had, either.

Late that evening Dallas was playing pool with Quinn when the telephone rang. Quinn went to answer it. He stilled, listening, knowing instinctively that it was Rachel. He'd been waiting for her call. When Quinn came in and announced it was Rachel for him, his father cast him a dark gaze.

"Aaron told me about the father-son dinner." Rachel's quiet voice came across the line, causing a knot to form again in his loins. "I'm very grateful to you for taking him."

"There's no need to be—he's my nephew. I'm glad to do it. And I'm glad you're not put out with me for not checking with you first."

"It was Aaron's choice," she said. "How's Ace taking it?"

"About like Aaron expected, but he'll get over it. He's consoling himself with expanding plans for a fishing trip during the spring break. How's Jasper?"

"He's disappointed, but I think he understands, too. Oh, Dallas, Aaron had a note about the dinner last week, but had hidden it from all of us. He was afraid to cause trouble between his grandfathers. He hadn't told me, and he's always come to me before." Her voice echoed with hurt.

Silence buzzed on the line as they both thought about this.

"He's growing, Rach," he said. "There's going to be some things you can't do for him."

"I know," she answered quietly.

"I'll pick him up Friday night a little before six."

"He'll be ready. And thanks again."

Friday morning a dozen long-stemmed yellow roses were delivered to Rachel's office. She knew even before opening the card that they were from Dallas. A bittersweet longing squeezed her heart.

After long minutes of gazing at the roses and sampling their fragrance, she opened the attached envelope and read the card.

I miss you—Dallas.

"Mmm," her father commented, poking his head in the door. "Jenny said you'd just gotten a mighty special delivery. 'Pears someone is right taken with my daughter." He gave his characteristic wink and stepped over to kiss her forehead. "Do I know him?"

She gazed into his eyes and smile, which were warm with love. "Yes," she answered slowly. "They're from Dallas."

His expression changed in a flash, turning cold and hard. "Why would Dallas send you roses?"

"I imagine because he wants to, Daddy." She tossed the card aside and turned toward a large crate leaning against the wall. "We've gotten in two more paintings by Blue Nightingale. Want to have first chance at them before I put them on display?"

If her father wanted to ask more, he restrained himself. He became absorbed with the paintings, deciding to purchase one. After he'd left, Rachel sat gazing at the roses.

Again and again throughout the afternoon, she found herself staring at them.

Dallas Cordell was one persistent man. One special man.

Their affair, which was the correct term, was beginning to take its toll on her. She was not a person suited for such a relationship. She couldn't go on living like this—feeling that she must hide a part of her life from those she dearly loved.

But she was beginning to believe that no matter how many people would be hurt, she couldn't give Dallas up. And the thought frightened her.

Rachel stood with her mother on the front porch and watched Aaron and Dallas walk away to the Lincoln. The resemblance between the two couldn't be overlooked. While combing Aaron's hair that evening, Rachel had realized that her son's hair was not only the same color as his uncle's, but had the same peak in the front.

Aaron waved gleefully as they drove away. He was so excited to be going to the dinner. The only thing to dim that excitement had been his grandfather's subtle criticism. Rachel had been glad when her father had retired to his study and hadn't come out when Dallas arrived. She didn't want this time spoiled for her son—nor for Dallas. She'd seen with great amusement and pleasure that Dallas was as excited as Aaron.

"Come walk out to the rose garden with me," her mother said, and slipped an arm through Rachel's.

They walked around the house and out across the lawn to the white-fenced area where her father grew his prized roses. The shrubs were beginning to put forth tiny green leaves.

"Daddy needs to get at the weeds," Rachel commented.

"He's busy with Aaron nowadays."

Rachel nodded with agreement.

"Your father told me that Dallas sent you roses—a dozen long-stemmed ones." Her mother studied her closely.

"Yes." She met her mother's gaze.

"You're my daughter...my only child," her mother said gently. "It isn't hard for me to sense when you're troubled. And after seeing yours and Dallas's faces tonight, I think I have a good idea of the problem."

There could be no lying to her mother, not ever. She leaned on the white board fence and looked out toward the barns. "I love him, Mama."

"And he loves you."

She nodded and cast her mother a pleading look. "Is that so awful?"

"What do you think?"

She bit her lip. "I'm ashamed . . . because I loved him before Coy died." She squeezed her eyes closed, then opened them. "I never betrayed Coy. Never. But Dallas and I had feelings for each other then. We didn't plan it—it just happened."

"And now you think you're not entitled to love him," her mother stated gently.

Rachel gazed into her mother's quiet, dark eyes. "Yes..." she said as the truth dawned on her for the first time. "I guess I do feel like I don't deserve to share a love with him. Especially one so . . . so special. Oh, Mama, it is special. I haven't cared for anyone in all these years. One of the reasons I had to come home was to see if our feelings for each other had died. I thought they had—really and truly. And then, that first day I saw him, it started all over again."

Her mother reached out and gathered her in an embrace. Rachel buried her face into her mother's neck for several long, comforting moments.

"Oh, Mama, I'm so sorry." Tears pushed between her closed lids, and she felt a small child again.

"Oh, my darling—what have you got to be sorry for? For loving someone?"

Rachel sniffed and stepped back. Her mother pulled a tissue from her sweater pocket and handed it to her. Rachel blew her nose, then said, "I don't want to let you and Daddy down again. Oh, Daddy will be furious with this."

"Rachel," her mother said firmly, "it was I and your father who let *you* down before, with Coy. You have a right to love whomever you please." Her mother's eyes sparked, then turned quietly curious. "Have you ever thought of such a love as a blessing?"

Amazed, she stared at her mother and shook her head.

Her mother smiled sadly. "I have a confession of my own." Her eyes resembled deep, dark pools. "Years ago, the first time I saw you with both Coy and Dallas, I thought even then that you were married to the wrong brother. Coy was so much like Dallas—both strong and handsome men, oozing sensuality. And don't look so wide-eyed. I'm a mother, but a woman first," she said, grinning, before again turning thoughtful. "But it was as if a piece had been left out of Coy, something important that left him weak in self-discipline.

"Still, the two were so much alike. And Dallas is the closest Aaron could ever come to his own true father, without his father's painful shortcomings. Dallas can give Aaron the father that he should have. And he loves you—and you love him. Such an opportunity doesn't come around to very many people. It is a blessing to you, to Aaron, to Dallas . . . and even to Ace, if he'll open his eyes to see it."

Rachel searched her mother's dark eyes. Then she gazed out at the bushes' first buds. The sun was dipping below the horizon; there were no shadows anymore, just a growing dimness.

Only her mother could look at the situation in such a light, she thought with wry amusement. She was given to finding the silver lining. Suddenly Rachel's heart felt lighter. Surely it could be a blessing, if they would let it be.

Then the doubts rallied. "But what about Daddy and Ace? Daddy won't see it as a blessing. And Ace may have a stroke."

"You must decide for yourself, for what you want and need. You won't be marrying your father or Ace, now will you?"

"There's still Aaron to consider. Already he was afraid to speak to anyone about the father-son dinner rather than get his grandfathers arguing. He'll hear things . . . about Dallas and me. People don't forget such juicy scandal. And now he'll be caught between both grandfathers and Dallas and me."

"You've done a great job with my grandson. He's secure in your love. He'll handle this." Her mother took her shoulders. "Talk to Aaron, Rachel. I think you'll find he may have already sensed more than you realize. He's a child—but not a blind one."

For long moments she and her mother stared at each other. Her mother was giving her blessing, she thought with wonder.

As if her mother read her thoughts, she said, "You are my daughter. Regardless of anything you may ever do, you are my daughter and I love you. I forgot that for a short time when you married Coy. I will never forget it again."

With a fervent motion Rachel reached out and wrapped her arms tight around her mother. "I love you, too, Mama."

Chapter Nine

Rachel was curled in the big chair in her bedroom late that night, enjoying a rare blend of specialty coffee and working on a new bead design, when her father knocked on the door with his customary four heavy raps. He poked his head around the door when she answered.

"Your mother said you'd decided not to go with us to the dog trials tomorrow," he said with a raised bushy eyebrow.

"No... I'd like to have a lazy day. It'll give me time to work on these moccasins—I'm trying a new design." She held the moccasin up to him.

He nodded. "You've been working awfully hard down at the store. You know, just because you're my daughter, you don't have to prove anything. You *can* take a day off once in a while."

"I'm going to—tomorrow," she said with a smile, and added, "I know I don't have to prove anything. I'm simply making certain you get your money's worth."

"Good." Then he looked vaguely sheepish. "Aaron had a swell time with Dallas tonight. It was good for the boy."

A rush of tenderness for him filled her. It must have been so hard for him to see it, much less to say it.

"Yes, it was," she agreed. "And I imagine it meant as much to him to be able to come home and tell his grandpa about it—and have you listen. And experiment with sticking a spoon to your nose." She chuckled.

"I can do that pretty good for an old man," he said with pride.

"It's not how old you are—it's how big your nose is," she teased.

He stepped over, bent down and kissed her cheek. "It's late. Don't stay up all night with that thing...." He inclined his head toward the beadwork in her lap. "You tend to get involved with it, like your mother."

"I'm heading for bed as soon as I finish my coffee."

"Good. And you might want to close your window. Rain's heading this way. Good, big storm, if my shoulder's a good indication. Good night."

"Good night," she answered softly, and watched his hefty frame leave the room.

Jasper Tyson was a big man, she thought. In more ways than one. It'd been hard for him when Dallas had brought Aaron home that evening. Unlike when Aaron had left, her father had not retired to the sanctity of his study, but had remained to listen to his grandson tell the tale of the important evening he'd spent with his uncle Dallas.

Of course, her father had made certain that Dallas had gotten no farther into the house than the entry hall and had almost been blatantly rude in the way he'd bid Dallas goodnight, giving Dallas no choice but to leave.

Her father had been a bear protecting his territory, she thought now with a sad shake of her head. She'd understood this even then, but Dallas had been excited from the evening, too, and she'd seen how he'd wanted to talk to her.

For an instant she'd almost insisted he come in for coffee, but then he'd bid them all good-night.

As she pushed the needle through the soft leather, she fondly recalled her son telling them all about his evening. Exuberantly he'd bubbled all about how he'd eaten five giant pieces of pizza, about how well he and Dallas had done at playing a game of naming basketball stars and about how his friend, Jimbo Brown, had taught him and Dallas to balance a spoon on their noses.

"Dallas can do it pretty good, too, 'cause his nose is big," he said. And then of course his grandfather had wanted to try.

Aaron and Dallas. Her mother had seen it right off—but then her mother had the gift of seeing into people's hearts. Dallas didn't spoil Aaron overmuch. He was probably the only male of the family who forced Aaron to do the things he should. And he didn't spend an inordinate amount of time with Aaron—the grandfathers had that claim. And yet Dallas and Aaron had formed an easy, familiar relationship. They instinctively liked one another. It could be because they were uncle and nephew, or simply one of those wonderful things that happens between certain people. Oh, she was so glad! Glad for her son and Dallas, and glad for herself.

"You like Dallas very much, don't you?" she said to Aaron when at last she'd gotten him tucked into bed and they were alone.

"Yeah," he'd said with a wide yawn and a sleepy nod. "Corky Williams's dad wouldn't put a spoon on his nose. Guess he felt stupid or somethin'. But Dallas didn't care. He had a contest with me and Jimbo and a couple of other guys—and he even played tag...." His voice trailed off with another yawn, and he turned over and closed his eyes.

"Mom?" he mumbled, eyes still closed as she smoothed the sheet. "Would my dad've done that—spoon on the nose and stuff?" He cocked one eye at her.

"Yes," she said without hesitation. "Oh, yes."

She'd stopped working now and stared across to where the small rose rock remained on the nightstand. Rising, she set aside the moccasin and went to pick it up. She ran a fingertip over its rough petals.

She'd wanted to ask her son about how he felt about her and Dallas marrying, but he'd been so tired—and she'd had neither nerve nor words. How was she to explain it all to him? And what if Dallas had changed his mind—no longer wanted her?

How she longed for Dallas. So much, she thought, clutching the rock. To be in his arms. She wanted him so much that she wondered whether he could feel it way across the meadows and trees and roads that separated them.

It wasn't wrong to love him. At last she could see that. And suddenly it seemed the true wrong would be in letting what they could share pass them by.

Her father's image filled her mind, and pain gripped her heart. She didn't want to hurt him. Would he hate her?

She recalled her mother's gentle words earlier that evening. Her mother was right. She couldn't live the way other people wanted her to—she had to do what was right for herself and Dallas. And Aaron. The time had come; she must make a decision one way or the other.

The following day the wind blew hard from the south, bringing a gray, misty day. It was the first moisture they'd had in the weeks since Dallas had broken off with Megan, and that time had been only an overnight thing. This day promised a soaking rain that had been a long time in coming. Like any other man who worked close to the earth, Dallas welcomed it, but for him it was even more welcome because it seemed to match his mood—cloudy and gray.

There wasn't much to be done. He puttered around the cow barn, doing some cleaning up in the storage room and a bit of paperwork in the office. Anything to keep his hands busy. But it wasn't enough to stop his thoughts.

He'd had a good time with Aaron, and his heart swelled knowing the boy had enjoyed himself, too. No doubt being so close to Aaron last night was why he kept thinking so much of Coy this day.

And Rachel. Oh, how he thought of Rachel—the way her big doe-eyes could start the warm throbbing in his groin and how her hair felt like rich silk threads in his hands. How he wanted her right now! His mind revolved with memories of her moving beneath his touch, of her warm, long hair flowing across his chest, of her pressing against him, spreading her legs to accept him.

He was standing at the far end of the barn, gazing out at the rain-soaked grass and trees, smoking a cigar, when he heard light footsteps on the concrete floor of the barn. Irritated at the interruption to his solitude, he twisted slightly, expecting to see Quinn. He saw instead Rachel walking toward him.

A tingle crossed his shoulders and shot down his spine as he turned fully to meet her. The hood of a dove-gray cape hid her hair; rivulets of water beaded and ran down the fabric. Her coffee-brown eyes dominated her pale face. Her footsteps grew slower, and she stopped about three yards away from him. He saw her searching his face, waiting for an invitation.

He tossed his smoke aside and opened his arms. In an instant she ran the rest of the way and hurled herself against him. Her cape was cool and damp against his flannel shirt, but her cheek was warm where it pressed his. She smelled of fresh rain and roses.

"Quinn told me you were out here." Her voice came breathless and hesitant. "I took a chance in coming over. I didn't know about Ace."

He pulled back and gazed at her, pulling the hood from her hair so he could see it and feel it. "He's gone into the city to see Megan."

She blinked those big brown eyes. "Quinn said." Her eyes searched his. "Aaron and my parents have gone up to the Dyer's ranch to see some working dogs perform."

He nodded. "Aaron told me last night."

They continued staring at each other, though Dallas wasn't quite certain why. An odd tension vibrated between them. He felt Rachel stiffen, resembling a mare poised for flight from some unseen threat. To run away from him, he realized with surprise as he recognized fear and doubt shadowing her eyes. It was a familiar look, and he'd give everything he possessed never to see it again—to eliminate the barriers between them forever and claim her as his own.

"What is it?" he asked. "Talk to me, Rach."

Rachel stared at him, hesitating. How did she say a belated "yes" to his marriage proposal? No doubt he would not ask again. What if he didn't want to marry her anymore? Of course such fear didn't make any sense—yet it lingered all the same.

His expression demanded an answer.

She lifted her chin. "Do you still want to marry me?" She held her breath.

What could only be described as shock flickered in his eyes a moment before being replaced by the twinkle of mischief. "I don't quite recall—did I want to?"

She pushed from his arms and took two rapid steps away. In a flash he followed and grabbed her arm, spinning her around.

"Rachel..." He gazed down at her finely chiseled features. Her cheeks were flushed, her moist, pink lips parted slightly. Her eyes searched his, bringing even more quickening to his pulse. He knew what she wanted, and because he loved her, he gave it. "Will you marry me?"

Gently her lips curved upward. "Yes." Her eyes shone up at him before being hidden by her lids as she raised her face to his. "I can't stand being separated from you any longer...."

Her huskily spoken words brought an immediate heating to his blood; her kiss was sweet and warm and wanting. He parted her lips and entered her with his tongue, sampling the erotic wet warmth of her. Though her cape was a bulky barrier between them, he felt her trembling. He pulled her against him, seeking some small relief for his swollen, aching organ.

They parted, both gasping for breath, and Rachel gazed again into Dallas's crystal eyes. Precious eyes. She put her palm to his cheek, feeling the stubble of a day-old beard. The nameless doubts that had gripped her hand melted away as late frost beneath a spring sun.

"I haven't talked to Aaron," she said. "I wanted to make certain that you still . . ."

"Did you really think I'd changed my mind?" He nibbled her ear, causing her head to spin and her breath to be almost nonexistent.

"I . . . I didn't know."

"Rachel—" he straightened and gazed pointedly into her eyes "—I'm not going to change my mind. I know you had a rough time with Coy. But it will be different with us."

"I know." Still, it was hard not to have fears. There was so much against them. She tightened her arms around his waist. "Mama knows. She sensed it—wasn't much for me to tell her."

"What did she say?"

"That we must do what's right for us," she answered. His eyes were so gray and clear, filled with love and desire.

"She's quite a lady."

"Yes."

"What are you crying about?" He wiped beneath her eye with his rough thumb.

"I didn't know I was. Oh, Dallas, I love you. I do. I want us to be happy. I—"

He stopped her words with his lips. His kiss was hard and demanding, his tongue sparring with hers, sending waves of emotion from her head to her toes. He brought his hands to cup her head and raked his fingers into her hair. Time stopped, and she felt her energy merging and exploding with his.

And then she sensed his body tighten, freeze. Through the mists clouding her mind, she heard a motion and knew they were no longer alone. Dallas turned his head toward the front of the barn, and slowly Rachel followed.

Ace stood there, smack in the middle of the large building. Even though he was fifty feet distant, she saw the fire in his eyes. His face was a stiff, rock-hard mask.

Rachel's mouth went dry, and she felt the blood drain from her face. Beside her, Dallas shifted smoothly, keeping a protective arm around her shoulders.

"I've asked Rachel to marry me, and she's accepted," he said, his deep voice exceedingly quiet.

Ace's sharp gaze flickered to her and then back to Dallas. "You have no shame—either of you! If you do this thing, you will no longer be my son."

With that, the older man pivoted and walked away through the barn and out into the rain.

Rachel saw the fury on Dallas's face and felt it shaking his body. She gripped his shirtfront.

"Go after him, Dallas."

He shook his head and averted his gaze. His arm tightened about her. "You heard him—I'm no longer his son. I've never been Coy," he added bitterly.

"He didn't mean it. He's simply shocked. Please go after him now," she said again. "He could get sick . . . and he won't tell anyone. You know that."

At last he seemed to trust himself enough to speak. "Okay . . ." He took a deep breath and brought his gaze to hers. He touched her cheek. "Come on. I'll walk you to your car first."

At the door he reached for his hat hanging on a hook. When they stepped out into the rain, Rachel shivered, though it wasn't really cold. Dallas glanced at her with concern, then walked faster, saying gruffly, "You need to get out of the rain."

"I'm all right." She squeezed his waist, trying to reassure him. It was him she was worried about. His pain was her pain, yet it seemed there was no real way she could help him share the burden.

He opened the station wagon door and handed her inside. "You'll call me and let me know how Ace is?" she asked.

He bent over, holding on to the door. Rain pattered on his hat. "I'll call you." He paused. "I'd like to talk to Jasper with you."

She shook her head. "It will be better if I see him alone. And I have to talk with Aaron first, Dal. We still don't know how he's going to take it."

Again his jawline tightened, and his face betrayed his reluctance, but he nodded in assent. "Tonight?"

"Yes." She reached up, touched his cheek and forced an encouraging smile.

"I'll try to reach Yancey and tell him to get his rear back here. We're going to have a wedding—as soon as possible."

He slammed the door closed, and she rolled down the window, calling as he hurried up the steps to the porch. "Go find Ace."

He gave her a quick salute, then watched as she drove away. With a glance in the rearview mirror, Rachel saw him gazing after her. She wished she didn't have to leave him now, didn't want him to face Ace alone—though it wouldn't help matters at all for her to stay.

The windshield wipers thumped in rhythm. A cold gripped her bones, refusing to be dispelled by the car heater. Dallas loved her. He wanted her. Oh, and how she loved him! But how long could their love survive when it meant turning their backs on their family and heritage, everything that made them who and what they were?

Once, long ago when she'd married Coy, she'd been young and naive. She hadn't realized how tightly their lives were woven with those of the others in the family. She hadn't anticipated the scope of the uproar their marriage would bring about. Her youth had believed anything was possible with love.

However, experience taught her what to expect now. Ace and her father were going to be furious. The animosity surrounding them would make things so hard, even for the innocents like Aaron, her mother, Quinn and Yancey. Every meeting, Sunday get-together and holiday celebration would be one tense battle of wills. Perhaps there wouldn't be any get-togethers. And then much of what she wished for her son would be impossible.

But he would have a good father. And she would have a good man who loved her.

A small glimmer of the youthful belief that love could surmount all tried to shine through. For comfort she clung to that glimmer. She thought of Dallas and Ace and prayed for them not to lose sight of their love.

"What's happened?" Quinn asked when Dallas met her in the hallway. "Daddy stormed through here and shut himself in his study."

"I told him I was going to marry Rachel."

Quinn's eyes widened with shock. "That would do it."

He tossed his wet hat to the table. His damp shirt was uncomfortable. "What did he look like? Do you think he's all right?"

She bit her bottom lip. "His face was very flushed, but he's been taking his medication. I just don't know, Dal."

"Stick around." He stepped toward the study. "I'm going to talk to him."

"Dallas..." she said, stopping him. A tiny smile touched her lips. "I'm very happy for you. You and Rachel should have done this a long time ago."

Her words were a balm to his flagging spirit. "Thanks, Sis. I think Rachel's going to need a bridesmaid."

"Good—it'll give me an excuse to buy another dress." Her expression sobered. "Be gentle with him, Dal—and with yourself."

He nodded slightly, then strode off to his father's study. He rapped and entered without waiting for a reply.

The old man sat in the high-backed chair behind his desk, lighting up a fat, forbidden cheroot. He puffed and glared up at Dallas. Only one expression was in his eyes—that of hate. It was a hard thing to see from his own father, but it wasn't unfamiliar. He'd seen it on more than one occasion since the morning he'd carried Coy's body back to the house.

Dallas shut the door quietly and crossed over to stand in front of the desk. "You're not supposed to have those things." He indicated the cigar.

His father didn't speak, simply regarded him steadily with his hard, black eyes.

"I'm not going to change my mind, Dad," Dallas said quietly. He watched his father's face for signs of weakness, anything to indicate the old man's health was in danger. "I love Rachel and I'm going to marry her."

"And try to take Coy's place?" his father said with a flat voice that cut like a knife.

"You know I can't do that. No one can take another man's place in this world." He breathed deeply and struggled to speak what he truly felt. "Dad, Coy's dead. He's not ever going to come striding up on that porch. And Rachel would marry sooner or later—she's young and healthy and has every right to a full life with a man. Aaron's is my brother's son—and I can be the next best thing to Coy for him. This way Aaron will continue for certain with the Cordell name and heritage. It's what you want, isn't it?"

"Not for you to do it!" His father barked the words and jumped to his feet. "You wanted Rachel when she was your brother's wife." He clamped his mouth against further words.

But Dallas didn't need to hear what else his father was going to say. He guessed he'd always known what his father thought and never said. And this time he was going to bring it out in the open.

"You think I killed Coy," he said flatly, feeling a pain beyond description.

His father glared at him. "Your brother needed you, and you weren't there to help him."

"I tried, damn it! I tried, but you've never believed me. I tried to catch the board that day—I tried to help Coy with whatever was tearing him apart during the years before. But he wouldn't let anybody help him. There was nothing anyone could do." Dallas's eyes burned with unshed tears. "I've loved Rachel for a long time, Dad—that's true, and I'm not ashamed of it any longer. I loved Coy, too. He was my brother. And he would be the first to wish me and Rachel well—he'd want me to love her and his son. He'd want me to give them everything that I could. And as selfish as he was, he never begrudged anyone all the happiness they could wring from this life.

"I'm not taking anything from Coy, Dad. He's gone. And I'm sorry you're against this, but Rachel and I are going to be married."

"Then you will no longer be a part of this family—nor have any part of this ranch. You can take your personal possessions and leave."

The silence that followed was deafening. Dallas had halfway expected this, and yet it came as a shock. Like a car accident—it was something that happened to someone else, not to him.

He was being told he no longer had an interest in something he'd spent his life thus far building. His entire heritage yanked out from under him in one instant.

"I'll be gone in an hour," he said through tight jaws, and turned to stride away across the plush wool carpet. He opened the door, walked out and closed it gently behind him.

Quinn was waiting in his hall. "Dallas?" Her voice rang with alarm.

"He's okay..." he ground out, and took the stairs two at a time.

He stopped inside his room. Take what he owned? The bed was the one he'd had since he was fourteen; his father had bought it, as well as the other furnishings. Dallas did own the grouping of photographs on the wall—all of him, Coy, Yancey, Quinn and his father. One with his mother, and another with Quinn's mother. Yancey's mother had left before they got any pictures of her.

He reached into the closet and yanked out two suitcases. They were his, too. He began pulling things from his drawers and tossing them into the cases.

Quinn appeared at his door when he'd almost finished.

"He'll get over it, Dal. Stay—give him a few days," she said.

"He's not going to change his mind. I've disappointed him, so I'm out. I'm not Coy—so there's no place around here for me."

"That's not true...."

He looked up from the suitcase, and she left off speaking. Her expression said that she knew the truth. He strode into the adjoining bath and grabbed up things, tossing them into his shaving bag. "You or Yance can bring me what I can't take now."

"Where will you go?" Her voice was so small.

"I'll be fine." He shot her a reassuring glance. "I've bought the O'Connor house for Rachel and me. She couldn't come back here to live, anyway."

"Oh."

He closed one of the suitcases, then paused. "How is he?"

"He's doing okay. His blood pressure is no doubt up—I'll keep an eye on him."

He stepped to the nightstand and scribbled a number on a piece of paper. "Here—I had a telephone put in down at the house last week. If you need me, call. I'll be out in the barn for a while to gather up a few more things. Then I'll head down to the O'Connor house.''

''Oh, Dal...'' She flung her arms around him. ''I love you.''

''I love you, too, Sis.''

He held her and realized that through the years, while they hadn't always had parents they could lean on, they'd all—he, Coy, Yancey and Quinn—had each other. ''I'll only be a few miles away. I'll always be there if you need me.''

''I know,'' she nodded, crying.

Dallas walked from the room and refused to allow his mind to think back.

Rachel had to wait until it was Aaron's bedtime to speak to him alone. Since leaving Dallas, she'd rehearsed what she would say to her son and later to her father. Her insides were now tight as an overwound watch spring as her mind spun with worries. She wondered how Ace and Dallas were. She knew how cruel Ace could be—and how hurt he must be feeling right now. It must seem to him as if she and Dallas didn't care about his feelings, and there wasn't much else in the world that could hurt a person more.

''Mom?'' She turned from where she stood gazing blankly into the closet. She'd put away Aaron's shoes and then gotten lost in thought. He gave her a quizzical look. ''What're ya lookin' at?''

She smiled. ''Oh, nothing. I was just thinking.''

He scrambled into bed. ''Can I watch the John Wayne movie? It goes off at eleven, and it isn't a school night, Mom.''

She sucked in a deep breath. ''I guess you can—but I want to talk to you first.''

She sat on the bed and smoothed up his covers, which he promptly wrinkled again with his feet to get them as he liked them. He gazed at her with his wide, gray eyes.

"What would you say to your uncle Dallas and me getting married?" Blunt but to the point.

His eyes widened even farther, and he stared at her for long seconds.

"We won't do it, Aaron, without your okay."

A hesitant, uncertain smile quirked his lips. "I guess it'd be okay. If you want to." His uncertain smile spread a fraction.

"I love him, Aaron. And he loves me. He isn't your father, but he is the next closest thing."

"Yeah."

She studied his face. He appeared pleased, if hesitant, but he was very good at hiding his feelings. "Can you elaborate on 'okay'? How do you feel about it?"

"I sorta figured you liked Uncle Dallas," he said, averting his gaze to the covers. "I mean, I saw him lookin' at you sometimes when he didn't think nobody was lookin'—and I saw you lookin' at him, too. You smile a whole lot when you're around him." He scratched his ear and shrugged. "Aw, I don't know. I . . . I think I'd like it, and he's a good guy, Mom. You should go for it."

Emotion choked her throat. "I should, huh?" She bent and hugged him to her. "You're some kind of kid, you know that?"

"Yeah . . . I know."

She pulled back and grew sober. "Things are going to change for us—a lot. And your Papa Ace and Grandpa J. aren't going to be too happy about this, honey. It's going to be a bit rough, at least at first."

He nodded, his gray eyes round and sober. "They weren't too happy when you married Dad."

"No, they weren't." She smoothed the hair from his forehead. "But they love you, Aaron. That will never change."

She spoke to him for a few more minutes about the house that Dallas had bought and how she would drive him to school for the rest of the year so he wouldn't have to change again.

Just before she left him watching the movie, he said with a wide grin, "We won't even have to change our last name, Mom. That's pretty neat."

"Yes . . . that's pretty neat."

She paused in the hallway and thought of her son with wonder. He was a most wonderful blessing in her life. Perhaps she and Coy hadn't succeeded in their marriage, but together they had produced a very special child. It seemed that all the past years when she'd worried about her mothering responsibilities, she hadn't been doing such a poor job, after all—thank God.

Aaron's love and acceptance gave her added support for facing her father now. Taking a deep breath, she went to do so.

They were in the family room, her father reading his gardening club newsletter, her mother studying a craft catalog.

Her father glanced up; the look on his face gave her pause. "Dallas called—for you," he said like an accusation. "Willow told him you were busy at the moment. He left a number where he can be reached." He extended a piece of notepaper.

"Thank you, Daddy." She took the paper and slipped it into the pocket of her slacks without looking at it. "I'll call him in a few minutes."

Her mother laid the catalog aside, folded her hands in her lap and sent her silent encouragement.

"Okay . . . are you two going to tell me what's going on?" her father said in a low bellow.

"Daddy . . ." She gazed into his scowling face and had the oddest thought of how dear even that scowl was to her. "Dallas and I are going to get married."

Watching her father's face in the silent seconds that followed was much the same as watching a violent thunderstorm gathering to the southwest.

"You are going to what?" His voice seemed to shake even the window blinds.

"Jasper, there's no need to wake the cows," her mother cautioned, and rose to slide close the double doors. "Listen . . . just listen."

"I'm listening!" He clamped his mouth shut and breathed heavily. "What is all this nonsense?"

Rachel stared at him, fear and anguish and anger spinning inside her chest.

"I love him, Daddy. He's asked me to marry him, and I've accepted."

"You *love* him? Wasn't it only a month ago that he was to marry some other woman? What does he do—change women like his socks?" As he spoke, her father tossed aside the paper in his hand and jerked to his feet. "By heaven, not again!" He paced across the room, rubbing the back of his neck.

Instinctively Rachel recoiled from his fury. Was there anything that she could say that would make a difference? This should be a happy time in her life—not a time of struggle.

"Dallas and I have been friends for a long time." She rose and moved the few steps toward him. "We share something special, Daddy—like you and Mom do."

"Don't compare it to me and your mother! Don't ever compare me to a Cordell!" he roared. "You loved Coy— and what did that get you?" He jabbed the air toward her; his thick burnished curls shook and caught the light. "Nothin' but trouble. Ace married three women and gave each one of 'em hell. Coy followed right along in his footsteps. You don't have the brains God gave a damn turkey if you're thinkin' of doin' it again. What is it? You go in heat whenever you get around Cordells? Coy's got another brother down the line. You goin' to try him out, too?"

"Jasper!" Her mother jumped to her feet.

The blood drained from Rachel's head, and a chill swept down her spine. She stared at her father.

"You owe your daughter an apology," her mother said firmly.

He snorted. "She knew how I would feel about this—but she's going ahead and doing just as she pleases, anyway. Just like the last time." He raised his head and pierced her with his pale gaze. "Never mind that you're a Tyson. It hasn't ever meant anything to you. You throw away our family heritage like you would a tissue."

Rachel swallowed the giant lump in her throat. "I do care, Daddy."

He turned away from her, saying, "If I'd had a son, this never would have happened."

His words were a hard slap in the face. "No . . . I'm not a son," she said between clenched teeth. "Whether you believe it or not—I'm sorry to disappoint you. And I'm sorrier still that you put your petty obsessions over my happiness and the happiness of your grandson."

"It's you who's putting yourself over Aaron's welfare," her father shot back. "The best thing would be for you to leave him here while you go on off with your lover."

"I'm not the only one thinking of himself!" she told him, her voice rising. "You've always wanted a son. Don't you think I know that? And because of this . . . stupid hate between you and Ace, you make everyone else miserable. I'm not going to live my life skirting your hates!"

"I'll tell you, daughter—" his eyes bore into her "—if you go off with Dallas Cordell, there won't be any coming home if things don't work out. Not ever again."

She felt as if her heart stopped. "I didn't come running home before, and I won't in the future." She kept her back straight. "Aaron and I will be leaving in the morning."

It was horribly painful to see the anguished look on her mother's face, but there was nothing she could do. Her father had his mind set—and he wasn't a man to change it.

She pivoted and headed for the door. Behind her she heard her mother's angry voice. "Jasper, she's my daughter, too."

But she didn't pause to hear more. She closed the door behind her and walked quickly away from the murmur of voices. She stopped to check on Aaron, hoping he hadn't heard any of the argument. It wasn't likely; the walls and doors were thick, making it exceedingly quiet in this end of the house.

He was asleep, curled into a ball. She moved stealthily to switch off his small television, then paused to touch his cheek. Her hands, her entire body shook with anger and fear. Because of the course she'd decided, he would be caught in the middle of such an uproar. She prayed to be able to spare him much of it—to make up for it.

In the sanctuary of her room she pulled out the paper her father had given her with Dallas's number. Why wasn't he at home? she wondered as she dialed with shaking fingers. Her vision blurred, and then a sob broke from her lips. Quickly she replaced the receiver and picked up her pillow, burying her face and cries. She couldn't talk to Dallas in such a state.

Her father had always wanted a boy; he and her mother had tried for years to have other children. But no boy had ever come to carry on the Tyson heritage. Still, she'd been there, and it'd been assumed she would marry a man she could bring home to the Golden Rose. Together this man and she would have children and keep the ranch and stores intact for future generations.

Then she'd married Coy—giving her father another great disappointment. And now she was about to spoil her father's second chance. He hated her for it.

She called out to Dallas in her mind, wishing she could pour out her hurts and fears right then and there. Wishing for him to hold her and tell her everything would be all right, tease her until she smiled, as he used to do.

She needed him; she loved him. She wished with all her heart that her father would share that joy with her and not try to take it away.

The telephone rang, and she moved quickly to answer it before it could ring a second time.

"Rachel?" Dallas's anxious voice came across the line.

"Yes." She sniffed and wiped at her eyes. She mustn't let on she'd been crying.

"Are you all right?"

"Yes...I just ran to the phone."

"I called earlier and left a number."

"I know—I got it and was just about to call you. Where are you?"

"Down at the house—the O'Connor place. I went ahead and moved down here. Did you speak to Aaron and your father?"

"Yes." *He'd moved out of the Cordell Ranch. Because of her.* "Aaron is pleased. Nervous and uncertain, but he's not opposed." She paused. "Daddy didn't fool me. He's furious. How's Ace?"

"He's doin' okay." There was an odd coldness in his voice that sent an alarm racing through her.

"What did he say?"

"He's mad—that's all. I spoke to Quinn a few minutes ago, and she said he'd gone to bed. He'll be okay, Rachel."

Yes, but will you? she thought.

"Dallas...can Aaron and I move down there with you tomorrow? I really don't want to expose him to the anger between Daddy and me...and...I simply can't stay around Daddy."

"I'll come for you."

"No. We can drive down. Just give me the directions."

"I'll come for you, Rach," he said firmly. "I want to talk to Jasper."

Yes, he would. It had to do with respect and honor. She wouldn't try to take it from him—no matter how much she wished to protect both him and her father from themselves.

"Okay. Make it around two. I'll try to be packed."

"I love you, Rach. It's going to be all right."

A tiny smile warmed the cold ache inside her. "I love you, too."

Chapter Ten

Dallas hung up the telephone and looked around the kitchen where he stood. The glistening plastic phone was the only thing in that room less than thirty years old.

The enamel white cabinets were chipped in a hundred places. Spots on the red counter were worn colorless. The linoleum was about a hundred years old, as was the gas cookstove.

He wandered out into the dining room and on into the living room. The only furnishings were two ladder-back chairs the O'Connors had left behind and the sleeping bag he'd brought down—unless he counted the bin full of wood beside the fireplace.

And he was asking Rachel to come down here to this.

She'd spent her entire life surrounded by shining silver, fine china, genuine silks and leathers and wools. While the Tysons didn't live extravagantly, they could afford to and did enjoy anything and everything they wanted. In addition to their ranch house, they owned a secluded cabin in

Colorado, a condominium in Hawaii and the exclusive town house in which Rachel and Aaron had lived in Phoenix.

Dallas looked around and thought wryly that they had furniture in all those homes.

Pulling a panatela from the packet in his shirt pocket, he walked out on the front porch. He lit the cigar, then leaned against the rock wall. The rain had stopped, leaving a wet scent heavy in the air.

He was mighty Ace Cordell's son, yet it counted for nothing now. He had little to offer Rachel and Aaron. He had no job, and his bank account wouldn't last four months. What money he'd saved had gone to put a heavy down payment on this house—which had no furniture in it. He owned his truck and a small tool kit he kept in it; he'd had to leave behind the mobile phone, which belonged to his father. This place had two barns, one made of old tin but solid, the other on the verge of falling in. He had nothing to put in those barns, no saws or hammers to make the smallest repairs. O'Connor had left behind a tractor, which he said ran and had been included in the price of the house, but Dallas wasn't certain it was worth counting as a possession.

For all his life he'd taken a lot for granted. He'd always had everything money could buy—the flashiest pickups, stock trailers that cost as much as he'd paid for this house and the latest in electronic equipment, from televisions to a complete computer setup for running the ranch to timed cattle feeders. He'd spent a great deal of time playing through college because he hadn't had to work to support himself, and in the end there'd been a job waiting for him— manager of one of the largest ranches in the state. He'd never thought of anything other than running the Cordell Ranch. It was all he'd ever desired, all he knew.

For an instant he thought he caught the sound of Coy's laughter. He listened, feeling foolish. But again he would have sworn he heard the gay, to-hell-with-it laugh his brother used to have. Somehow it made him smile.

It was late when he finally went back inside to bed down on the hardwood floor. He vowed to find at least a couple of beds tomorrow. He supposed his name would still get him credit somewhere. Then he remembered that tomorrow was Sunday; it wasn't going to be easy.

The last thing he thought of before falling asleep was Rachel and how disappointed she'd probably be when she saw the house. She might turn right around and run home. He'd never felt more alone in his life.

The following morning he was up at dawn. Though it wasn't raining, gray clouds hung heavy. He drove to the small local store for a cup of coffee and packaged doughnuts. It was barely past seven when he returned and called Quinn.

"No, I haven't seen Daddy. You woke me up!" she railed at him when she could finally get some words out.

"Look, Quinn, I want you to check on him, then I want you to call me back."

"Damn you, Dal," she mumbled. "I don't get up with the chickens! Oh, all right. I'm awake now, anyway."

"Call me back."

"I will . . . I will."

While he waited, he checked the attic for a table he thought he remembered seeing. There was one—gray and chrome covered with ten years of grime. One of the legs had come off but was repairable.

"Daddy's fine," Quinn told him when she called back. "Except he got up and had breakfast and went back to bed."

Dallas didn't like the sound of that. "He never sleeps during the day."

"I know. He's not sleeping. He's just lying in there, snoozing, he said. But he's okay, Dal. What else do you need?"

He gave her his list, ending with his need for her to come down and help him clean. "I'm picking Rachel and Aaron up at two o'clock."

"Then what you need is a marriage license, or Jasper's going to come after you with a shotgun."

"Very funny, little sister. Have your laughs but come on down here. I don't want Rachel to see the house like this. It's going to look bad enough as it is."

"Okay. I'll do my best. But I'm not doing anything to break my nails."

"I'll leave the door open. I'm off to find some furniture."

He hung up and wondered where to begin, his mind ticking through names of people he knew. He seemed to remember that Tom Sager's father owned a furniture store in Chickasha. He'd start with Tom.

It had been hard to tell Aaron they were leaving that day.

"Can I take Wheeler?" had been his first question, his voice tight and small.

"Of course you can," she'd answered. "And your television and computer, too. We can easily fit those in the station wagon. We'll get your bed and other furniture later." *After things have calmed down—I hope.*

She thought now, as she maneuvered the heavy computer, that it wasn't easy to fit very much into a station wagon the size of theirs. She leaned against the car and took several deep breaths. The cool mist bathed her face; at least it hadn't out-and-out rained.

Her gaze strayed to her father's study window, and she saw him standing there, studying her. She refused to be the one to look away. After a minute he moved, dropping the curtain back into place.

He was the one who was wrong. He was the one who needed to apologize.

Still, regret clutched her heart. Because of what she was doing, because of her desires—her father, her mother and her son were having their world turned upside down. *She* was the cause now of the rift between her parents.

She had the impulse to call a halt to everything, to some-how put everything back in place, put the clothes back into the closets, the television to its stand, the computer to its desk. But while that could be done, there was no putting feelings back exactly as they had been. Her father might forgive her if she stayed and broke off with Dallas, but things still wouldn't be the same. The hurtful words couldn't be wiped from the air. The rift between her parents wouldn't be solved. The confusion and insecurity Aaron was no doubt feeling wouldn't vanish. And neither would her longing for Dallas.

She experienced the tremendous urge to turn and run away from all of it—and everyone.

"This is all of Aaron's clothes," her mother said, hurry-ing toward the car. After a glance at Rachel, she forced a smile. "It's a blessing the rain's holding off. The weather-man is calling for more ahead."

Rachel took the suitcase and large box from her mother, wondering exactly where to fit them into the car. Tears that had been threatening all morning pushed forward again. Then she realized the box was unfamiliar.

"What's this, Mom?"

"Your wedding gown."

Rachel jerked her head upward.

Her mother smiled softly. "It was your grandmother Ty-son's. She gave it to me when your father and I married, and I'd always hoped you could wear it. You didn't have a chance to with Coy. Now you do."

Rachel carefully placed the box in the car, then turned to embrace her mother. "I'm so sorry, Mom."

"Sorry for what—for doing what your heart tells you?"

"I'm sorry to cause all of this—" she lifted her hand and let it fall "—you and Daddy arguing, Aaron wondering where he'll sleep tonight."

"Aaron knows where he'll sleep—he'll be with you, and that's enough for him." She smiled. "I think he's rather excited. His basic concern was to take Wheeler. As for me and your father—you are not the cause. Our difference in opinion is the cause. Now, in the words of your grandmother—thee come have coffee and thee will feel much better.''

Rachel smiled at the old, familiar words no longer heard much in their family since the passing of her feisty grandmother.

"Yes," she agreed, falling in step beside her mother, "we need bracing to tackle my closet."

She thought of Dallas and wondered what he was doing. Perhaps he, like herself, was having second thoughts. Her pulse quickened. She was having her doubts, but every time she thought of giving it up—of giving Dallas up—she felt such pain and fear she couldn't bear it. She longed to see his slow smile and to put her hand into his tight clasp. And she would see him soon.

Her heart lifted with anticipation.

Dallas returned just before noon to find Stella hard at work cleaning and her husband, Henry, puttering around making repairs.

"Quinn sent me," Stella said, shaking the rag in her hand. "She didn't want to leave Ace."

"Is Dad okay?" he asked, alarm shooting through him.

"He's playing for sympathy is my opinion. He had our Quinn call Doc Priddy to come out to the house." She wrapped a hand around his waist. "It'll take more than a bit of high blood pressure to get Ace Cordell down—don't you worry. And I'm so happy for you, son. You and Rachel will make a good match, and Aaron will have a good daddy. Now, how'd you make out with furniture?"

He'd managed to get two cheap double-bed frames with mattresses and box springs, along with a used refrigerator and a big platform rocker that had caught his eye. He'd bought a few staples, a coffeemaker and a set of pots and pans at the grocery store, but there'd been no place open earlier to buy linens.

Like a fairy godmother Stella produced linens and the best down-filled pillows, filched from the closet at the ranch, as well as necessities like dishes, silverware, cleaning supplies, and a small clock radio. "Every woman needs a radio in her kitchen," she said smartly.

"All these years, and I didn't know you had talent as a thief," Dallas teased.

"There's a lot you don't know about me, young man," she quipped in return. "Now get yourself busy."

Tom had come to help, and along with him and Henry, Dallas got the refrigerator and beds into place. The rocker went beside the fireplace in the living room. Though that room was small, it looked mighty empty with only that one piece in it.

An hour and a half later Dallas glanced around. The house looked much better. Henry had cleaned and repaired the table from the attic and placed it in the kitchen. The oak floors shone in places, the windows were cleaned streakless, the fingerprints and smudges wiped from the woodwork and not a dusty cobweb was to be found.

"You'd best get going," Stella told him. She jerked off the bandanna she'd had covering her hair. "We'll finish here and clear out."

"Thanks." He bent to give her an awkward kiss, realizing the number of years he'd taken her presence in his life for granted. She'd cooked his meals, washed his clothes and fussed over him, and he could probably count on one hand the times he'd told her how much he appreciated it.

"Go on with you. Rachel and Aaron'll be waiting."

He drove away with the three of them, precious friends, waving from the porch. In that instant Dallas felt a very rich man.

The thought that Rachel was waiting for him sent a rush through his body. He would be able to touch her hair, feel her warmth next to him. It was a heady realization, didn't seem real. He felt as though things were spinning past him much too fast and that he needed to grasp hold of something or he was going to lose it all. He would lose Rachel.

He jerked his mind away from such thoughts and focused on what lay ahead. He had to talk to Jasper. The big man was making one hell of a mistake, for himself as well as everyone else. Maybe they would do okay without Ace's approval, but if Jasper withdrew from Rachel's life, it would kill her. And Dallas feared that eventually she would come to resent him for the loss.

The skies were clearing slightly when he pulled beneath the arched entry to the Golden Rose. Rachel's car in front of the sprawling house came into view; it was packed full with hers and Aaron's belongings.

She was coming with him; she hadn't changed her mind.

Dallas pulled his pickup to a stop and slowly got out and walked to the front door. He knocked and waited, listening to heavy footsteps approach. Jasper's footsteps. His pulse quickened as he prepared himself.

The door was jerked open, and Jasper filled the entry. His pale eyes blazed. The next instant Dallas saw the older man's big fist coming at his face. In reaction, he moved, but shock slowed him down. The fist smashed into his face, and he went stumbling backward.

"Daddy! Oh, my... Dallas... oh, Dallas."

Rachel pushed around her father and ran to Dallas leaning against the outside brick wall. Dallas blinked rapidly and shook his head. His jawline tightened with fury. *Because of her... because of her...*

She touched his chest, and he glanced down at her, anger and regret mingling in his eyes. Then he looked back up at her father. Rachel, too, still nestled against Dallas, twisted to angrily regard her father. His face was a ruddy mask of rage, and his fist was again poised in the air.

"I won't fight you, Jasper," Dallas ground out hoarsely. His chest shook beneath Rachel's hand. "You're Rachel's father, Aaron's grandfather. I won't fight you."

Her father's massive chest sagged, and his fist slowly dropped to his side. He turned, and Rachel saw him pause as his gaze met her mother's and fell downward to where Aaron peeked around from behind her. Then he walked away into the house.

"It's all right, Rachel." Dallas pulled away from her touch.

"Let me see it."

He gave in then and bent his head for her to examine his face. The punch had caught him on the cheekbone, just below the eye, busting open the skin. The area was dotted with blood and was bright pink with swelling; by nightfall it would no doubt be a purple shiner. Because of her, she thought again.

"Here, Rachel."

Her mother handed her a tissue, and she dabbed at the blood with shaky fingers. Then Dallas took the tissue.

"I've had worse," he said, dismissing it. "Are you and Aaron ready?" He studied her with an intense gaze, as if searching her soul.

She nodded. "I just have to get my purse—and Aaron must get Wheeler."

"He's right here, Mom," Aaron said in an unusually shrill voice. "I'll get him in the car."

"I'll help you, cowboy."

Rachel got her purse off the entry table. "Mom, I..." She couldn't find words for the turmoil in her heart. Her mother opened her arms, and she went to her. "I've left the number by the phone," she whispered hoarsely. "You know where—"

"I know where the O'Connor place is," her mother whispered back. "And I expect to see you and Aaron soon and often."

"Yes..."

"I'm your mother and I love you. Give your father a bit of time, and he'll remember that, too."

Rachel had her doubts but didn't voice them. Her mother was dealing with enough disappointment already.

Dallas stepped to the door. "Aaron and Wheeler are in the car. You go on, and I'll be out in a minute. I want to speak to Jasper alone."

She stared at him. Did he want to get punched in the other eye? "He's probably gone to the kitchen—I'll go with you."

He rested a hand to the side of her neck. "Let me speak to him alone, Rach."

"You want to relegate me to the car while you discuss *me* with my father?" She'd had about enough of the foolishness of the men in her life.

"I have a couple of things to say to him, and I'd like to say them in private."

He wasn't going to be dissuaded. Reluctantly she nodded, and he caressed her neck quickly before removing his hand and stepping past her into the house.

"Through here," her mother directed.

Rachel was tempted to stand there with her mother and listen for sounds of violence. Then she smiled resolutely and squeezed her mother's hand. "Aaron's no doubt wondering what's going on, so I'd better get out there. I'll call soon, Mom."

Her mother smiled, though the smile didn't reach her dark eyes.

Dallas pushed gently through the swinging door into the kitchen. It was a spacious room, reminiscent of old-world Spanish kitchens, with brick and brightly colored tile walls, genuine wood counters and copper pots hanging from hooks. Jasper stood with a cup in hand, gazing out the giant bay window. He turned at the sound of Dallas's footstep on the clay tile. His bushy eyebrows rose in surprise, followed by burning anger.

"I thought you would have the decency to leave quickly." He smacked the cup to the counter and placed both hands to his hips.

Dallas came forward until he could rest his hands on a chair back. "I want to assure you, Jasper, that I love your daughter—and your grandson. I intend to marry Rachel and to do my best to make her happy."

"Your brother made her life miserable. Living at the Cordell ranch made her miserable. Why should it be any different with you?"

"Because I'm not Coy," Dallas said between clenched teeth. "And we won't be living with Dad. I've bought a place to the south—the old O'Connor ranch."

"Mira told me about the house. Where you and Rachel live won't change things. You're still a Cordell."

Dallas gazed at the older man's face, which remained etched with hatred. "You've probably told Rachel and yourself that your objections to our marriage has to do with your concern for her happiness—but it really has more to do with you not liking our families joined, just as my father doesn't. And for you the loss is greater because this will mean eventually the Golden Rose will be joined to the Cordell Ranch, something that has never been, that no one in either family has wanted to see for way over one hundred years."

The thunder gathered on Jasper's ruddy face, but Dallas continued.

"Well, Rachel and I can't live our lives based on hates and prejudices that long since passed reasoning. We fell in love, Jasper—like you and Mira. That's a rare thing, seems to me, something I'm not going to throw away just because you and Dad are intent on carrying your feud to your graves."

"You've got her," the older man ground out. "It's what you want, isn't it?"

"Do I, Jasper?" He eyed the big man. "Rachel and Aaron and I can't ignore where we come from, no matter how much we try. It's there with us. And Rachel loves and needs you, Jasper. Marrying me isn't going to change that. And instead of me, this time it'll be you making her life miserable if you cut her out of your life. Maybe you can forget she's your daughter, but she can't forget it. And if you turn your back on her, I know that eventually she'll resent not only you but me. We'll all lose, Jasper.''

"You're better with words than your father," the older man said with disdain.

"With all these words I'm asking you to give Rachel your blessing. You don't have to include me—just her and Aaron. I'll go so far as to beg you, Jasper." The older man's gaze narrowed. "Because I love her and I don't want to see you break her heart.''

"It's you that's causin' all this!"

"I'm marrying your daughter just as soon as we can get together a small wedding," Dallas said evenly. "I hope you'll come."

For long seconds the two men stared at each other. Jasper's forbidding expression did not lessen. Quietly Dallas turned to the door. Mira stood there. She touched his arm with a gentle gesture as he passed.

They stopped for pizza on the way. Dallas gave Aaron over two dollars in quarters to feed the jukebox and held Rachel's hand beneath the table. She gazed at his handsome face, seeing the fatigue and ever-swelling blue-black eye. They smiled at each other, but a strange wariness lingered between them.

Rachel wanted desperately to know what had transpired with Ace, but there could be no talking of it in front of Aaron—nor of what Dallas and her father had said to each other. She wondered whether that was what was causing the tension between them—something that her father had said. She wished she knew, and was irritated that Dallas hadn't allowed her to be beside him when he'd spoken to her father.

The O'Connor place was a small rock house much like a thousand others dotting the state. Rachel had always liked the look of them—rugged Oklahoma sandstone that made the structure belong to the land.

"This is Little Blue Creek," he said, leading her through the wet, tall bluestem prairie grass to a stream that cut deep into the earth about three hundred yards from the house. He was a rancher; the land would come first. "It branches out of the Washita eight miles to the north and waters the pastures and woods from there to here, our land."

"Can I check it out, Mom?"

She nodded. "Only a few minutes. It looks like it'll rain again."

Dallas escorted her through the house, an action that took barely fifteen minutes, even with his taking extra time to explain about the new beds and refrigerator he'd bought just that day. She saw the peeling paint, rotted windowsills and aged sinks and tub. One ancient bathroom, when she'd never lived with less than two of the most modern. Actually she hadn't been in a house of this sort since her high-school days when visiting friends.

"It's small—just two bedrooms," he said. "And it needs work, but eventually we can enlarge it or build another one exactly how we want it."

She saw the worry in his stiff expression—concern that she wouldn't like his offering. Her heart squeezed, and she did what she'd been wanting to do since seeing him— stepped over and wrapped her arms around his waist and laid her head on his chest.

"I don't mind about the house, Dallas. It's a charming place, and any woman would die over that refrigerator." She squeezed her eyes shut against tears. "I just want...us."

He held her and rocked slightly on his heels. His arms were strong and warm, and gradually that warmth generated to Rachel. She inhaled the scent of him and listened to his heartbeat beneath her ear.

"Rachel," he said, his chin moving on her silky warm hair. He had to get it said. "I don't have a job anymore...not a lot of money, and—"

She'd jerked her head upward, and her brown eyes widened in shock. "What do you mean, you don't have a job?"

"The old man threw me off the place." He gave a wry grin, trying to lighten what he had to tell her. "I've been fired." The shame poured over him. How could he ask her to marry him now, when he had no security to offer her and Aaron?

"Ace...but you're his son. You've always taken care of the ranch." The enormity of it hit her. She'd been such a fool not to think of that before! She'd known Ace would be angry, would undoubtedly condemn Dallas, but she'd never thought he would take away his birthright. *Because of her...*

"I'll get a job, Rach. And I've got some money to tide us through."

But she was shaking her head and pulling away. "That ranch is yours by right. Oh, Dallas! It's because of me—*me*! And you can't ever build up another place like it. It'll take a lifetime of—"

He gripped her by the shoulders. "Okay, Rach, okay." He forced her to look at him. "But it's not the end of the world. And maybe it's the best thing that could happen. This way I can build my own—from the bottom up. Just like the Cordells did when they first came to Indian territory." His tone softened. "And I'll have you, which is what I want more than anything else."

She studied his precious gray eyes. He meant what he said; she saw the love and longing in his face and felt it echo in her heart. But at what price? she asked herself, guilt weighing her soul. At what price?

"Mom?"

With Aaron's voice the intimate moment popped and fizzled away. Rachel glanced to the back door, where Aaron's voice had come from. He stood on the porch, looking through the screen, an uncertain expression on his face. "Me and Wheeler...we're awfully sorry...but we fell in the creek."

She stepped to the doorway and peered out at her son. He was covered from his waist down in bright orange oozy clay. All four of Wheeler's legs were likewise coated. Rachel's heart turned to lead, and she experienced a return of the urge to run away.

While Rachel saw to getting Aaron and Wheeler cleaned up, Dallas tried to get the furnace going; it had become quite cool and damp in the house. The furnace, however, refused to work. Dallas lit a roaring fire in the fireplace, and Rachel made Aaron sit in front of it, wrapped in a blanket from one of the beds.

A heavy thunderstorm passed over, and they discovered that the water stains on the ceilings were recent ones when water began dripping on Rachel's head as she stood at the kitchen sink. Up in the attic Dallas discovered four leaks; they had only three pans to catch the water. Rachel took the salad crisper out of the refrigerator to use under the fourth.

Then there was the car to be unloaded. Rachel insisted on bringing everything in, even through the heavy rain. "I want it tonight," she said sharply when Dallas suggested they wait until morning. It had become suddenly so important for what few belongings she had to be close at hand. She wanted to see and touch them—her hair dryer and bathrobe and slippers and big, round brass clock that she could hear ticking in the night.

Dallas clamped his mouth shut and strode out in the pouring rain to continue the job. Rachel followed, refusing to get any less wet than he did, though she commanded Aaron to remain in the house, wrapped in the blanket.

"Mom, I'm suffocating." He elaborated with a forced gag.

"Stay there. I don't need you getting pneumonia."

"He's a healthy boy, Rach, not a—"

She shot him a warning look and strode out for another load from the car. She didn't need him telling her how to care for her son.

As soon as everything was in the house, Dallas disappeared, leaving Rachel to put it away as she chose.

"He went out the back," Aaron said when Rachel asked.

He always did that, she remembered. Went off alone when something was bothering him. She leaned her head against the kitchen cabinet. She didn't mean to snap, to act so shrewish. He'd lost his birthright. Dear God, the ranch that was his whole life—and all because of her. Tears threatened, and she wished for a damn good cry—she owed it to herself, she thought angrily.

But of course there was neither time nor place for emotional hysterics.

She made Aaron a snack of milk and jelly bread, then tucked him into bed. Dallas still hadn't come in by the time she'd washed her face and changed into a gown and robe, and she began to vacillate between anger and worry. He was sulking, and it was rude. Perhaps he wished himself free of all this, and who could blame him?

She didn't know what to do and hated the feeling. It was like a cruel replay of what had happened between her and Coy. She hadn't known what to do then when the silence slammed down between them; she hadn't been used to such treatment. In her own family, problems had been talked out, but Coy wouldn't talk, and gradually the pain had forced Rachel into a protective shell—one she hadn't been able to break out of.

Dallas was so like Coy. She'd known this. Maybe this strangeness between them was a warning—her life was about to repeat itself. The idea terrified her.

She thought of Dallas outside alone, and a tiny flicker of determination tingled in her shoulders. Drawing on that tenuous determination, she stepped toward the porch.

Dallas heard the porch screen squeak and then a soft bang, and knew Rachel was coming after him. Still, he stood where he was in the dark barn. The end of his panatela glowed brightly as he puffed on it.

"Dallas?" She'd reached the wide barn entry.

"I'll be in after a while." He was immediately sorry to sound so short.

He heard her breathing, waiting, but he remained where he was, feeling perversely mixed up. He longed to go and sweep her into his arms and at the same time keep a distance just to punish her for shutting him out earlier.

"I'm sharing with Aaron," she said softly, almost apologetically. Something that didn't need saying.

"Fine." His pride won out.

He listened to her quiet movements recede, and then the screen door tapped softly.

He was glad she'd come out to speak to him, so why in the hell had he acted like such an ass? He leaned his head back against the barn pole. Lord, he was scared. Suddenly reality was clearly before him like bright neon lights: he was taking on a wife and son at the age of thirty-seven.

Rachel had made it plain that night that she didn't want his interference with Aaron. They had a hurdle in balancing that out. And how was he going to support them? He'd never looked for a job in his life. Rachel had given up all she had to come and be plunked down into this. She was probably wondering why she'd done it right about now, and if anyone questioned him, he'd have to say he was wondering, too. They'd gone and done exactly what she and Coy had done years before—let irresistible passion carry them away. The love they'd felt had blinded them to cold, hard facts.

He thought for several long minutes of how good it would be to make love with Rachel. He recalled with aching vividness her satiny skin and her hair that he loved so much. He recalled how she'd come to him that first crisp, fresh morning, given every secret part of herself to him. He couldn't have put into words how he'd known this, only that he had—and that such was a rare blessing to a man.

With a deep breath he tried to push down the throbbing in his gut. It wasn't possible to take comfort with Rachel now—one more thing that he found unreasonably galling.

There would be no checking out the stock at the Cordell Ranch in the morning; he wouldn't be issuing orders to the men, wouldn't be handling the buying and the selling ever again. Even his mare, Shadow, belonged to the ranch, so he wouldn't be riding her. A crack a mile wide opened inside him.

How had everything gotten so crazy? He and Rachel loved each other—why couldn't they simply come together and live happily ever after?

When he finally went back to the house, he found Rachel had left the hall light on for him. He peeked into the room Aaron had chosen for his own. Rachel was curled with her back to Aaron. Her dark hair spilled across the pillow and over her shoulders. Dimly the light from the hall illuminated her features, showing her asleep yet frowning.

He moved into the room with the urge to stroke away the frown, then checked himself, not wanting to wake her. His gaze fell to the big brass clock sitting on a box. Beside it lay the rose rock he'd given her that morning weeks ago. He'd meant it as a promise—that his love would be as everlasting as that rock.

He stretched out on the bed in the other room. The extrafirm mattress proved as hard as sleeping on the floor. There came a heavy downpour on the roof. The sound was pleasantly lulling, and Dallas had just drifted off when something cold smacked him on the forehead. It came again . . . and again. Drips. Jerking his pillow, he moved to the far side of the bed.

Chapter Eleven

The big brass clock's jangling alarm woke Rachel. At first disoriented, she lay there a moment after she'd shut it off. Then she remembered, the fear and longing washing over her again. Quietly but swiftly she slipped from the bed and padded into the kitchen, flinging back her hair as she went, femininely hoping to shake it into order. Her heartbeat quickened at the light spilling out the doorway and the aroma of coffee. She smiled, imagining Dallas there and how she wanted to run into his arms in this precious moment of privacy.

But the room was empty. Even as she stepped to the window to look, she knew she'd find his pickup gone. Her heart plummeted. She'd wanted to make up with him, to weave again the threads between them that seemed to be coming unraveled. Why had he left without waiting to speak with her?

Her gaze fell to a piece of paper lying on the counter beside the coffeemaker—a scrap from a brown paper bag.

"Have gone job hunting," he'd written. *"Will be back by evening—Dallas."*

If possible, her heart fell even further. She needed him, needed to talk to him and hear him say he still loved her—even if she had been a shrew the night before. Didn't they have that—a love strong enough to go through the hard times? She reread his note. He hadn't even mentioned love, simply signed his name. More like an acquaintance than a lover, she thought resentfully.

"Where's Dallas?"

Twisting around, she saw Aaron standing in the doorway, rubbing his eyes.

"He's gone already." She moved to get a cup from the cabinet and reached for the coffeepot. Aaron walked over and studied the note.

"A job?" His eyebrows came together. "What does he need a job for?"

"To pay the bills, of course."

"But he has the ranch...doesn't he?"

Rachel shook her head. "The Cordell ranch belongs to Papa Ace," she said gently, "and Papa isn't very happy with Dallas right now."

"Oh." He frowned. "Because of us?"

"No, darling," she said firmly, "not because of you."

"How do you know?" He set his jaw stubbornly, looking very much like either of his grandpas.

She reached for the telephone and dialed the Cordell number. At this early hour the chances were that it would be Ace who answered. It was. "Ace, your grandson would like to speak to you," she said, not bothering with a "hello," which would give him a chance to hang up. Her heart pounded, and she prayed she wasn't wrong.

"Well, put him on." Ace growled the words.

With a small smile she handed the telephone to Aaron and went to get dressed. She was braiding her hair when Aaron came to the doorway.

"How was Papa?" she asked.

He gave a reluctant but true grin. "He's okay. He said to come this afternoon to work Scout. It's about time for the show, ya know. He said he'd get me from school and Pete could bring me home around eight."

She nodded and smiled. "That'll be fine."

He remained standing there. "I guess you ain't gonna work for the store anymore, huh?" She turned to see him eyeing her denim slacks and oversize cotton sweater.

Rachel shook her head. "No, I won't."

It was a sad thought. She shared her father's pride in the family stores, enjoyed her work and friends she'd made there. And when being truthful, she very much enjoyed the luxuries of being the boss's daughter—the executive office, unlimited funds. She turned from the images.

"I'll kinda like it," he said, "you being around awhile after I get out of school."

"I think I'll kinda like that, too." She grinned and gave him a gentle shove. "I've laid out your clothes. Go on and get dressed. I don't want you late for school."

Aaron was worried about Wheeler being at a strange home, so they shut him up in one of the empty stalls in the barn before taking off. The sun was well over the horizon, but the air remained heavy with the possibility of more rain.

"Mom, are you and Dallas still getting married?" Aaron asked on the drive.

"Yes, of course," Rachel answered, casting her son a quick, curious glance. "Why would you ask that?"

"Well, you sure didn't seem like you were last night."

"We didn't?"

"No, you seemed sorta mad at each other."

It came on the tip of her tongue to say that wasn't so, but she stopped. It was so, she realized. She'd been hurt and frightened and uncertain, and had taken it out on Dallas.

"I guess we did, sweetheart, but it's like that, sometimes. We were both tired and upset."

"Doesn't make much sense to me."

"No," she said softly, "it certainly doesn't."

On the way home she drove automatically, her mind focused on what her son had said. He'd thought maybe she and Dallas weren't going to marry, because they'd seemed anything but lovers the past night.

Things had just gotten so...so out of focus. She'd focused on the things she didn't have instead of the one magnificent thing she did: Dallas's love.

All of it, the fight with her father, Aaron falling into the creek, the faulty furnace, leaking ceilings—and selfish pride—had piled up, sucking dry the spirit of love.

She pulled the car to a stop in the driveway and walked out to let Wheeler out of the stall. At the barn door she paused and gazed at the house, seeing instead first her father's face and then Ace's.

Their fathers didn't want them to succeed—for their own selfish reasons. Yet Ace and Jasper could only be blamed so far—what she and Dallas made of their love was up to them.

She did love him. *Oh, Lord, she loved him so much!* And *that* was what she needed to focus on and be thankful for. They shouldn't let that love get lost, buried under all the trials.

The bright morning sun peeked through a billowy cloud, washing the sandstone house with golden rays, like a promise. Her heart filling with hope and purpose, she strode out for the house. Wheeler cavorted alongside her, and savoring the warmth breaking over her heart, Rachel allowed him inside with her.

"Are you feeling a bit lost, too, fella?" She scratched behind his ear. "Well, this is home. This is home."

First she made the necessary call to the store. Just as she'd suspected, her father had not spoken to Oran. When she told him, as gently as possible, that she wouldn't be returning to work and sketched in bare details, regret squeezed her heart. But, she told herself, she and Dallas had much ahead. She would get another job—being his wife. Next she took a luxurious bath in fragrant bath soap and washed her hair, a woman preparing for her lover. Perhaps, she hoped as she carefully chose deep-blue slacks and a sweater, he would return before evening, giving them time alone to talk, among other things.

Though she feared being away when Dallas came, she went to get groceries, buying everything to make him one scrumptious steak dinner. Alone in the house again, she busied herself with putting away the food. That done, she made beds and straightened up, then reverently took out the wedding dress her mother had given her.

Quickly she shed her clothes and tried it on, wishing for a mirror to see it better. It was quite tight in the waist but fit perfectly everywhere else, even the length. It was delicate ivory silk, with lace that had come from France, she remembered her mother telling her long ago. Her father's mother had designed it herself with pale turquoise beads sewn in a pattern around the waist and up the sleeves to add a traditional Indian touch. Rachel had wished to have it when she and Coy had run off and been married by a justice. At last she hung it on the back of the closet door because there was no other place high enough.

The telephone rang, and she raced to answer it, hoping to hear Dallas's voice. It was Yancey.

"Hi, beautiful!" he said in his warm and jovial tone. "This is a pleasant surprise. Hey...you two haven't tied the knot yet, have you? Dallas promised I could get to see this."

"I thought you didn't like weddings."

"This is one I'm busting my butt to see. For this I'll gladly wear a suit and tie. Is he there?"

"No. He's gone job hunting," she added after an instant.

The line buzzed softly. "Dad cut him off?" Bitterness rang in his voice.

"Yes."

"Well, you tell him I'm held up here in Chicago, but I'm headed home. Flights are delayed because of heavy storms, and nothing's posted yet, but the storms can't go on forever. I should be there by early morning before sunup, providing we don't get diverted—again. I'm coming out of Canada, been hitting spring storms everywhere.''

''We'll wait for you, Yancey,'' she promised.

She hung up, and her heart longed more than ever for Dallas. They were going to get married but hadn't even discussed when, where, anything.

To dispel the empty feeling, she turned on the radio. Sitting at the shaky kitchen table, she occupied herself by planning a small wedding on paper. It was midafternoon when she heard a pickup pulling into the drive.

Dallas tried to convince himself he'd done well that day—because he had. He had two good offers of ranch-managing jobs down in Texas, one locally. Bill Simmons at the Black Angus Association wanted him to work for them in research, and Lyle Richards, editor of the *Western Rancher* magazine and whom he'd run into at the Angus offices, offered him a good salary to write for them.

All good jobs, making decent money—but not doing what he loved, which was working for himself. He silently chastised himself for being ungrateful. He would work for himself one day—and it would be all his, built from the ground up.

He heard the screen door slam and looked up to see Rachel running toward him. Her hair was loose, flying out behind her like black silk rippling in the wind. His heart jumped with joy; she obviously hadn't changed her mind. He'd half-expected to find her making preparations to move back home.

She pressed herself against him. He tilted her face with both hands and brought his mouth to hers, sudden desire firing his blood. He kissed her hungrily, all thoughts of what he'd been doing that day blowing away with the wind.

At last he lifted his head and gasped for breath. ''I could learn to like greetings like this,'' he said huskily, allowing his sensual intentions to show in his eyes.

"Dallas..." She touched his cheek. "Where have you been so long?"

"We'll talk about it...later. We are alone, aren't we?"

"Yes, but—"

He stopped her words with his lips. He'd been thinking of her all day while he talked to men about cattle and breeding and prices and weather.

"Dallas?" She laughed as he scooped her up and strode toward the house.

"Just hold on. This isn't as easy as it looks in the movies." It was good to carry her—made him feel strong and virile.

He strode through to the bedroom where he'd slept the night before and deposited her on the bed, pushing her back on the pillows.

"Did you know there's a big wet spot..." She caught her breath as he kissed her neck.

"Leaked last night."

He slid his hands beneath her sweater, and she quivered at his touch. She wasn't wearing a bra and smiled saucily when he discovered that fact. Her skin was warm as sunshine through glass, her nipples hard with wanting—of him. To have a woman react like this was every man's dream. He stroked her and watched the heat gather in her eyes until his own blood reached the boiling point. Sitting up, he began to unbutton his shirt.

"I'll help you with your boots," she said, her lips curving coyly.

She took his leg between her legs and bent her bottom to him. Her silky hair waved in the air. He enjoyed gazing at her shape while he carefully placed his boot there for leverage. First one boot and then the other came off, and then he pulled her into his lap. Her hip rubbed his swollen manhood.

Quickly he slipped her sweater over her head and tossed it aside. Caressing her skin, he gazed at her pale beauty. Her dark hair tumbled like a black cloud over her shoulders and breasts. The sweet, enticing scent of her engulfed him.

With two fingers he moved her hair aside and stared at her creamy breasts, nourishment for one hungry man. Then her hands gently cradled his face and forced him to look at her. She gave him a slow, sensual smile.

While she finished unbuttoning his shirt, he stroked her back and kissed the sensitive places of her neck, taking pleasure in making her breath catch in the back of her throat. And then her hands were caressing his chest, bring his own breath fast. He lost it completely when her fingers moved to his belt buckle. She hadn't done this to him in the past—been so bold and brassy. It set him off balance.

"Where'd you learn this?" he whispered.

"What?" she asked breathlessly, and unzipped his jeans.

He leaned backward to give her free access. "To take command."

"You don't like it?" She studied him and moved her hands beneath his shorts, encircling him with her hand.

"I didn't say that . . . Oh, no, I didn't say that." And he reached for the front catch of her slacks.

They were both filled with pent-up longing of days of wanting and not being able to have each other. Every cell in Rachel's body throbbed from Dallas's touching and stroking. Soon she abandoned her wanton advances to being overcome by his. He kissed her roughly and moved his hand with agonizing slowness lower and lower on her body until she thought she would die with wanting.

Then at last he entered her. Quick, hard it came for them both. Her heart filled to overflowing with love for the man filling her. Then came the pure exploding peak of fulfillment so dazzling it blotted out conscious thought.

Dallas reclined on the two big feather pillows propped against the headboard. Rachel lay in the crook of his arm, surrounded with the wonderful afterglow of their love. Listening to his heartbeat and wondering whether she'd conceived—she smiled at the thought.

"What are you smiling about?" he asked around the cigar between his teeth.

"We didn't use birth control."

The slow smile traced his lips, and the glint in his eye turned sensual "No..." He stroked her bare arm and looked rather pleased with himself. Then he glanced to his watch. "Aren't we supposed to get Aaron?"

She shook her head. "Ace's picking him up for the evening. Pete will bring him home."

He nodded, and a somber mask descended across his face. Then his lips quirked again, and he suddenly sat up, reaching for his clothes. "Get dressed, woman, and if you're real sweet to me, I'll take you for a steak dinner," he said with an exaggerated drawl.

"I have steak in the refrigerator."

"Save it. Come on..." He tossed her sweater to her.

Catching his mood, she dressed quickly and pulled her hair up into a neat chignon.

"Yancey called." She remembered to tell him as he took her hand and led her out the door. "He's stuck in Chicago because of weather but expects to get in sometime after midnight."

"Good." He handed her up into the seat of his pickup and got in beside her. From the glove box he pulled a small bundle of deep-blue velvet tied with a white satin ribbon. He held it toward her.

It was a traditional engagement bundle. With the realization came awe as she watched him place it into her palm. Ancient Chickasaw custom had been for the man to bring a gift wrapped in a bundle to the woman he wished to wed. Her acceptance of the gift meant her acceptance of the man, and the two were engaged.

She stared at the bundle and fingered the soft velvet. Suddenly it was as if she could feel the essence of all her ancestors welling up within her—their pride and strength and fortitude. The intangible wealth of these traits ran in her blood and in Dallas's.

Her vision blurred by unshed tears, she raised her eyes to him.

"You're supposed to open it," he said hoarsely.

Slowly she pulled the end of the ribbon. It came loose, and the velvet spread apart. There, lying on the soft fabric, was a tiny, exquisitely formed rose rock set in gold filigree and attached to a gold chain. She blinked, and a tear dropped to the velvet. Then she saw that the gold filigree was actually the entwining of hers and Dallas's initials in fancy script. He'd had the necklace made for her.

"Does it please you?"

She sniffed. "Of course it does...." She leaned toward him, and he held her tight.

He took the necklace from her and placed it around her neck, fastening it. She felt his fingers fumbling with the unaccustomed action. She turned so he could see it against her neck. He raised his eyes to hers.

"Now you are my woman."

She nodded. "Yes."

He eased away and smiled. "Let's get to the courthouse for the marriage license. I've been inviting people to our wedding most of the day. Must be at least twenty people who've already said they'd come, and we don't want to disappoint them."

"Twenty..." She gaped at him as he started the engine. "But I thought we'd just have a small ceremony when Yancey got here—tomorrow or the next day."

"The people I've talked to have all agreed that Friday would be a great day." He turned the truck.

"Friday?" It was now Monday. "What kind of a wedding were you planning, Mr. Cordell?"

"The usual. Preacher, bride and groom, food and dancing, right here at the house." His eyes twinkled merrily as he headed the truck out on the road.

"Here?" They had only two chairs. "But the arrangements..."

"Quinn's handling it, said she's had lots of practice. Something like this will be a breeze. Stella's bringing her almond delights that are crowding the freezer."

Rachel sat there, stunned.

Suddenly, right on the bridge over the creek, Dallas stopped the pickup and turned to her. "I want to marry you publicly," he said seriously. "I want to say to the world that I love you and I'm proud of it. I want Aaron to see this."

"I want that, too," she said quietly.

On the way to the courthouse Rachel questioned Dallas, and he told her about several job offers. They were all good ones with sizeable salaries; he had the education and experience to command such. Yet he didn't appear enthused about any. And she knew why—none of them was what he truly loved to do, which was work his own land.

"Dallas," she said slowly, "I have money. Enough to get us started on this place. And there's also Coy's insurance money. I've saved most all of it for Aaron."

He scowled. "I'm not touching Coy's insurance. That'll be for Aaron." The scowl faded, and he tenderly rubbed his thumb on her neck and shook his head. "And I'm not taking your savings."

"I no longer have my savings—it is *ours* as husband and wife," she pointed out.

He shook his head again. "It'll take a lot of money to start an operation and even more time before we would turn a profit. We have nothing—no decent tractors or machinery for haying, no stock trailers. A number of fences need repairing. Even if we did begin, we'd need another income to live on until we made enough money to be self-supporting."

"I intend to get a job," she told him, "which would enable you to concentrate on the ranch." She knew she made perfect sense.

"I'll support this family." His voice was tight.

"I have no doubt of that," she said, then added softly, "If you come home some day and there's cows in the yard, you can't send them back."

He frowned but didn't speak.

When Pete brought Aaron home that night, he also brought Dallas's horse.

"Big Ace said the mare belongs to you," Pete said, self-consciously averting his eyes as he unlatched the trailer door.

Dallas couldn't deny his pleasure. He was damn glad to have Shadow. He got her out of the trailer and stood caressing her neck.

"We got your saddle and bridle, too, Uncle Dallas," Aaron said. Dallas looked over to see Aaron smiling broadly.

"Thanks. You, too, Pete."

Pete gave a toothy grin.

"How is Dad?" Dallas asked.

"Seems pert' near hisself to me. Don't think he's likin' handlin' the whole operation, though. He had a go-round with Wes, and he quit. Big Ace didn't know 'bout Jones and Hobart not gettin' on and sent them out together. They spent the better part of yesterday mornin' fightin'. And he's hirin' some woman to come work the computer for him—he needed to know the head count today and nobody on the place knew, 'cept the machine, and none of us can work it. Things ain't quite the same with computers runnin' the show."

"Yancey'll be home by tomorrow," Dallas said. "He can help out."

After they bid Pete goodbye, Rachel took Aaron in to get ready for bed while Dallas led Shadow toward the night-black pasture. He let her loose, though the old girl walked only a few feet away and began grazing. Dallas lit a panatela and leaned against a fence post, listening to distant thunder. It was going to rain again. Minutes later he heard the screen door bang—Rachel coming to join him.

"I've told Aaron about our wedding." The back porch light shone on her face enough for him to see her smile.

He nodded. "Thought I'd ask him to stand up with me, if it's okay with you. Yancey'll understand."

She hugged him. "He'd love it." She stayed in the crook of his arm.

"Guess the old man wants to be really done with me," he commented, watching the mare move into the deep darkness where he could only hear her. "He didn't even want Shadow around the place." He told himself it didn't matter, that he'd never had the best relationship with his father. But it still felt like a piece was being torn from his heart.

"I don't see that," Rachel said in a voice that drew his gaze to her shadowed features. "He knows you love that horse, so he sent her to you."

"Maybe," he allowed after a moment, and he felt better.

The following day the sky was heavy with gray clouds— more rain on the way. Rachel and Dallas heard on the morning radio weather report that heavy storms were moving across New Mexico and west Texas, and many areas were reporting flooding. Yancey telephoned to say he'd made it home, though it was foul weather to the north, as well.

Dallas left early to speak to a man about a job. He appeared more interested in working with this man, P. J. Stone, than in any of the offers he'd had previously. Mr. Stone was an old friend, and one he highly respected.

Left to her own devices after she took Aaron to school, Rachel stopped by her parents' home, braving a chance meeting with her father because she wanted to visit with her mother and to pick up more of her things.

Her father was just coming out of the house when she pulled the car to a stop.

"Hello, Daddy."

He paused and nodded at her, crooking a bushy eyebrow. "I don't suppose you've come to your senses."

"I don't suppose you've come to yours," she retorted.

He strode away to his Mercedes-Benz, which had already been taken from the garage, and something drove her to holler after him, "You're going to let your grandchild attend his mother's wedding alone."

"That's his mother's doin'," he shot back.

Stubborn ass, she thought as she turned for the door and heard gravel flying where her father sped angrily away. Well, she was his daughter and could be equally stubborn. She would show him that much!

Her mother's greeting brought tears to her eyes. They clung to each other for long minutes before her mother said, "Come in for coffee. I want to know everything—about Aaron, Dallas, the house and the wedding."

Though she hadn't intended to, Rachel found herself pouring it all out to her mother, the joy of being with Dallas, of what she'd learned about being grateful, showing the gift he'd given her in the Chickasaw tradition. She spoke also of how Ace had cut Dallas off from the ranch, his inheritance, how she worried Dallas wouldn't be able to be happy without it and how she wished it could be different with Ace and her father.

Her mother listened, which was exactly what Rachel had needed. When she'd finally wound down after nearly an hour, she felt much relieved and stronger.

Together, she, her mother and Willow packed hers and Aaron's remaining belongs, putting as much into the station wagon as would fit. Then Rachel contacted a moving company about coming for her furniture, agreeing to pay a small fortune if they could move her things by Wednesday. She was determined to have her house as lovely as possible on her wedding day.

It had begun to rain when she drove away just after lunch. Though anxious to get home to see whether Dallas was there, on impulse she turned into the Cordell ranch.

"My goodness," Stella said when she opened the door. "Get in here and let me hug you."

Rachel obliged. "Thank you so much for what you did down at the house."

"It wasn't nothin' at all." Stella's smile widened. "We're looking forward to coming down on Friday. Weather permitting."

"Please pray for clear skies," Rachel said, then asked hesitantly, "Is Ace in?"

"In his study." Stella looked curious.

Rachel stepped toward the study door. "I'm just going to speak to him a moment."

She entered at Ace's "Come in." For long seconds they stared at each other, Ace definitely surprised at first. Then his expression settled into a cold, stoic mask.

"You've obviously come to say something," he said, "so say it."

Rachel swallowed the intimidation he'd always managed to raise in her. "I want to thank you for sending Shadow down to Dallas."

"The mare's his. He helped in her birth and trained her."

"Couldn't you say the same about this ranch?" she asked quietly. "Isn't it his as much as yours?"

He just looked at her, his features remaining coldly forbidding. She wanted to turn and walk away from the confrontation but kept her feet rooted to the floor. All those years with Coy she'd never spoken up, fearful of making the situation worse. But patient suffering in silence hadn't helped. Right or wrong, she would say what she must in this instance and not live with the regret that she should have spoken but hadn't.

"Ever since he was a child, Dallas has worked on this ranch. At nine he was driving a tractor and haying with the men. In his teens he was helping deliver calves at midnight, rain or no. For the past twelve years he's been your right-hand man. This ranch wouldn't be what it is today without him, and you know it." She regarded him imploringly. "Don't take it away from him, Ace. Please don't do that."

"If he can forget his brother and his heritage so easily that he can take his brother's wife, I don't care to have him in my sight, ever." His words fell hard as rocks against rocks.

Anger at the stupidity of it flashed within her. She balled her fists at her sides and struggled not to scream. "I am no longer Coy's wife. He is gone. I don't intend to live my life as a monument to your warped memory of him, and neither does Dallas.

"And because you won't see, you're going to lose the son who, above your other children, has remained the most loyal to you. He's your firstborn, Ace. He feels such loyalty to you, though God only knows why, when you've always clearly favored Coy. Have you ever considered how good this will be for all of us? Have you ever considered that Dallas, your son, too, Ace, is happy with me—happy to raise Coy's son? No..." She shook her head, no longer truly seeing his face. "You're only concerned with yourself and to make things as *you* wish them."

Trembling, she backed toward the door. "We'll miss you and my father, but you two can just finish your days surrounded by your own selfish stubbornness, since you obviously prize it so much."

She pivoted and walked out.

It wasn't until she was halfway home that Ace's high blood pressure came to mind. She pushed the car faster along the slick, wet roads, intent on getting home to the telephone.

Dallas's pickup wasn't in the drive, and she was grateful. She didn't want him to know she'd been to Ace or to see her so upset.

Through the sprinkling rain she ran into the house and straight to the phone, her boots making puddles on the floor as she dialed the Cordell number. She had no idea what she would say if it was Ace who answered.

Quinn answered. Ace was fine, Quinn assured her after Rachel had gotten out her garbled question. She'd just spoken with him before he'd walked out to the barn.

"Thanks..."

Rachel slowly hung up the telephone, then sat at the old table and cried.

Chapter Twelve

When Rachel returned with Aaron from school, she was amazed to see the movers with her furniture waiting in the driveway. She hadn't expected them until the following afternoon at the earliest.

"Had to squeeze ya in when we could," the one in charge told her, then spit out a dip of tobacco. "It's good that this rain's stopped for a while, 'cause it's supposed to hit again tomorrow."

Rachel was so excited to see hers and Aaron's beds, her precious dining table and chairs, Navaho rugs and the boxes she knew contained antique brass lamps—and oh, the painted tiles her mother had given her—that she could have kissed the man's whiskery face!

There wasn't much, so in a matter of forty-five minutes the three men had not only piled everything into the middle of the living room, but had also dismantled and carried to the attic the beds already in the rooms and moved hers and Aaron's into their place. By dark when Dallas arrived, she and Aaron were happily singing in the kitchen as they put her dishes away into the cabinets.

The delighted surprise on his face brought joy to Rachel's heart—as did the warm, intimate gaze he shot her. Though he gave her a very chaste kiss in Aaron's presence, his hand caressed her back seductively.

The three of them dined by candlelight in the dining room on Rachel's table, complete with tablecloth and her best china and silver. Talk was lively of Aaron's getting an A on his math test, Rachel's plans for decorating the house and of the coming wedding. Dallas had again been inviting people, and Aaron, too, admitted he'd invited several friends.

Lastly, quietly, Dallas told of his new partnership with P. J. Stone. He had agreed to breed prize Tarentaise cattle for Mr. Stone. Dallas would be supplying his vast knowledge and the land; Mr. Stone would supply the cattle and capital—his share of the profits would be larger.

Rachel watched the excited light in Dallas's eyes as he told of the Tarentaise cattle. In recent years considered an exotic breed, they were proving to be extremely hardy and to outweigh other breeds by hundreds of pounds. It was plainly evident Dallas found them an interesting challenge. It further warmed her heart to sit back quietly while Aaron questioned Dallas, and the two of them became deeply engrossed in something so ugly and boring as a cow. Yet they were both Cordells, she told herself, smiling as they didn't even notice she'd risen to clear the table.

Dallas had found a way to work his own land, and she was very grateful.

Later, after Aaron was in bed and they were sharing coffee at the kitchen table, Dallas said slowly, "This thing with P.J. has a good future, but we're going to be starting out lean." He hesitated. "So I guess we could use that savings of yours—but we'll put it back double. I don't want you to go out to work, Rach, if that's okay with you. I could build you a workroom up in the attic for you to have a private place to do your beadwork and such.''

She smiled at his tender, hesitant expression. ''I'd like that.'' She kept to herself the fact that her needlework had become quite a lucrative endeavor. It would be fun to see the look on his face later.

''Talked to Yancey today on the phone,'' he said. ''He's willing to stay around for a few months and help me when he can with fences and other things around here to set up for the cattle. It's best I get him while he doesn't have any broken bones.''

Gazing at his grin, Rachel thought of her meeting with Ace. She'd better tell him about it, though she feared he'd be angry with her.

''I went to see Ace today,'' she said slowly.

His eyes turned sharp. ''What about?''

''I wanted to thank him for sending Shadow down, for one thing.''

''I doubted that he needed to be thanked for wanting to get rid of her.''

''I just wanted to speak to him,'' she said after a long second. ''The same way you wanted to speak to my father.''

He gazed at her with a dark expression that she couldn't truly read.

''I just had to appeal to him, Dallas. I couldn't *not* do it. It didn't do any good, and I truly didn't expect it to, but I had to try.''

He nodded, his expression a closed mask, and got up to pour another cup of coffee. Feeling very distant from him and not liking it, Rachel rose, put her arms around his waist and leaned against his back. He rubbed the backs of her hands with his rough palm, then turned and encircled her against him.

''You're not angry with me, are you?'' she mumbled into his shirt.

"I can't be, and you know it." His chest shook slightly with a chuckle.

With a deliberately sultry look, she lifted her face. He kissed her deeply, then drew back and held her to him. His heart pounded against hers.

"You'd better go on to bed with Aaron before I get carried away and we get caught doing something we don't want him doing," he whispered hoarsely.

Yet for a moment longer she clung to him, inhaling his scent and savoring his warmth. One last time she kissed him lightly, then slipped away without a backward glance, for she felt entirely too tempted to brave one.

Dallas sat with another cup of coffee and a cigar, listening to the soft sounds of Rachel moving around down the hall and the radio behind him on the counter. He was tired but needed time alone—to calm down from the slow heat Rachel had just ignited, for one thing, and to go over the plans he'd been making with P.J. He also wanted to hear the weather report. The ground had taken about as much water as it could soak up, and he'd heard reports of severe flooding out in west Texas.

The weatherman called for rain the following day, lots of it.

After locating a flashlight, Dallas walked out back and headed across the pasture for the creek. Wheeler came bounding along beside him when he chose to walk rather than drive over.

Training the flashlight into the creek bed, he could see that the water had risen about halfway up the deep sides and was running fast. He cursed himself for not checking earlier and making certain he forbade Aaron to come near it. Boys were naturally drawn by such.

An uneasiness gripped his shoulders as he walked back to the house. O'Connor and others he'd talked to had said this land had never seriously flooded. And the house was a good distance away, atop a rising slope. Still, he remembered one friend whose house had been a half mile from the Canadian River one year when it not only swelled out of its banks but decided to change course. It'd taken the house with it.

The following morning Dallas and Aaron joined forces to persuade Rachel to let Aaron stay out of school so that the two could go up to P. J. Stone's and see the fabled Tarentaise cattle. Rachel played her part well—hesitating because she knew they wouldn't enjoy it if she gave in too quickly. At last she gave her permission.

"You sure you don't mind us leaving you alone most of the day?" Dallas asked as he reached out and drew her to him, kissing her neck.

She shook her head and smiled. "No...you go and enjoy yourself with Aaron. I think I'll call Mom to see if she can come down to help me with the house. And I need to speak with Quinn—there's a lot to be done before Friday."

Aaron entered, grinning when he saw them.

"You go get your raincoat, young man."

"Aw, Mom...it's for sissies."

"I've got two slickers in the truck, Rach," Dallas said. "And I promise we'll use them—if we need them," he added with a sly grin.

It drizzled most of the day, and Dallas and Aaron obediently used the slickers when they walked out to view the Tarentaise with P.J. Dallas had intended to make a day of it with Aaron, from their breakfast out together to introducing him to P.J. and visiting a rancher up toward Tulsa, who had raised Tarentaise for some time. But shortly after lunch he experienced the odd, irresistible inclination to head home.

He turned on the radio as he sped down the highway and listened for reports of the rain.

"Is somethin' wrong, Uncle Dallas?" Aaron asked suddenly.

Dallas glanced over and realized he must have been scowling. He shook his head and lightened his expression. "No...I just don't want your mother alone with this heavy rain. She might not be able to find enough pans to put under the leaks," he joked.

He was already going as fast as he dared on the rain-slicked roads, and impatience gripped him. When they were twenty minutes from home, the dark clouds opened up and poured forth a torrent of water, forcing him to slow.

Rachel and her mother had taken a break from washing walls and hanging pictures and were discussing preparations for the wedding over coffee when Dallas and Aaron drove up.

"Dallas said they were going to be gone all day," Rachel commented as she peered curiously through the driving rain at their approaching figures. The two were wearing the slickers, as promised.

"I want to check the creek," Dallas said as he stood dripping just inside the back door. Rachel pressed a cup of coffee into his hands.

"Is there a problem with it flooding?"

He nodded as he swallowed a sip of coffee. "It's to be expected, but I'd like to keep an eye on it. We're breaking records all across the state with this rain. Mira," he said to her mother, "it isn't that I don't want your company, but you'd better be heading home. The radio's been announcing flooding roads everywhere—the highway patrol is advising people to stay home if possible."

He drained his cup and set it on the counter, giving her and her mother a nod before securing his hat on his head. "I'll take Shadow. I can get to more places with her than with the truck." He walked out into the downpour.

She stepped to the door to watch him striding toward the barn, shoulders hunched against the rain. A sudden anxiety clutched her heart. Pushing it away, she turned back to Aaron, who sat at the table, allowing his grandmother to help remove his soaked leather boots. After he had his boots off, Rachel sent him to get dry pants and socks.

The latest weather report came on the radio, and both Rachel and her mother stilled to listen.

"Mom," Rachel said when the announcer finished, "I think you'd better call Dad to come get you in the truck."

"Rachel, dear, I've been driving these roads for better than thirty years—and in the rain, too."

Rachel lifted the receiver and extended it to the older woman, who gave a tolerant smile. Leaving her mother to the call, she went to check the pans beneath the leaks in the attic.

Aaron found her there. "Mom, I called Wheeler and he didn't come."

"He probably doesn't want to come out of the barn in this rain."

"How do you know he's in the barn?"

"A dog naturally takes cover when there's rain, sweetheart."

"Have you seen him since I left this morning?" His eyebrows knotted with worry.

"I saw him and fed him a dog biscuit," she assured him, laying an arm around his shoulders. "We'll go out to the barn when the rain lets up some, just to make sure."

He nodded his reluctant acceptance.

"Your father's coming directly," her mother told her when she got back to the kitchen. Her mother looked concerned. "He said the South Canadian is almost at flood stage and is rising faster than has ever been recorded."

Rachel didn't like the sound of that, would rather neither of her parents be out on the roads. But she said, "He'll be okay, Mom. The roads between the Golden Rose and here generally don't flood too badly, and the truck's four-wheel drive will get him through."

Together she and her mother stepped to the window and gazed out at the rain. Though only just past two o'clock, it was exceedingly dim, night coming early with the thick, low-hanging purple clouds.

Dallas was drenched when he came in. Immediately Rachel scoffed at the mud and insisted he sit down for her to remove his boots. Her mother went to the living room to light a fire in the fireplace. Aaron hung back, gazing wide-eyed at Dallas.

"Did you see Wheeler in the barn?" he asked.

Dallas shook his head. "But then I didn't look."

Rachel set his boots aside and stood to pour him a cup of coffee. His face was drawn with worry. "Your mother didn't leave."

"Daddy's coming for her. I was afraid for her to drive home by herself in this."

He nodded and focused on the cup she handed him. He took a drink, then lifted his eyes to hers. "The creek's over its bounds and flooding into the low pasture, about a mile back. It's still rising."

"How's the bridge?"

He looked solemn. "The water's flowing just under it. It'll go over in another hour."

"Is it strong enough to hold?"

"It has been."

Rachel took a deep breath. For her father to get to them, he'd have to cross over that bridge. Unless he'd thought to go the long way around, though there was no reason for him to consider doing such.

Dallas asked Aaron to take a towel out to the barn and remove his saddle from Shadow and dry her, then to grain her. Aaron scurried away to get dry sneakers and the sweatshirt Rachel insisted he wear underneath the slicker.

Then Dallas stood and dialed a number on the phone, speaking to someone named Tom. Rachel listened to him ask to borrow Tom's bulldozer.

"Okay," he said, frowning into the receiver. "I'll make out. Yeah . . . I'll get back to you."

"Why do you need a bulldozer?" she asked as she re-filled his cup.

"To move dirt up to act as a dam behind the barns and maybe dig a holding hole for the water. Tom's rented his out, though."

She stared at him. "You think the water's going to come that far?"

He gazed pointedly at her and nodded. "If it keeps raining like it is now. The water's rolling off the hills to the low-lying areas. If it gathers enough, it's going to surge and that creek's going to turn into one hell of an angry river."

"You think it'll reach the barns?"

"It may reach the house."

Her heart thumped. This was all he had now—all they both had.

He stood up and raked his fingers through his wet hair. "I'm going to try to get O'Connor's old tractor going. I can use the box blade on the back of it to move dirt from the pasture."

"Daddy has a bulldozer," she said.

But Dallas shook his head. "No doubt he's already halfway here—and the Golden Rose is too far away, anyway. Call Yancey and tell him to get down here to help me."

"Does the ranch have a bulldozer?" She was already reaching for the phone.

He nodded. "But it belongs to Dad."

"Does that matter now?"

"It matters," he said flatly. "Just ask Yancey to come." He paused. "Tell him to try Jennings's and Massey's for a dozer. Their places are on the way."

"What about the bridge?" She dialed as Dallas moved toward the hall.

"He'll make it if he comes right away," he said, and dis-appeared down the hall.

Rachel made the call and reached Quinn, who said Yan-cey was out in the barn, tending to water problems of his own. Rachel explained the situation to Quinn and asked her to relay the message to Yancey. When she hung up, she caught a report on the radio—they were now reporting the flooding to be the worst ever in recorded history in the state. Stalled cars were jamming streets in the city, and one car was known to have been swept away by rushing water over in Caddo County. A number of roads were being closed.

Rachel glanced to the doorway to see her mother standing there; she'd caught the report, too.

"Dallas says the creek is flooding badly," Rachel said. "He's afraid it may reach up to here." She caught her bottom lip between her teeth a moment, then strode forward. "Help me look through those boxes. I've got a pair of rubber boots and a slicker in there somewhere."

She was standing in the rain, pointing a flashlight at the greasy depths of the tractor engine with one hand and holding an umbrella over her and Dallas as best she could with the other when her father arrived. She heard him call above the pounding rain and the sound of rushing water.

Glancing over, she saw him stalking forward. She blinked as water dripped into her eyes. Her teeth began to chatter.

"You got to get outta here," her father bellowed when he reached them. Water drops flung from his Stetson as his head moved with his speech. "The water's splashing over the bridge—it'll be in your front yard next! This dang flood is the worst in history—they've even closed one of the bridges over the Washita out in Caddo County."

Dallas appeared not even to notice her father's presence. He finished fiddling with the carburetor and reached to press the starter. The engine tried. It sputtered and coughed, and for an instant Rachel held her breath, willing it to start. Then it died. Dallas sprayed the carburetor with ether and fiddled again.

Her father took hold of Dallas's arm. "Did you hear me, boy? We've got to get out of here while we still can. That water could cut down through here in a flash. We'd be lucky to make the bluffs over there." He pointed toward the wooded hills.

Dallas shook Jasper's arm away. "I'm not leaving." He paused and met Rachel's gaze. "You and Aaron go with Jasper," he ordered, inclining his head.

"And leave you?"

"I'll be okay, Rach. If things get bad, I can hit the bluff, like Jasper said."

"You listen to him, daughter!"

Rachel ignored her father and gazed at Dallas, setting her jaw and her will. "I'm not leaving without you." For an instant they stared at each other. Then Jasper jerked the flashlight from her hand.

"Get up to the house to dry out," he bellowed, gesturing with the light. He turned to Dallas. "Come on, let's get Poppin' John goin'. I'll spray. You press that starter—and keep the hell out of the way if we get flame."

Rachel backed away, holding the all-but-useless umbrella over her head, and watched. Her father sprayed the ether liberally and boldly—seemingly heedless of the fire he'd warned of. On the third try the tractor came to life. Dallas tested the gears. They changed with deep grinds, but they did change. Her father jumped up to stand on the platform beside Dallas on the seat, and with a series of jerks Dallas started the rusty green tractor off out behind the barn toward the swollen creek's edge. Water rolled off the brim of his hat and splattered on his back; her father's yellow slicker whipped out behind him in the wind.

Rachel lowered the umbrella. Water drops slipped down her face and seeped into her mouth. Tasting salt, she realized they were tears.

When Dallas reached the water's edge, he stopped the tractor and surveyed the scene. The water had entered the old rickety barn that sat the farthest from the house and closest to the creek. It was rising at an unbelievable rate and was spreading ever wider across the pasture.

"You'd best begin digging here," Jasper called into his ear. "That barn's lost already."

Dallas nodded. He didn't think the old wooden barn was strong enough to stand the surging water. But maybe, just maybe he could save the other, stouter steel barn. *We need that barn,* he prayed.

Jasper jumped to the ground and stepped aside as Dallas shifted the tractor into gear and began scooping earth with the box blade.

It was slow work, scraping the ground and piling it. More than holding back the water with earth, he hoped to dig the ground deep enough to change the flow of the stream—to at least lessen the force with which it ran by the house.

He didn't know how long he'd worked, with water pouring down his face and Jasper standing aside watching in the same pouring rain, when he heard a familiar shout. Glancing up, he saw a figure in a yellow slicker striding out across the pasture. In amazement he recognized his father's stride. Four men bearing shovels came close behind. And behind them rumbled the massive bulldozer, Yancey in the driver's seat, waving at him.

The old man had come! How in the hell had they gotten the bulldozer down and across the bridge? The thoughts raced through his mind, but there wasn't time to dwell on them. It didn't matter how they had gotten there, only that they had. Renewed energy surged through him, and Dallas forgot all else but saving what belonged to him and his from the raging floodwater.

Rachel stood with her hands resting on Aaron's shoulders. Her head was covered by her slicker hood, but still her hair beneath was more wet than dry. She blinked as the rain pelted her face and slipped down her cheeks.

Beside her stood her father, on the other side, Ace. Quinn and her mother were there, too. All of them stared at the rising murky water. Far out in the main stream, debris—branches, whole tree trunks, boards—rushed past. Rachel caught a glimpse of what she thought was a cow's body, but averted her gaze, not wanting to know. Daylight was all but gone.

Dallas and Yancey were cutting into the pasture, taking the dirt to pile up behind and around to the side of the barn toward the house. The hands from the Cordell ranch went out in the pasture to the side of the house and began packing and shifting the dirt that the machines had dug and digging more of their own, working furiously.

"What about those posts, Ace?" her father bellowed, and pointed to a small stack of aged cedar tree trunks stacked beside the barn. "They'd help in shoring, and I ain't too old to be doin' the job if you're not."

Rachel drew in a sharp breath, not certain whether she should believe her eyes and ears.

Ace slowly turned to look at her father. "You're on, Jasper."

Rachel heard him with astonishment—and worry. She reached out to stop Ace. He wasn't in any condition to be doing such labor. Not under these circumstances. No barn or house or material thing of any kind was worth jeopardizing his health.

But Quinn laid a hand on her arm and shook her head.

Then her father said, "Mira...Rachel, you women get anything of value into our truck. Then you all and Aaron drive on up the road to wait. Just in case."

"But—"

"You do as I said! We'll all work here, but we may have to head for that higher ground. Don't let us be havin' to worry about you."

"Jasper is right," Ace put in. "I've seen this kind of flooding more times than I can count—and I ain't never seen it worse."

Rachel wanted desperately to join the men—to join Dallas in fighting for what belonged to them. But there were no more tools. The best thing she could do was support the men.

She nodded and turned toward the house with the others. With every step she prayed for the men's safety. Nothing, not possessions, not land, not pride—nothing was more important than their lives.

"How can we help?" Quinn asked when they reached the kitchen.

Rachel gazed at her and didn't know what to say. She glanced over to her mother, who was removing her soggy coat, and then to the counter where Dallas's empty coffee mug still sat.

What few items out of all the material things she possessed could she choose? There was her antique oak dining table, which couldn't be considered—and which meant so very much to her. There was her sterling silver tea set, the tiles her mother had given her, which were priceless. There were her needlework designs, which were worth ten years' work, but she wasn't certain which box they were packed in. She adored her antique chiming clock, her collection of moccasins from various Indian tribes. One pair from the Comanche people was over one hundred years old and beyond price. The rest of the collection was worth at least four thousand dollars. What about her coyote-fur coat, which she'd had especially made from her own design? There wasn't another like it anywhere.

Aaron touched her arm. "Mom, we still haven't found Wheeler. He wasn't in the barn or under the house. If he could have, he would have come to be with us. He might need help." His voice broke with the last.

She looked down into his worried eyes and thought of the carcass she'd seen floating by and tried to figure out what to say.

"I don't know about Wheeler, sweetheart, and there's nothing we can do now." It broke her heart to see the pain gather in his gray eyes. "We're going to have to hope and pray. He's an awfully smart dog. He may have gotten stuck on the other side of the creek and knows not to try to get back."

"Your mother's right," her mother put in. "You know Wheeler is smart. He's no doubt found a good place to take shelter until he can get home again. There's no profit in supposing the worst, yet," she added firmly, and rose to hug him to her.

Aaron nodded reluctantly, and Rachel knew with a sinking heart that there was nothing anyone could say to console him.

"Go and get any special thing from your room that you wish to make certain not to lose," she told him. "Put it in Grandpa's truck."

He walked slowly away down the hall.

"Dallas's mare..." Rachel said, turning to Quinn with squared shoulders. "Could you shoo her over toward the bluff? That way she can easily take to higher ground if she needs to."

Quinn nodded. "No problem." She was already turning toward the door.

"Wait!" Rachel tossed her the flashlight from the counter. "We've got a couple more."

"Rachel," her mother said, "I'm going to start carting things up to the attic. If the water should come, it may not do any more than enter this first floor."

Rachel nodded and called after her, "Get my coyote coat first!"

She was losing her mind, she thought. Worrying over a stupid fur coat when she could lose so much more.

She went to get the few things she would put into Dallas's truck: her purse containing their marriage license, the small box of important papers containing Aaron's birth certificate, vehicle papers and such, the box of photo albums and the rose rock Dallas had given her that day beneath the cottonwoods. These small, irreplaceable things summed up her life. She plopped them on the truck seat and discarded thought of the expensive things she left behind.

Next she walked out to the barn to get Dallas's saddle. It was one Ace'd given to Dallas on his twenty-eighth birthday. He'd had it especially made to fit both Shadow and Dallas. She tried to gather up the saddle blankets, too, but all of it was too heavy with water, so she settled for the saddle and bridle alone. As she struggled across the wet, tall grass toward the pickup, she heard the rapid chugging of the two machines, Dallas and Yancey still moving earth, the shouts of men and the rushing of water.

Then suddenly she heard one shout above all the others. Though she couldn't understand the words, there was an urgent tone in the call. She dropped the saddle into the pickup bed and turned to run back to the creek. There came a tremendous groaning and cracking. Peering into the gloom, she saw the old wooden barn falling as if in slow motion. The old building listed to the side, then in the blink of an eye collapsed into the water and disappeared, swept away.

Rachel's gaze swung around to see Dallas furiously trying to restart the tractor that had apparently stalled. It chugged, and puffs of smoke popped out of the exhaust pipe, but the machine didn't start.

She'd reached the muddy piling of dirt and heard Ace calling to both Dallas and Yancey.

"Get out of there, boys! She's coming fast." He waved frantically. "Come on, Dallas! Leave it be!"

Then her father was calling to her, and the men were moving up toward the yard. "Get back, Rach—get your mother! Get back!" He raced toward her.

She stared at the swelling, churning water. *Oh, Lord, the flood! It was coming in a wave!*

She stood rooted to the spot, watching Dallas jump from the dead tractor and run across to where Yancey still persisted in moving the earth, the rear tracks of the dozer churning in the rushing water. Dallas gestured and screamed up at his brother, though what he spoke was garbled to

Rachel's ears. Her attention riveted on him, she began running toward him.

Dallas heard Jasper shout and turned to see Rachel stumbling toward him down the lumpy embankment they'd made. Giving up on Yancey, who'd shifted to drive the bulldozer away from him anyway, Dallas ran toward Rachel. He had to get her up and out of there. He could hear the water right behind him.

"Dallas..."

"Get out of here!" He grabbed her arm and started hauling her up the embankment and over the wet, dark ground toward the yard. With his free hand he waved to the others. He wasn't certain they could see him. He called at the top of his lungs. "That's enough! Get to the house! It's coming!"

Rachel stumbled beside him, and he lifted her, heedless of where he walked, unable to see in the dimness and only concerned with putting distance between them and the raging water. There was no controlling the creek now. Either they'd succeeded in doing enough to turn the water, or they hadn't. His only concern now was for saving those most precious to him. Quite suddenly he had no thought at all for the barn or the house—only for Rachel, Aaron, the others of their family. That was all that mattered.

He pulled Rachel close and yelled, "Get the others from the house. We're heading for the bluff!" For an instant he stared down into her shadowy, precious face.

She nodded and turned to run across the wide yard for the house. He saw the rain in the light of the back pole lamp. Several of the hands were there at the back porch. He saw his father and Jasper approaching, waving and calling to him.

Damn Yancey! He had to get him off that bulldozer.

The next instant the ground rumbled beneath his feet, and he twisted around to see the bulldozer chugging at record speed around the corner of the barn, tearing through the wire fencing as he came, heading for the creek. Yancey's white teeth gleamed as he smiled and motioned for Dallas to get out of the way.

Dallas hurried toward the house and stood with the others, watching as Yancey scraped a path through the backyard toward the creek. The dozer bogged down with the load of earth piling in front of it. It wasn't a big dozer, but Yancey kept the engine roaring enough to blow it. When it died, he jumped from the seat, leaving it jammed like a plug in a hole in a dike.

Yancey ran to join the group gathered beneath the pole light, and as he approached, Dallas heard his father call, "You can take that dozer out of your share of the ranch!"

Yancey grinned at Dallas.

"Dallas!" Quinn came flying out of the house, the screen door flapping behind her. "Oh, Dallas!" she cried frantically, sending a chill down his spine. "Aaron's missing!"

His gaze had already swept to Rachel, who came behind his sister. The pole light shone upon her pale, drawn face.

"We can't find Aaron," she said in a tight voice. Her lower lip trembled.

Chapter Thirteen

By unspoken agreement they'd fanned out. Mira and Jasper had headed west in their pickup, following the creek and searching the narrowed pasture and tree line. Ace and the others had driven off south and were combing the wooded bluffs, while Dallas and Rachel followed the swollen creek eastward.

They left the glow of the backyard pole light behind them. Dallas didn't know what was to be the fate of their barn and house, but as Rachel directed the powerful battery-powered spotlight along the water's edge, he saw that the small creek had swollen into a great rushing sea, flooding far into the land.

Dallas braked. "I'm going to get out and walk. You follow me with the truck." Rachel's face was strained and greenish-white in the dim glow cast from the dash lights. "Can you drive a stick shift, Rach?" Funny—she was his woman, but he didn't know something as basic as that about her.

She nodded. "Yes." Her voice was hoarse.

He touched her cold hand. "We'll find him, Rachel." God, it was such an empty promise—one she knew damn well he couldn't keep. *Oh, God, let him be okay. She won't be able to stand it. Dad, Jasper, Mira...none of us can bear it.*

The thoughts ran through his mind as he took the spotlight from Rachel and stepped out into the rain. It had let up some, but the water, unbelievably, still appeared to be rising. It passed up over the toes of his boots within seconds, and he pointed, directing Rachel to move farther inland.

He paused, catching a shout. South of him, he gauged, and searched the darkness, finding the lights of his father's pickup and hearing again the men calling out for Aaron.

He started off again and shone the spotlight in an arc in front of them, from the land out into the rushing water. The beam played upon an object, and his breath stopped for an instant. Then he recognized the carcass of a cow before it spun away into the murky dimness. Rachel called for Aaron through the open truck window.

Where would Aaron have gone? Dallas asked himself, trying to put himself in the boy's place. Rachel had explained about Wheeler being missing, and there was no doubt that Aaron was looking for the dog. He couldn't have gone far; there hadn't been but maybe twenty minutes at the most. And Dallas didn't like the thought, but he felt certain Aaron would have followed the floodwater, fearing, and rightly so, that the dog could be caught and need help.

"Aaron!" he called, then listened. Nothing. He continued to walk and search with the spotlight as well as the truck's headlights, alternately calling and listening.

Rachel's heart pounded, and she tried to pray, but she could do little more than repeat feverishly, *Let him be safe... Oh, please let him be safe....*

Suddenly the ground before them dipped, and the headlights played upon a sparse line of twisted tree trunks and debris, deposited there when the floodwater had veered into a low area of the pasture. Dallas held up his hand, and Rachel braked, her eyes examining the area illuminated by the headlights.

Surely Aaron couldn't have gone much farther. Perhaps he'd gone over the way her father and mother were looking. Or over into the hilly woods.

Her eyes strained so hard to see something, anything, that they hurt. *No! She refused to think about him in the water....*

"Aaron! Aaron!" Leaning her head out the window, she shouted, then listened, desperately hoping to hear his small, precious voice. It was a young boy's voice, only loud when he was enclosed by four walls. How would they possibly hear it out here?

Ace's and the others' voices could be heard, she reasoned. Sound carried for great distances at night out in the country.

Dallas walked over to the truck. "We'll go a bit more this way, then backtrack," he said. "I don't think he would have gone farther."

She nodded and again inched the pickup forward, veering away form the swirling water and debris. Maybe he'd already returned to the house or was trying to find it. It was so dark now. The thought of him alone in the darkness cut sharply into her heart. Aaron wasn't afraid of the dark, and he had good, common sense—but he was only ten years old.

She listened to Dallas calling and wondered about the house. Had the water flooded up into it? Had it been swept away? Aaron would be terrified to return and find it gone, water flowing where their house was supposed to be. Surely the barrier the men had managed to build would keep the water from rushing the house, she thought, calming herself. And Quinn and one of the hands had stayed behind to be there should Aaron come. They'd take shelter in Rachel's car, moving it to the pasture south of the house, where the ground was a bit higher.

Where are you, Aaron?

Dallas suddenly stopped and held up a hand. "Cut the engine," he called back to her.

She did so immediately, an icy chill stabbing down her back like a razor-sharp knife. Leaning her head out the window, she listened, as did Dallas. She heard the water flowing, rippling. And there came the distant thumping of an old oil well. She caught a faint call, and her heart pounded. It could have been Ace and the men still in the woods. She strained to follow the bright beam of light that Dallas was directing out into the water.

Again Dallas called out. There came a faint answer.

Rachel's heart leaped. *It was Aaron!* Maybe. She thought she recognized his voice and quickly slipped from the seat and ran ahead to catch up with Dallas, who was hurrying forward, skirting the water and flashing the light across its murky depths.

Oh, please let it be Aaron . . . please . . . please.

Trees. Dallas played the light quickly across them—willows and big old cottonwoods. A rise in the land. The rushing water had split and cut a swath through the pasture, flowing around the rise, making it an island.

"Aaron! Aaron!" she called, then strained to listen and willed for an answer.

"Mom . . ."

It was Aaron! Dallas heard him, too, and directed the light again across the trees, slower this time.

Aaron . . . Oh, God . . . my son . . .

When the light found Aaron, he appeared as a growth attached to a tree trunk at the fork of several small, low-growing branches.

"Here!" He waved an arm. "Mom . . . Mom . . ." His childish voice echoed with a sob.

"Hang on!" Dallas cried, his heart pounding in his chest. He pressed the flashlight at Rachel. "Stay put." With long strides he sprinted for the pickup, hearing Rachel call reassurances to Aaron behind him.

"We're coming, Aaron.... We're going to get you."

Rope... Had he remembered to put it back into the truck?

He jerked open the door, smacked the horn, giving three loud blasts as a signal to the others, then checked behind the seat for the long length of nylon rope he liked to keep there.

It wasn't there.

He hurriedly and desperately checked beneath the seat, but his memory saw the rope clearly—he'd left it on the porch after unloading the beds and refrigerator that day, had been in too much of a hurry at the time to return it to its place—and hadn't done so since.

"Damn!" He hit the horn again, two loud, hard blasts. An instant later he heard his father's answering honk.

He gunned the pickup to life and drove it to the edge of the water, aiming the headlights to the tree where Aaron clung. When he got out of the truck, he heard Aaron calling for him. "Dallas... Mama..." His terrified scream pierced the air, followed by loud sobbing cries.

"Hang on, cowboy!" Dallas called back, and reached out to grab Rachel, who'd waded up to her knees in the dark, rushing water.

"Don't go any farther, Rach," he ordered, and tugged her out of the water.

"Snakes, Dallas..." Her voice vibrated with revulsion and fear. "He says there's snakes all over the place!"

"Lookin' for higher ground like every other living thing."

In a flash he analyzed the situation. He didn't know what the water would do in the next minutes. By all rights it should level off at least—but it was still rising. And it was highly likely that at least one or more of those snakes were poisonous copperheads. He couldn't wait. Right or wrong, he just couldn't wait.

"Hang tight!" he called to Aaron. "Just be still—I'm comin' for you, son!"

He plopped to the ground and began tugging off his boots.

"Dad's comin'," he shot back over his shoulder to Rachel. "Get back in the truck and start honking the horn to make certain he can find us."

For a split second she didn't move, her face and form a black silhouette illuminated by the headlights behind her. He felt her desperation and her love. He turned toward Aaron and pushed out into the water. *God, it was cold!*

The strength of the current amazed him. He'd always heard that rushing floodwater could easily tug a person under; now he experienced it firsthand as his foot slipped and he went down. Immediately his body was jerked around like a rag doll. Water flooded his nostrils, choking him.

He fought for and regained his footing. He broke the surface coughing and struggling to keep his head up. Pausing, he gasped for breath and refocused on Aaron. The soil beneath his feet was washed away, and he pushed off, found footing and half walked, half swam, fighting the tremendous current that kept pushing him farther and farther downstream from Aaron.

The truck headlights illuminated Dallas's head and shoulders as he pushed through the murky flowing water. Watching him, Rachel held her breath, praying and willing him to safety. Just as her ears picked up the sound of Ace's approaching truck, she caught sight of a large, dark log bearing down on Dallas.

She screamed. A second set of headlights illuminated the twisting water. The log hit Dallas, and he went down as the log swirled around and disappeared downstream.

"Dallas!" She ran for the water, splashing out into it, not knowing or caring about the cold and wet, the fear and helplessness gripping her bones. *Oh, God, help him! Help him!* It was a demand. Suddenly Ace and Yancey were at her side, Ace's hand closing around her arm. "He's gone on after Aaron...and a log..." She pointed, barely able to get the words out.

"There he is!" Yancey shouted. "Up on the bank. He's made it!"

"Get the rope from the truck," Ace ordered, but one of the men was already bringing it, another driving the pickup forward. "Here you go, son." Ace handed Yancey the stiff rope. "Let's see some of your fancy ropin'."

Between them Rachel stood, her gaze riveted on the figures silhouetted across the water. *Please let them be all right.*

All Dallas thought of was getting Aaron. He could see the boy's shadowy face gripped with terror. The water had now edged up to the base of the tree trunks, and Dallas splashed through it. Instinctively he scanned the tree where Aaron sat for snakes, catching sight of a slithery tail hanging from a small branch.

Aaron stretched out a hand, and Dallas lifted both of his arms. "Come on, son," Dallas said. "Just move slow, and we'll leave those snakes in peace." He hoped.

Aaron gave out a small whimper, then clamped his mouth shut, visibly concentrating on his motions. Seconds later, Dallas clutched Aaron to him; Aaron gripped hard around his neck.

"It's okay, son. It's okay."

"I'm sorry, Uncle Dallas..."

"Hush...just hold on."

Dallas saw Yancey standing well out into the water, his big frame silhouetted by the headlights. Dallas waved, then watched his brother's arm swing the rope up in the air. Tightly holding Aaron, Dallas moved cautiously out into the water as far as he dared. "Hold your arm out, Aaron, to give Yance something to aim at.

Once...twice...three times Yancey's arm twirled, and then the rope came flying through the night, across the wide expanse of rippling water. It struck Aaron's arm, but slipped off to the water. Frantically both Aaron and Dallas splashed around for it.

"I got it!" Aaron cried, holding it up.

"Good boy! Okay... help me get it around us."

They were pulled across by Yancey and the men. Luckily no more logs or branches came floating by, and in minutes Dallas was finding a solid footing beneath him. Then Rachel was there.

"Oh, Dallas... Aaron..." She was touching him and Aaron over and over. "Are you okay?"

Dallas nodded and tried to catch his breath as he stared down into Rachel's anxious face. He touched her cheek, his other hand remaining tight around Aaron. For some odd reason he didn't want to let go of the boy, who'd laid his head on his shoulder and still clung to him.

He lifted his eyes from Rachel's to his father's. In wonder, he recognized a tear slipping from the old man's eye—it could be nothing else. His father's mouth spread into a trembling grin, and his hand fell upon Dallas's shoulder.

"Well, get them over here to the truck," Jasper's voice bellowed, and for the first time Dallas realized Mira and Jasper's truck had joined them and everyone was hovering. "Here, take my coat...."

Dallas, with Aaron on his lap, sat on the tailgate of Ace's pickup. Rachel sat beside them, and Aaron turned to let her hold him. *Her baby... Oh, thank you, God.* Her son was safe.

She stroked his head, ran her hands down his shoulders and peered at his face. "No snake bites... or anything?"

He shook his head, then threw himself on her chest. "I'm sorry, Mom. I just had to look for Wheeler. I just had to."

"Shush."

"It's okay, son." Dallas slipped his arm around Rachel and leaned close. "You had to do what you thought was right. It was somethin' that just happened."

Aaron sniffed and wiped his nose on his wet sleeve. "I heard the water comin', and I lit out for the tree. I guess I went the wrong way."

"You found a tree," Rachel said, keeping back the sob in her throat. "And you're both safe. That's all that matters."

"I didn't find Wheeler," Aaron whispered hoarsely.

Rachel clutched him to her, hurting for him and giving thanks at the same time.

Finally, in the early hours of Thursday, Rachel lay in bed, Dallas on one side, Aaron on the other. They'd all felt the need to be together. Aaron and Dallas had fallen asleep almost as soon as their heads had hit the pillows. Rachel lay awake, listening to the two breathing.

It had been nearing midnight when the men and the radio reports had concurred that the floodwater had crested and was receding by fractions. It hadn't taken the house—or even reached it. When the water had rushed, it had quickly eroded the earth piled at the rear of the steel barn, washing out the foundation and causing the barn to collapse to the side, into the mound of earth Yancey and Dallas had piled there. The metal and timbers stuck into the ground, helping to form a tight levee that kept the water from the house and yard.

The others had been forced to circle around to the south when they'd left for home because the bridge was still under water. Ace and Jasper had each telephoned to say that they'd made it safely. It appeared the only casualty of that day was going to be Wheeler, poor thing.

Lying there, Rachel remembered the look in Ace's eyes after Dallas had rescued Aaron. Relief and love such as she'd never seen had been in his expression. He'd repeatedly touched Dallas; she'd never seen him do this. It had taken an awful incident to bring it out, but at last the barrier had been broken, and Ace had not only realized how much he loved his eldest son but had been able to convey it.

And her own father. She smiled, remembering now how he'd thrown himself into helping them—and how he and Ace had worked side by side. Drawn there by their children's need.

Carefully, not wanting to wake her guys, Rachel twisted to look into Dallas's face. He slept peacefully. Seeing his injured eye remained several shades of pale purple brought a bitter sweetness to her heart. She turned and caressed Aaron's warm hair.

She had no idea what the following days would bring— perhaps her father and Ace would be staunch enemies again tomorrow, there was a barn to be rebuilt, a leaky roof to be fixed, pasture to be repaired, bills for it all to be paid—and a wedding to celebrate. But any time she began to feel irritated and overwhelmed, she vowed to remember how thankful she felt for her life in that moment. Right there in that bed she had her wealth and her life—all that mattered.

The following morning the destruction the flood had wrought was in full view beneath a gray sky. Dallas was already up and standing out at the back fence—where the fence had been before Yancey had torn through it—when Rachel rose and went to the back porch. Aaron was poking around the edge of the water. The creek was still up in the pasture, though down a number of feet from where it had been, leaving behind thick mud and mashed grass. The barn looked like a tumbled house of cards.

Stepping gingerly across the wet ground in her slippers, Rachel went to put an arm about Dallas's waist. His eyes were shadowed and doleful.

"We'll build another barn," she said, wanting to ease his disappointment.

He nodded. "And put back the pasture. The dozer's still here, so Yance won't have to pay Dad for it."

He looked down at her and gave a small smile. She smiled back.

"We're okay."

His smile widened. "We're okay," he agreed, and shook his head, squeezing her against him, holding her for long seconds.

Calling to Aaron, they walked slowly back to the house for breakfast. They'd just sat down to eat when a car pulled into the drive.

"It's Papa Ace," Aaron called from where he went to spy out the window. He sent them a wide-eyed look of speculation.

"Got some extra coffee?" Ace said when Dallas opened the door for him. The old man walked into the house as if he'd been doing so for the past ten years. He continued right on in front of Dallas through the dining room and into the kitchen. "Mornin', Rachel."

Rachel stood in the middle of the room, her eyes wide with shock. "Good morning, Ace," she answered haltingly. Then she smiled. "May I pour you a cup of coffee?"

"Yep, you can."

"Would you like some breakfast, Dad?" Dallas asked. It seemed the thing to say.

Ace shook his head as he took a seat, somehow seeming like a king taking his throne. "I had breakfast already."

Rachel set a cup in front of him and brought the cream from the refrigerator.

Ace fixed his coffee as he liked it, passed his gaze from Dallas to Rachel to Aaron and back again. "Look, this place is a mess. I think you two should move the wedding on up to the ranch. You don't want to be putting it off, and we sure as hell have a lot more room."

Rachel dropped her cup; it shattered on the floor.

Dallas moved to help her clean up the mess. From the window, Aaron called out, "Grandpa J. is here." He turned to look at them all with much the same expression as a boy waiting for a fireworks show—part apprehension, part gleeful anticipation.

Dallas thought the world was about to come to an end when he stood in the same room with mighty Ace Cordell and dynamic Jasper Tyson.

Jasper had come in through the back door without knocking. He'd paused only a fraction upon seeing Ace, then went and kissed Rachel. "Good morning, daughter." He rubbed Aaron's head fondly, then hugged him, as if he couldn't help himself. "Mornin', Dallas." Then at last, "Mornin', Ace."

"Mornin', Jasper."

The two big men stared at each other as if they were trying to read each other's minds. When Dallas offered Jasper his chair across from Ace, Jasper hesitated, then took it. The room was quiet, and then Jasper began making small-talk comments about last night's events and what the conditions were now locally and across the state.

"Heard they found this woman up in a tree this mornin', Aaron. She'd been there all night and with snakes, too. She was fine, though."

"Fella found he'd suddenly gotten lakefront property down at Texoma," Ace put in, not to be outdone on tales. "And before the rains he was two blocks from the lake."

This went on for a few more minutes, and then Jasper apparently got tired of waiting for Ace to leave. "Well now," he said, rubbing his round stomach. "I came here to see about this wedding. It seems to me it'd be a good idea to move it up the Golden Rose."

Dallas's father plunked his cup to the table. His eyes flashed. "I've already offered for them to have the wedding at the Cordell Ranch, Jasper."

Dallas glanced at Rachel. He didn't think he wanted to be stepping between the two men after what happened to him last time. His eye remained quite colorful from Jasper's punch on Sunday. But seeing her worried expression, he reluctantly made ready to step into it.

"I'm the bride's father," Jasper was saying. "We're supposed to give the wedding."

"That's a lot of baloney, and you know it. I've got just as much right to be givin' them a wedding."

"Wait a minute," Rachel said.

The two men looked at her. Slowly she moved to get the coffeepot and refill cups all around, saying, "This is my wedding, and I want to have it here."

"This place isn't only a mess, daughter," Jasper said, "it's too small. We've got plenty of room up at the Golden Rose—and the wedding would look awfully nice out on the back lawn."

"We've got plenty of room up at our ranch, too. And we've held many a party out on that big patio we've got. Perfect place."

Dallas figured this could go on forever. "We will have it here," he said firmly. "We just won't have so many people. We'll keep it to a small service in the living room. Just the family. We can invite all our friends to a party afterward at the Hall up in Hoving."

"Might not be able to get the use of the Hall on such short notice," Jasper observed, and Ace nodded.

"Clyde Jennings would lend us his barn."

"Your mother might like you to say the vows at the meetinghouse," Jasper tried, looking at Rachel.

"We'll have the wedding here," she repeated. "Now, Daddy, I've made biscuits. Surely you won't leave without having some. Ace?"

Both men enjoyed a plate of biscuits and sausage gravy, though said no more than a very polite please-pass-the-salt and thank-you to each other.

"Three o'clock tomorrow afternoon?" Ace asked as he prepared to leave, his face very somber.

"Yes, Dad." Dallas studied him. The old man simply nodded.

Jasper came right behind him. He flicked a glance to Dallas, then bent to hug Rachel. "Your mother and I would like to give away the bride."

Rachel pulled back and gazed through tears at his flushed, precious face. "I'd love that."

With high curiosity Rachel and Dallas watched the two men pause and speak briefly to each other on the puddled gravel driveway before getting into their respective vehicles and driving off. Neither seemed to be arguing.

"What do you suppose that was all about?" Rachel asked, turning a questioning gaze to Dallas.

He shook his head, his expression equally perplexed. Then a wide grin slipped across his lips.

Rachel grinned joyously in return. "They're both coming," she said hoarsely. "Both of them!"

Dallas felt the same glorious emotion echoing within him. He guessed he'd seen a few miracles last night, but they were tiny compared to this: his father and Jasper accepting the marriage.

With a sudden motion he reached out and grabbed Rachel around the waist and twirled her in the air. "Whooee!" He simply had to do something, had to express the emotions boiling up in his chest.

Rachel's beautiful eyes widened with surprise, and then she was laughing down at him.

Oh, God, how he loved her! And she was his... his!

"I love you," Rachel said, cupping Dallas's face as he slowly lowered her to the porch floor. Every cell in her body echoed the feeling.

"I love you, too."

"Mom! Dallas!"

They turned their heads in unison. Aaron was running up the drive with a small, muddy creature running beside him. Wheeler!

* * *

That afternoon two large flatbed trucks of lumber arrived along with a crew of eight men.

"This the Cordell place?" a big burly man asked Dallas just as Rachel joined him on the front porch.

"I'm Dallas Cordell, if that's who you're looking for."

"You're the one. Ace Cordell hired us," the big man said, eyeing the wet ground skeptically. "He said to cover this here front yard with a wood floor—today. It's going to be a job." With that he lumbered off and began shouting orders.

Rachel took Dallas's hand and stood with him, staring at the workmen. "Since we won't go to the ranch for our wedding," he said, "I guess Ace intends to bring us a patio here." In wonder she lifted her gaze to his. He was grinning broadly.

They hadn't gotten over that surprise when two young women arrived in a van—caterers, the most sought-after in the city, sent by Jasper Tyson. They wanted Rachel's approval on the food they'd contracted to provide and to check out the facilities. Nothing was too small, they assured a very dazed Rachel, and they would also be providing waiters, in suits, and a rolling bar, if Rachel would like. She was still talking to them when the florist arrived—she couldn't be certain who'd hired him.

Next came Quinn and Mira, who proceeded to take command of all the arrangements, saying that Rachel was not to lift a hand, except to begin preparing herself as the bride.

That evening, after everyone had left and Rachel was just getting her breath, another truck pulled into the drive—a roofer sent by Mira. Rachel directed the man to Dallas, who was up on the roof working.

Approximately sixty people came to see Rachel and Dallas wed. A crowd too small to suit Ace and Jasper, too large for Rachel and Dallas.

As Rachel stood inside the front door, preparing to walk down the red-carpeted aisle, she looked at the faces. A few she recognized, many she did not. A number of the people had come out of sheer curiosity—that was plainly evident on their faces.

But there was also love from those who mattered most—their family. Ace had never looked more distinguished; Yancey was exceedingly striking—as were the two beautiful women standing on either side of him. Stella dabbed at her eyes; Rafe and Pete and the other hands picked at their collars and ties. Quinn walked beautifully down the aisle in a new dress of yellow silk.

"Ready?" her father asked, extending his arm as the organist changed the music.

Between them, her father and Ace had thought of everything, from red carpet for the aisle to the huge yellow roses that graced not only Rachel's bouquet but every corner available, to the organist and the famous country band that waited to play at the reception. The living room also had furniture—temporary, her father had assured her.

Rachel smoothed at the skirt of her wedding gown, then extended her arm toward her mother. "Mama." Her mother smiled tenderly.

"I'm so proud of you, my darling."

The three of them started out. Rachel did not shake; she'd never felt more certain in her life. Her gaze lingered on Aaron, standing beside Dallas. For a rare moment she recognized a bit of Coy in his twinkling eyes. He smiled at her and gave her a subtle thumbs-up sign.

Her gaze moved upward to Dallas's. Only his eyes were smiling, sending her his love in a very private manner.

I love you. . . . She allowed her eyes to tell him, her heart to call to his.

I love you, he answered without speaking.

The sun broke through the clouds as her father placed her hand into Dallas's, giving them his public blessing.

Rachel held it all in her heart; the vows she and Dallas spoke to each other before receiving a blessing from the pastor, her mother kissing both her father and a very flabbergasted Ace, and the pandemonium of hugs and kisses and tears all around.

All in all it was the wedding of the decade, giving everyone something to talk about for months to come. It would be reported that the bride was as beautiful and shining as a rare jewel, and that her husband stared shamelessly at her with love. That two state senators and the richest oilman left in the West, who landed in his private helicopter, attended, would no doubt make the television evening news. The size of the giant cake would no doubt triple with the telling, as would the number of presents that filled the back bedroom. That Dallas received a top-of-the-line, airconditioned cab tractor from Ace, and Rachel a plush sable coat from her father would go far.

People would laugh over how a scrubby blue heeler dog managed to knock over one table of food and eat half of it, and also over Clyde Jennings falling off the wooden floor and wrenching his ankle while dancing the two-step. Never to be forgotten would be Bob Monroe and Jessie Walker being discovered in a most compromising position in the front seat of Bob's car—by his wife. Aaron's claim to fame was joining two young accomplices in the wonderful delight of throwing firecrackers beneath the wooden floor and scaring the daylights out of everyone.

Perhaps what would top it all in memory was Ace and Jasper managing to argue almost every time they came within spitting distance of each other but not to come to blows. No one counted the time Yancey had to step between them.

It would be said that Rachel Tyson Cordell had married Coy's brother to give her son the nearest thing to his real father—and this would be true, in part. It would be said that Dallas Cordell had always lusted after his sister-in-law, or

that he'd felt obligated to marry his brother's widow—and
both of these suppositions would be true, in part. It would
be said the marriage was to join two giant ranches and dy-
nasties—something that both Jasper and Ace would never
learn to like but, being shrewd men, could perhaps learn to
profit by. But the closest truth would be that Dallas and
Rachel were in love and had been for years. A rare love
found by few people.

Five hours later Rachel sat encircled by Dallas's arms on
the plush seat of a private jet her father had hired to take
them to the family lodge in the Colorado mountains. They'd
flown directly from the still-soggy pasture beside their house
to the airport in the helicopter Ace had ordered.

Dallas kissed her lingeringly and caressed the tender skin
of her neck. The warm, moist wanting throbbed sweetly
between her legs as she pulled loose his ribbon tie.

He took her hand into his, gazed at her, then gave her a
quick, soft kiss.

"Dad offered me my job back at the ranch," he said
hoarsely into the top of her head.

She stilled. "And?"

"I hope it's okay with you, but I told him no."

She pulled back and studied his eyes, then lifted her finger to touch the fading purple bruise. "You told him no?"

He nodded. "I know we'll be short on money for a few
years, Rach, but it won't be forever." His brows came together. "I never realized before how easy I'd had it. Never
having to look for a job. Having everything handed to me."

"You've built that ranch, Dallas. Yes, it was big, but you
brought it up-to-date—made it even bigger."

"Yes, but now I want to prove I can make it on my own.
I want to build something of my own—from the ground up.
I want to see if I can do it."

Rachel had no doubt he could do it. "I don't care about the money." She nuzzled his neck and knew it was her turn to tell about high-handed fathers. "Dad offered to build us a house—any plan, any price."

He stilled. She pulled back and gazed into his eyes.

"What did you tell him?" he said, his expression totally impassive.

"No," she said with high uncertainty.

He grinned and hugged her, and she mumbled into his shirt. "I told him we'd build our own house—but that I would return to working at the store, at least part-time. Oran's lost there, Dal. He needs me."

He chuckled and stroked her back. "Okay—but I need you, too."

She sighed and relaxed in his arms.

"There's no halfway measures for either of them, you know," Dallas said, speaking of their fathers.

"Not at all," she agreed. "I guess now they'll shower us with 'help.' And they'll each always be trying to outdo the other, just like they have with Aaron." She paused. "And there'll be fights to come."

Dallas's chest rumbled with chuckling agreement. "You know what will please the hell out of them?" A sly tone traced his voice. Rachel looked up to see bright twinkling in his beautiful, pale eyes.

"What?" She breathed the word; her heartbeat quickened.

"Grandchildren. The more we give them, the better they'll both like it."

"Oh...then we'd better get started," Rachel said in a silky voice, and began to unbutton his shirt.

Grinning broadly, Dallas reached for the nearby phone. "How long until we land?" he asked the pilot. "Well, stretch it out as long as possible. And Mrs. Cordell and I don't wish to be disturbed until then—for any reason."

He replaced the receiver, then laid Rachel back into the soft folds of the long couch. His panetela was left smoldering in the ashtray.

* * * * *

COMING NEXT MONTH

#595 TEA AND DESTINY—Sherryl Woods
Ann Davies had always taken in strays—but never one as wild as playboy Hank Riley! She usually offered tea and sympathy, but handsome Hank seemed to expect a whole lot more....

#596 DEAR DIARY—Natalie Bishop
Adam Shard was falling hard for his childhood pal. But beneath the straightforward, sardonic woman Adam knew so well lay a Kerry Camden yearning for love...and only her diary knew!

#597 IT HAPPENED ONE NIGHT—Marie Ferrarella
When their fathers' comedy act broke up, impulsive Paula and straitlaced Alex grudgingly joined forces to reunite the pair. But after much muddled meddling by everyone concerned, it was hard to say exactly *who* was matchmaking whom...

#598 TREASURE DEEP—Bevlyn Marshall
A sunken galleon, a tropical isle and dashing plunderer Gregory Chase... Could these fanciful fixings finally topple Nicole Webster's decidedly *un*romantic theory on basic biological urges?

#599 STRICTLY FOR HIRE—Maggi Charles
An accident brought unwanted luxury to take-charge Christopher Kendall's fast-paced life—a lady with a limo! And soon bubbly, rambunctious, adorable Tory Morgan was driving him to utter amorous distraction!

#600 SOMETHING SPECIAL—Victoria Pade
With her pink hearse, her elderly companion and her dubious past, there was something mighty suspicious about Patrick Drake's new neighbor, beautiful Mitch Cuddy. Something suspicious, something sexy...something pretty damn special!

AVAILABLE THIS MONTH:

Just when you thought all the good men had gotten away, along comes ...

SILHOUETTE® Desire™

MAN OF THE MONTH 1990

Twelve magnificent stories by twelve of your favorite authors.

In January, FIRE AND RAIN by Elizabeth Lowell
In February, A LOVING SPIRIT by Annette Broadrick
In March, RULE BREAKER by Barbara Boswell
In April, SCANDAL'S CHILD by Ann Major
In May, KISS ME KATE by Helen R. Myers
In June, SHOWDOWN by Nancy Martin
In July, HOTSHOT by Kathleen Korbel
In August, TWICE IN A BLUE MOON by Dixie Browning
In September, THE LONER by Lass Small
In October, SLOW DANCE by Jennifer Greene
In November, HUNTER by Diana Palmer
In December, HANDSOME DEVIL by Joan Hohl

Every man is someone you'll want to get to know ... and love. So get out there and find your man!

MOM90-1A

® *Silhouette Romances*.

DIAMOND JUBILEE
CELEBRATION!

It's Silhouette Books' tenth anniversary, and what better way to celebrate than to toast *you*, our readers, for making it all possible. Each month in 1990, we'll present you with a DIAMOND JUBILEE Silhouette Romance written by an all-time favorite author!

Welcome the new year with *Ethan*—a LONG, TALL TEXANS book by Diana Palmer. February brings Brittany Young's *The Ambassador's Daughter*. Look for *Never on Sundae* by Rita Rainville in March, and in April you'll find *Harvey's Missing* by Peggy Webb. Victoria Glenn, Lucy Gordon, Annette Broadrick, Dixie Browning and many more have special gifts of love waiting for you with their DIAMOND JUBILEE Romances.

Be sure to look for the distinctive DIAMOND JUBILEE emblem, and share in Silhouette's celebration. Saying thanks has never been so romantic....

SILHOUETTE DESIRE™
presents
AUNT EUGENIA'S TREASURES
by CELESTE HAMILTON

Liz, Cassandra and Maggie are the honored recipients of Aunt Eugenia's heirloom jewels...but Eugenia knows the real prizes are the young women themselves. Read about Aunt Eugenia's quest to find them everlasting love. Each book shines on its own, but together, they're priceless!

Available in December:
THE DIAMOND'S SPARKLE (SD #537)

Altruistic Liz Patterson wants nothing to do with Nathan Hollister, but as the fast-lane PR man tells Liz, love is something he's willing to take *very* slowly.

Available in February:
RUBY FIRE (SD #549)

Impulsive Cassandra Martin returns from her travels... ready to rekindle the flame with the man she never forgot, Daniel O'Grady.

Available in April:
THE HIDDEN PEARL (SD #561)

Cautious Maggie O'Grady comes out of her shell...and glows in the precious warmth of love when brazen Jonah Pendleton moves in next door.